SILENT WEAPON

Also by Andy McNab

THE STREET SOLDIER SERIES
Street Soldier
Silent Weapon

THE LIAM SCOTT SERIES
The New Recruit
The New Patrol
The New Enemy

DROPZONE
Dropzone
Dropzone: Terminal Velocity

BOY SOLDIER (with Robert Rigby)
Boy Soldier
Payback
Avenger
Meltdown

OTHER NOVELS:

Aggressor	*Fortress*
Battle Lines (with Kym Jordan)	*For Valour*
Brute Force	*Last Light*
Crisis Four	*Liberation Day*
Crossfire	*Recoil*
Dark Winter	*Red Notice*
Dead Centre	*Remote Control*
Deep Black	*Silencer*
Detonator	*State of Emergency*
Exit Wound	*War Torn* (with Kym Jordan)
Firewall	*Zero Hour*

NON-FICTION:
Bravo Two Zero
Immediate Action
On the Rock
Seven Troop
Sorted!: The Good Psychopath's Guide to Bossing your Life
(with Professor Kevin Dutton)
Spoken from the Front
The Good Psychopath's Guide to Success (with Professor Kevin Dutton)
Today Everything Changes

ANDY McNAB

SILENT WEAPON

A **STREET SOLDIER** NOVEL

DOUBLEDAY

DOUBLEDAY

UK | USA | Canada | Ireland | Australia
India | New Zealand | South Africa

Doubleday is part of the Penguin Random House group of companies
whose addresses can be found at global.penguinrandomhouse.com.

www.penguin.co.uk
www.puffin.co.uk
www.ladybird.co.uk

First published 2017

001

Text copyright © Andy McNab, 2017

With thanks to Ben Jeapes

The moral right of the author has been asserted

Typeset in 13/17.5 pt Adobe Garamond Pro by Jouve (UK), Milton Keynes
Printed in Great Britain by Clays Ltd, St Ives plc

A CIP catalogue record for this book is available from the British Library

HARDBACK ISBN: 978–0–857–53467–5
INTERNATIONAL PAPERBACK ISBN: 978–0–857–53468–2

All correspondence to:
Doubleday
Penguin Random House Children's
80 Strand, London WC2R 0RL

GLOSSARY

ACOG – Advanced Combat Optical Gunsight, providing up to six times fixed-power magnification, illuminated at night by an internal phosphor

AK-47 Kalashnikov – a selective-fire (semi-automatic and automatic), gas-operated 7.62mm by 39mm assault rifle

ANFO – Ammonium Nitrate, Fuel Oil – one of the most popular low-explosive lifting charges in use today

Biorepository – a place that collects, processes, stores and distributes biological specimens for future research

Boko Haram – an Islamic extremist group in Nigeria

C-17 Globemaster – a large military transport aircraft

CamelBak – back-worn hydration pack

COBRA – Cabinet Office Briefing Room: the location for a type of crisis-response committee set up to respond to instances of national or regional crisis

GLOSSARY

EOD – Explosive Ordnance Disposal. Sits alongside improvised explosive device disposal (IEDD) as a particular form of bomb disposal

Fusiliers – an infantry regiment of the British Army, part of the Queen's Division

GSW – Gun Shot Wound

Guerrilla – a member of an unauthorized military unit, usually with a political objective such as to overthrow a government

Heckler & Koch MP5 – 9mm submachine gun built by Heckler & Koch

HG85 grenade – a spherical grenade that, on detonation, fragments the outer shell

IED – an Improvised Explosive Device, which can be placed on the ground or used by suicide bombers; sometimes activated by remote control

Int – army term for intelligence: information collected on, for example, enemy movements

Lancers – The Royal Lancers, a cavalry regiment of the British Army

MC – Military Cross: a medal awarded to officers and other ranks in the British Armed Forces, in recognition of acts of bravery during active service

MI5 – a British intelligence agency working to protect the UK's national security against threats such as terrorism and espionage

Mk 7 helmet – a general-issue combat helmet for the British Armed Forces

MO – Medical Officer

MoD – Ministry of Defence. Their aim is to protect the security, independence and interests of our country at home and abroad. They ensure that the armed forces have the training, equipment and support necessary for their work

Molotov cocktail – generic name for a variety of bottle-based improvised incendiary weapons; more commonly known as a petrol bomb

NATO – North Atlantic Treaty Organization: an organization whose essential purpose is to safeguard the freedom and security of its members through political and military means

NCO – Non-Commissioned Officer, for instance a corporal or sergeant

No. 8 Temperate Combat Dress – this replaced the Nos. 5 and 9 Dress, in what is known as the Personal Clothing System (PCS). It is based around a Multi-Terrain Pattern (MTP) windproof smock, a lightweight jacket and trousers with a range of ancillaries such as thermals and waterproofs

NSP – Normal Safety Procedure

OP – Observation Post

GLOSSARY

PCS – Personal Clothing System: the new uniform for the British military phased in after 2011

Phosphorous smoke bombs – a smoke bomb that spreads quickly, burning white phosphorous and creating a dense cloud of concealment

PLCE – Personal Load Carrying Equipment: the current tactical webbing system of the British Armed Forces

Pressel switch – a switch operated by a push-button, usually hanging from a wire and used especially on radios and other communication equipment

PRR – Personal Role Radio: small transmitter–receiver radio that enables soldiers to communicate over short distances, and through buildings and walls

PTSD – Post Traumatic Stress Disorder: a condition of persistent mental and emotional stress occurring as a result of injury or severe psychological shock

RPG – Rocket-Propelled Grenade

SA80 – semi-automatic rifle made by Heckler & Koch, the standard British Army rifle

SAS – Special Air Service, tasked to operate in difficult and often changing circumstances, within situations that have significant operational and strategic importance

SCO19 – a Specialist Crime & Operations branch within Greater London's Metropolitan Police

Service. The Command is responsible for providing a firearms-response capability, assisting the rest of the service, which is not routinely armed

Sitrep – Situation report

Special Branch – units responsible for matters of national security in the British and Commonwealth police forces

TLDR – Too long, didn't read

Warrior – a series of British armoured vehicles, originally developed to replace the older FV430 series of armoured vehicles

Wolf – a light military Land Rover

YOI – Young Offender Institution, a type of British prison intended for offenders between eighteen and twenty, although some prisons cater for younger offenders from ages fifteen to seventeen, who are classed as juvenile offenders

Chapter 1

Sean Harker saw the danger racing towards them in the headlights.

'Target is fifty – that's five zero—'

'*Brace!*' Sean shouted. He kept his grip on the steering wheel – too late, too dangerous to swerve – and felt the bone-crunching thud run through his body as the Land Rover Wolf hit the pothole. He lurched into his seat belt. In the split second before the engine caught up with the fact that the vehicle had slowed down, Sean had jammed his foot on the clutch, shoved the stick one gear too low and released the clutch again. His foot stayed on the accelerator. The engine howled and the whole vehicle lunged forward, hurling him and a section of seven heavily armed bastards down the streets of night-time Lagos in pursuit of two fleeing terrorist suspects.

'Bloody *hell*, Stenders!' That was Johnny 'Shitey'

Bright, one member of his human cargo clinging on in the back. None of them had belts.

Corporal Joe Wolston, next to him in the front, tugged at his seat belt to loosen its death grip on his body.

'Try not to lose the lads, Harker?' he grunted with all the cool and authority of a man who had faced worse shit than Sean ever had. He tugged the mike of his PRR back towards his mouth and finished his report. 'Target is fifty – that's five zero metres ahead.'

Sean bared his teeth. Even at this speed, the blast of warm tropical night air in his face made sweat trickle down beneath the rim of his domed Mk 7 helmet. He shook his head to keep the drops from stinging his eyes as he fixed them on the swerving tail light of the target ahead. His arms ached from hauling the powerful vehicle round the rubbish heaps, and clapped-out cars, and crowds of Nigerians out to enjoy the city nightlife.

But it felt good. After six months of taking care – looking twice at every shadow in case it contained an insurgent, at every bump in the road in case it concealed an IED – the British Army were now the ones in pursuit. Pity the two guys ahead. If the lads could just catch up with this pair, then they would be on the receiving end of six months' pent-up tension.

And the Wolf was gaining. The two suspects were

on a scooter, and its little putt-putt engine could never compete with a 300Tdi – on the straight and level, that is. Earlier they had tried to make a break down Lagos's A1 highway, and the Wolf had come within metres of them. Then they had veered off onto a side road, and the game got harder again. The Wolf had power, but it also had bulk. It couldn't just dance round any obstacles in the way, and it couldn't just go through them, either.

But, Sean told himself as the speedo crept up and the revs crept down, all things considered, a fifty-metre gap swerving about in this traffic stream was pretty fucking good. None of the other lads could have done it. It wasn't the first car chase he had been in, though it was the first where he was the one doing the chasing. He wondered if the cops he had so often led a dance round the North Circular in a wired Beamer or Merc had got as much of a blast as he was getting now.

And speaking of cops, there they were – a fence of flashing blue and red lights racing down the road towards them. Within a couple of minutes the suspects would have to turn off again. Left or right? Sean braced himself, ready to match whichever way they went.

Wolston spoke into the PRR. 'Hound One, what is your position?'

'*On Herbert Macaulay Road, heading south. Estimate*

we are running parallel to your course, probably half a k behind.'

The platoon's other section was in a Wolf like theirs, under the command of Sergeant Phil Adams. Adams's voice was crackly in their ears. PRR was designed to hold platoons together on foot, not coordinate vehicle chases, and the second Wolf must have been right on the edge of the radio's 500-metre range.

'Roger that, Hound One,' Wolston confirmed. 'You going to come and join us?'

'Negative – local int suggests that any moment now your lads are going to hang a left, and then we will converge—'

The scooter's red tail light suddenly ducked off to the left, darting between a bus and an ancient VW Beetle.

'There they go!' Sean shouted. He just managed to bring the speeding two-tonne vehicle round without turning it over. The tyres ground against the road surface, digging into the loose grit and gravel and spitting them behind as the Wolf took to its new course.

'Hound One, that's the players heading towards Herbert Macaulay, ETA one minute. How did you know it would be left?' Wolston asked.

'Local liaison says they'll be heading for Makoko. That is a shanty town – half of it's on stilts over the lagoon.'

Sean filled in the blanks, and coaxed another five

mph out of the engine without being asked. They had to get the suspects before they reached Makoko. A Wolf could never follow a scooter into a town built on stilts.

The Wolf shuddered so much on the bad road that it was like driving into a succession of brick walls, but now its powerful headlamps were close enough to light up the scooter. The next few things happened almost simultaneously. The pillion passenger on the scooter twisted round and raised his right arm in a gesture Sean recognized.

Fuck!

It took all his self-control not to stamp on the brakes or twist the wheel over – following the basic human instinct to avoid death. The windshield in front of his face starred and cracked, and he was squinting at the embedded lump of lead that would have drilled right between his eyes but for the Wolf's armoured glass.

The part of his mind not concentrating on navigating took a moment to realize that the shit had finally got real. In nearly two years of army service – in nearly nineteen years of life – it was the first shot ever fired at Sean in anger. It made a subtle but very important change to their situation. The section was no longer just in pursuit of suspects. It could now reasonably say that it was in danger, and take the appropriate action to defend itself.

'We're taking hits!' Wolston shouted. 'Abort!'

Sean had learned to obey orders quickly – do first and think later. But this order, coming from Wolston of all people, didn't feel right. It surprised him enough to delay him for half a second. And then it was countermanded by a voice that Sean would never disobey in a thousand years.

'*Negative! Keep going!*' Adams bellowed in fury. '*Step up the pace! The more they shake, rattle and roll, the more they'll cling on for dear life and not take pops at anyone. Harker, I want you breaking the fucking land speed record!*'

'Yes, Sergeant!' Sean shouted.

Dimly he realized he had no idea what was happening. The NCOs were disagreeing. People were shooting at him. He did the only thing a soldier can: follow orders and keep going.

He had the brief impression of something heavy swooping in the humid air above him, and suddenly a bright white light from the sky was pinpointing the scooter like a death ray from a skyscraper-busting alien spaceship. Over the roar of the Wolf's engine he caught the *thud-thud-thud* of heli blades.

Shit, the air force were in on this too. *Everyone* was in on it. Sean could almost feel sorry for the suspects.

Almost.

*

The pair had done almost everything right – until they were spotted emerging from a hole cut in the army base fence. They had been round the back, away from the main gate, and had obviously timed it between sentry patrols to give themselves maximum opportunity. But they had done it just as two Wolfs full of British soldiers, a whole platoon of Fusiliers, were coming back from exercise, fully kitted and tooled up.

Two days earlier, insurgents had raided a village between Lagos and Ibadan, less than thirty miles from their present position. Boko Haram were meant to be holed up in the mountains on the other side of the country. The possibility that they were making a comeback – or, worse, that a new force was emerging to replace them – meant that the battalion had been on full alert ever since.

The suspects hadn't had a chance. The chase was on the moment they were clocked.

Commands and responses shot back and forth over the PRR. Adams's speed-up strategy had worked – there was no way the suspects could afford the luxury of firing back *and* keeping hold of their ride at the same time. The heli searchlight still impaled them from above.

'If it looks like they're getting away, ram them,' Wolston ordered.

Sean gripped the wheel a little more tightly and forced extra power out of the engine.

It would be impossible to open fire safely from the Wolf without endangering civilians. The best weapon they could use was the vehicle itself. It wasn't something Sean wanted to do, but it beat being killed.

And then the scooter was barrelling down an alley, piles of rotting rubbish on either side and a wheel-less Toyota partly blocking the way. The Wolf was barely twenty metres behind when the lamps of Hound One swung into the alleyway ahead, silhouetting the players in a neon outline. The suspects were trapped – they weren't going anywhere. As the scooter skidded to a halt, Sean swung the Wolf to a halt across the alley so that their retreat was completely blocked.

The sections were already piling out of the Wolfs, SA80 rifles in their shoulders, ACOG gunsights fixed unerringly on the two suspects' *heads* – a body shot could set off a suicide vest. Only Sean and Tommy Penfold, Hound One's driver, stayed in their places. Sean gripped the wheel, bracing himself for whatever was to come as he clocked the two suspects. Their eyes were wide, their faces stamped with looks of terror. They weren't much more than kids.

The two sections advanced from either direction, with Adams and Wolston at the front. The suspects raised their hands above their heads, resigned to their fates. The scooter toppled over. Sean took in their battered jeans and faded multi-coloured shirts, and stared closely at each upraised hand. They had all heard scenarios of a cornered bomber surrounded by infidels taking the quick way out to Paradise. One little switch concealed in the palm was all it needed.

The driver's shirt clung to his body, damp with sweat, and Sean couldn't see any outline of a suicide vest. But the other one had a backpack and was still gripping the pistol he had used to fire at the Wolf.

Adams grabbed him first and pushed him to his knees, relieving him of the weapon in the same move. The other one was pushed down too, both of them frisked while they kept their hands on their heads. The boys stared wide-eyed at the half-circle of rifles aimed at them.

Adams studied the backpack, then slowly lifted the flap. Sean's fingers tensed on the wheel, which would have made sod-all difference if several pounds of explosive had suddenly gone off. But Adams must have already decided it wasn't a bomb. He barked a harsh laugh, and roughly pulled the pack off the boy's back before turning it upside down. Several round metal objects tumbled out.

Someone shouted, '*Grenade!*'

But only a couple of lads flinched. Most of them

stood their ground, on the basis that their sergeant wouldn't be chucking explosive ordnance around.

Adams shot a withering look at the soldier who had shouted, and stooped to pick up one of the objects. He held it in front of the thief's eyes, then up for everyone to see.

'Insecticide spray,' he said loudly. 'Nice one. First thing they got their hands on that they thought would sell, no questions asked, at the local market. Only' – he rapped the thief on the head – 'it's *British MoD issue insecticide*, you dickhead! Clearly labelled! You know this would instantly be identified as stolen? That you could have only got it from one place in the whole country? Pillock.'

He looked around. 'They're just kids. Chancers.'

The tension in the air evaporated.

Of course, as Sean and everyone knew, being a kid didn't stop you being one of Boko Haram's finest. The extremist group – a constant thorn in the side of the Nigerian Army, which was why the British Army was out here training them – was perfectly capable of sticking an AK-47 Kalashnikov in the hands of a ten-year-old, pointing them at the enemy and telling them to pull the trigger or have their throat cut. But the insecticide was kind of a giveaway. These two were just a pair of opportunists trying to lift supplies from the camp. Local kids, not too bothered about issues of ownership if it helped them get ahead.

A pair of young African Sean Harkers, in fact.

The police sirens were drawing near.

'Wood, Jardim, keep an eye on them,' Adams snapped. 'We'll hand them over to the local plod when they show up.' He jerked his head at Wolston, summoning him to one side. 'So, Joe,' he said with quiet intensity. 'Abort? What the fuck was that all about? You've been fired at before, for Christ's sake. Did you abort then?'

Sean couldn't help earwigging. Now he'd had time to breathe and think, he reckoned that abort command had been uncharacteristic. Wolston had served with distinction in Afghanistan and had the Military Cross to prove it.

'No, I did not,' Wolston said hotly, 'because in Afghanistan I was allowed to shoot back. Rules of Engagement, Sergeant – they were taking wild potshots with a popgun. It didn't justify responding with half a doz SA80s.'

'Hmm.' Adams grunted and looked at him sideways, then patted him on the shoulder. 'Your hot seat, your call. Just remember that the key word in the Rules of Engagement is still *engagement*. These ones were innocent. Doesn't mean the next ones will be. And I see the popgun still scored a hit.'

He ran his fingers over the starred glass and stared down at Sean. 'Bit of a first for you, Fusilier. How are you feeling?'

Sean still had adrenalin pumping through his system. 'Just fucking grateful for armoured glass, Sergeant,' he said.

Adams grinned. 'Excellent. I always appreciate a straight, honest answer. And it won't be the last time someone takes a shot at you.'

He turned away and addressed both sections. 'We'll wait here until the cops show up, then proceed back to base in convoy. And just in case you're all thinking tonight has had a happy ending, think on this . . .' He had his hands on his hips, and a flat grin that always meant he was being deadly serious. 'Thanks to this little op, word will be out all around Lagos that two sections of the Royal Regiment of Fusiliers are on the edge of Makoko and will now be heading back to their base, so if anyone fancies having a pop, now's their chance. And once we're back on base, don't any of you lot think that, just because we're going home in twenty-four hours, tomorrow's going to be any easier. Not a chance!'

Chapter 2

The canteen was full of chat and unfamiliar faces. Sean shuffled along the breakfast queue, with Bright close behind him.

He snuck a look at all the newbies. Everyone was in the same khaki T-shirts and PCS trousers – the multi-terrain pattern of light greens and greys – but somehow you could spot the ones who hadn't spent half a year in a tropical climate. He guessed he must have looked that fresh in his own first week.

After a six-month tour in Lagos Sean's battalion had already handed over to its replacement and departed for home – all except for Nine Platoon, who were the ones chosen to stay behind and complete the transition. Their job was to show the newcomers the ranges and the training areas, introduce them to the locals, hand the camp over – and go out with them on their first patrol. Sean's own experience had told him that it was one thing poncing around on Salisbury Plain pretending there were insurgents behind every bush; it was another out here, where Boko Haram really were an issue.

'Back in Tidworth tomorrow,' Sean said. 'I almost miss it. Apparently there's a heatwave hitting back home.'

'Mate, Tidworth is the place God would put the tube if he gave Salisbury Plain an enema,' Bright said as he dumped his plate down to receive a double helping of scrambled eggs. 'Roll on Tenerife!'

Which was where they expected to be the day after the day after tomorrow. The lads had a lot of leave piled up and a lot of dosh in the bank, and they were putting it to the best possible use. Forget the UK's heatwave – this would be the real thing, and none of Nigeria's tropical crap, either, with its summer rainy season and mosquitoes and flies and humidity. Nothing but sun, sea, señoritas and other things starting with S that Sean had been looking forward to for the last six months.

They took their breakfasts and sat down at the nearest table. They had both gone for the full English – sod the heat, there were traditions, and they would need the energy because they both knew that Adams hadn't been lying about today.

One thing that Sean had liked about Bright from

the start was his attitude to food. It was for eating, not talking. So, as they concentrated on throwing their breakfast down their necks, it took them a moment to clock the new kid standing nearby.

'Can I . . . ?' The kid indicated the seat next to them with his tray.

Sean just grunted in a way that said 'Sure', so the lad slid his tray down next to him.

'So, you guys were in that bust last night?'

Sean and Bright exchanged glances. *Uh-oh, talker.*

'Listen . . . can you help me out? I could really do with some guidance. You know, from the guys who know.' The kid seemed to be concentrating on Bright, maybe because he was obviously the older of the two.

Bright wiped his mouth and glanced at Sean. 'Mind if I take this one?'

Sean gave a *Go-ahead* wave, his mouth still full.

'Always buy them a drink first, only give your phone number if you're serious, and no means no.'

'Heh. Sure. No, I meant about . . . out here.'

Bright burped with a force that gave Sean and the kid fresh partings. 'You missed the orientation lectures?'

'Well, no, but . . . there's always a shortcut, isn't there? And there's always older, wiser guys who know it. Help me get on the inside track, lads?'

Sean and Bright looked at each other again, for half a second longer. Sean hid a smile as Bright regarded the kid thoughtfully.

'OK. You got all that stuff about malaria? And about taking the anti-malarials, for a start?'

'Uh – sure. The mosquito bites you and then injects parasites into you as it drinks your blood. The parasites multiply inside you. You get a fever, then you feel sick, then you get the squits and start throwing up. And it can come back again at different times throughout your life. And the anti-malarials? One a day, without fail. And you keep on taking them for weeks after you get back, because the malaria parasite stays in your blood-stream.' The kid looked pleased with himself.

'Correctamundo.' Bright nodded in approval. 'But what they don't tell you is, they're only fifty per cent effective.'

'Eh?' The kid looked sideways from Bright to Sean, not sure if he was being ragged.

Sean thought he should help. 'Maybe seventy-five per cent?' he said.

Bright shrugged. 'Maybe. It's all in the DNA. But the thing is, antibiotic resistance. Every year they're less and less effective, and the MoD always lags behind the rest of the health industry. There's defence cuts, and there's health cuts, so we're on the receiving end of two sets of cuts, for double the pleasure. True fact. But despair not, Grasshopper.' He pulled a blister pack from his pocket and popped one of the blue doxycycline tablets onto the table top. 'Thing is, you have to increase absorption through the mouth membranes. In other words, chew it well and good, don't just swallow it straight down.' He popped it into his mouth, and Sean heard crunching as his jaws worked together.

Sean kept his face straight and followed suit with a pill of his own. He chucked it straight down his throat and ground his teeth, though he couldn't produce the same sound effects as his mate.

The kid looked from one to the other, then took out his own blister pack, popped a tablet and crunched his teeth down on it. His face twisted in revulsion and he almost gagged. 'Christ, that's disgusting!'

Sean and Bright hooted and bumped fists over the table. The kid glared at them.

'Mate.' Sean shook his head and cheerfully went back to hacking up a sausage. 'Can't believe you fell for that one.'

'OK.' Bright put his serious face on. 'Inside-track lesson number one: pay attention in your briefings, try and learn something new every day, and work things out with your mates so that you're all equally proficient. And don't listen to what anyone says in the canteen at breakfast. As for the pills – like they say, take one a day and keep doing it, and you'll be fine. Malaria free. But swallow them whole because, as you now know, they taste like crap.' Bright grinned. 'Plus, doxycycline is good for all kinds of other shit too. Like zits. That's why Harker's skin is so silky smooth you just want to rub your face against it.'

'And STDs,' Sean added, giving Bright the finger, 'which is why Bright no longer wakes us all up with his groans whenever he takes a midnight slash.'

'Shit, yeah.' Bright pulled a face. 'That was not fun.'

He tapped the kid's plate where his breakfast – a small helping of eggs and a couple of sausages – was slowly going cold. 'And eat up. Get second helpings. You're going to need plenty of energy on patrol.'

'It's a twenty-k tab,' the kid said. 'I read the briefing. I can *run* twenty k on this.'

Sean grinned. OK, so the kid was a cocky tosser. Let him learn.

'Twenty k *wading through a swamp*,' Bright said. 'Think two or three times the effort you'd need normally. Plus tropical heat, sweat, every malarial mosquito you could ever hope to meet . . . and, you know, the possibility that reports of Boko Haram insurgents might actually be real.'

'Boko Haram are stuck up in the mountains,' the kid said. 'They're defeated. I read that.'

Bright shook his head. 'Jesus, it's like I'm talking another language.'

The kid looked puzzled and Sean had to fill him in.

'This is a free country, mate. So insurgents can jump on a train and get from one side to another, just like you and me back home. And they don't wear T-shirts saying *Proud to Be a Fundie, Die Infidel*. They look like anyone else. So, sure, BH might officially be over *there*. Just that some of them are over *here*. Right beside you. Looking at you.'

Bright made cross hairs out of his fingers, and squinted through them across the table at the kid with one eye closed. 'And they're thinking, *Ooh, I'll have that one*,' he said. 'That's what we're getting into in' – he checked his watch – 'fifty-three minutes' time.'

'Right . . .' The kid thought for a moment, then pushed his chair back and took his plate to the canteen for an extra helping.

Chapter 3

The dark brown water of the mangrove swamp came up to Sean's knees and swirled in big, lazy whirlpools with every step. The light colours of his MTP trousers were stained dark by the water and the rotting leaves that floated on top.

Something particularly powerful bubbled around his knees. Oily water splashed up his legs and a smell like Satan's diarrhoea hit his nose. He caught the muffled gasp of disgust from the soldier he had been paired with. It was the kid from the canteen, whose name he had learned was Private Cooke. The patrol was meant to be silent, and if an NCO's finely tuned ears had caught it, then Cooke would be in for a bollocking.

Sweat dripped into Sean's eyes and he gave his head a firm shake to clear them. It was the only way that didn't involve taking your hands off your weapon, and sometimes it could look like the whole platoon were coming down with nervous twitches. Which would probably look funny to a civilian, but Sean had long since stopped caring what civilians thought.

He took a firmer hold of his SA80A2 assault rifle and pressed on.

The two platoons patrolled side by side, Nine Platoon and the new lot. Ruperts – what the rest of the world called officers – at the front, sergeants at the back and other ranks in between. Sean's peripheral vision kept a fix on Bright's back as the patrol waded further down the channel, keeping his distance – not so close as to ram his mate up the arse and not so far away as to leave a fatal gap in the patrol's strength. And meanwhile he scanned the vegetation on either side for signs of danger. As a kid growing up in the crappiest parts of London, Sean had learned to pay attention to his environment at a very early age. The slightest thing out of place or unexpected could be a clue – a sign of an imminent ambush or attack. He hadn't lost the habit in the jungle. You no longer looked at buildings and lampposts and shadowy corners. You looked at the vegetation, the nearness of the trees, the thickness of the undergrowth around you.

The swamp was a maze of water channels between tangled clusters of trees and roots. Hundreds of square miles of water with God knew what floating about in it and rotting leaves underneath. Kamikaze mozzies that zipped past your head like rounds – and felt like one when they landed – and the certain knowledge that two or three leeches would have attached themselves to you as you waded through the water.

An endless stretch of trees provided enough shade and shadow to hide a regiment of insurgents brave enough to try an attack. They just had to hope that two platoons' worth of British Army would make them think twice.

The SA80A2 carried by each lad was the finest infantry rifle known to man. Below the helmets, cam cream was smeared randomly on their faces to break up the shine of human skin so that they could blend into any background. The upper halves of their bodies were wrapped in PLCE webbing that held ammunition, bayonet, food, CamelBaks of water, cooking equipment, communications equipment and other essentials for an introductory twelve-hour patrol.

And under it all were the bits the insurgents would never see but which made the swamp bearable. The British Army's PCS clothing took even more care of you than your mum had. Every lad on the patrol wore anti-microbial underpants and knee-length socks. The anti-microbial component meant that they could be worn for days on end without turning your private parts and feet into fungal plague zones. Even if they didn't keep the leeches out.

Up ahead, the three officers – Nine Platoon's Second Lieutenant Franklin, the new platoon's Lieutenant Hanson, and the Nigerian liaison, Captain Kokumo – turned a corner and started to clamber up the side of the bank. The rest of the lads swung after them and, two by two, the patrol gratefully left the water behind. Now that they were out of the swamp Sean felt himself relaxing – and immediately made himself pay even more attention to his surroundings. A false sense of security might be the last sense of security you ever had.

The more or less solid ground beneath their feet was not much more than a sandbar, but as they walked, it spread out on either side, becoming firmer as the trees thinned out. What at first looked like an animal trail through the trees was turning into something more. It was still lined with trees, but it was wider and straighter than before. The ground was getting harder. Just as Sean realized that it was a track, kind of, the broken but regular shapes of a ruined village started to emerge from the undergrowth.

Orders rattled back down the line. A wave of snaps and clicks ran through them as selector levers on weapons were flicked from safety to single shot. Sean brought his rifle smoothly up to nestle in his shoulder, caressing the smooth plastic of the pistol grip, the front pad of his index finger resting lightly on the trigger, both eyes wide open with an unblinking stare to take in both the natural view and the enhanced view through the ACOG clamped to the top of the weapon.

The patrol advanced slowly, weapons fanning from side to side.

The village had once been in a clearing. There had been streets of mud-brick houses, single storey, pale yellow walls, with low roofs of corrugated iron. Now the trees had half reclaimed it – which made it twice as dangerous. Two different environments where insurgents could lurk and plot their ambushes. Two different skill sets required for smoking them out.

The platoons broke into their sections, each taking a different part of the deserted village to check out. Wolston's section got a group of houses on the edge that had been half retaken by the trees. He led Sean, Lance Corporal Marshall, Bright, Mitra, Burnell and West over, communicating with the sign language that they had learned to read fluently. They paired up – Sean and Bright, Marshall and West, Burnell and Mitra – and each couple approached their designated hut, eyes peeled for any movement inside the dark, empty windows, or any other sign that someone had been here recently. Wolston joined up with Mitra and Burnell, and gave the signal. Each pair burst into their hut, rifle butts in their shoulders and fingers on triggers, ready for whatever was waiting.

Sean found himself staring at a tangled mass of leaves and branches advancing through the opposite wall. Branches and roots didn't have to try very hard to worm their way through the mud bricks, and the sheets of rusty iron on the roof had been casually pushed aside.

The single-room interior didn't take long to scan. Flaky mud walls, an earth floor, a cracked bathtub, debris blown in from the jungle. Signs to look for were disturbances in the soil or the leaves, or anything that looked like it had been moved or not been there as long as the rest. After a couple of seconds Sean and Bright felt they could relax – a fraction. But they didn't give the all-clear for their hut until they had checked out the invading jungle at the back for any signs of cut wood, or branches running the wrong way. They had experience of lurking in the undergrowth, bare metres away from an enemy (usually another platoon) that was looking for them, so there was no reason the local branch of Boko Haram shouldn't have developed the same skill.

But there was no one there.

With two platoons at work it didn't take long to declare the place clear, section by section. They rendezvoused in the open area at the front of the village. It had stood right at the edge of the mangrove swamp, on the shores of a saltwater lake which Sean's sense of direction told him must join up with the sea somewhere to the south. The waters of the lake lapped at the foot of a small, sharp bank. The rotting remains of a wooden jetty – not something anyone would want to trust their weight to – stuck out into the water. A couple of long, thin boats had been pulled up and left upside down to protect them from the rain – but not from the termites. The hulls were half eaten. One had a football-sized hole in it; the other just looked like it might collapse if anyone breathed on it. The ground had once been dry, beaten earth, kept free of vegetation by the feet of the people of the village. Now it was knee-high grass.

At the signal from Franklin, everyone sat down on the ground. He gave them all a minute to chug down half a litre of water from their CamelBaks, then gave the nod to Captain Kokumo.

'So.' Kokumo stood at ease in front of both platoons. 'You're wondering why we're here? I wanted you to see what our country is up against. What do you think cleared this place out, almost overnight?'

A hand went up from one of the new guys. 'Boko Haram, sir?'

Kokumo gave a smile to let him down gently, but it

didn't reach his eyes. He left it to the NCOs to indicate by silent glares that Private Pillock ought to pay more attention in briefings.

'Boko Haram were a powerful military force in the north-east of the country, but this far south they can only send small groups on small operations. A bomb here, an ambush there. Not good, no, but also not enough to clear out an entire community. Anyone else?'

And Sean suddenly realized, to his surprise, that he knew the answer. He had paid attention in the MO's lectures. He put up his hand.

'Disease, sir?'

'Disease,' Kokumo confirmed with a nod. 'To be precise, cholera. The people here grew complacent. This is a malarial zone, and they knew how to deal with that. You sleep inside nets soaked in insecticide, you make sure no stagnant water accumulates where the mosquitoes can breed, and you can reduce the risk of malaria right down. But then you forget that there are other diseases out there too. Such as cholera, which comes from drinking water contaminated by human faeces, so really ought to be easy to avoid. The cause of death is severe diarrhoea which can lead to fatal dehydration within hours – and is impossible to treat without the right drugs, because even drinking clean water will make you vomit it straight up again.'

He gestured around them. 'This used to be a thriving fishing village, home to a couple of hundred people. A comfortable living, all things considered. But they forgot to keep their water clean. They forgot to keep their drinking water and waste water separate. It only takes a small contamination.'

He swept them all with a grave look. 'The phone lines were down due to a storm. The roads were blocked by fallen trees. There was no way of calling for help apart from going and getting it. It took forty-eight hours after the first recognized case for medics to arrive. By then it was too late.'

The platoons were quiet while the reality of an entire village population being destroyed over two days sank in. Sean tried to picture it. A village hit so badly they couldn't do anything to save themselves, while they vommed and shat themselves to death.

Shit. A few bad bugs could do in days what terrorists dreamed of doing in years.

'This place symbolizes everything that can so easily go wrong here,' Kokumo went on. 'One small slip, and an unforgiving environment is poised to strike. Someone once said that the price of liberty is eternal vigilance. And that is what we do, and *why* we do what we do . . .'

The pep talk went on. It was a good introduction to

the realities of life here. Sean's own introduction had been a patrol of the Lagos slums. The same lessons had been learned. Eternal vigilance.

Boko Haram were officially defeated – at least, the president said so, which was what made it official – but that was absolutely no reason to let go. With their scorched-earth tactics BH had displaced two million people, clearing whole communities – attacking at night, then murdering, raping, kidnapping and looting before pulling out again. Military operations with a new, improved, de-corrupted army and the help of several hundred South African mercenaries had pushed them back.

But they were still there, lurking in the mountains on the border with Cameroon.

Sean understood the comparison with disease. One little slip-up, one moment taking your eye off the ball, and back in the shit you went.

It concentrated the mind.

Finally, with the talk over, and with the area checked out, the stage everyone had been waiting for could go ahead. The stripping off and de-leeching.

Sean wasn't a leech-virgin but the little buggers still made him shudder. On his first jungle patrol he had innocently assumed that none of them had got him because he had kept his trousers tucked into his boots and hadn't felt anything. Then the trousers came off, just to be sure – and there were four of the tossers, three on one leg and one on the other. When they bit you, they injected a natural anaesthetic, so you didn't feel your life blood being glugged by vampire slugs.

Ravi 'Kama Sutra' Mitra, nineteen years old and the second-youngest member of the platoon, was humming 'YMCA' as he pulled his T-shirt over his head. They caught each other's eyes and grinned. Mitra turned round. 'Check me out, Stenders?'

No one could see their own back, so Sean checked that Mitra was leech-free there and Mitra returned the favour. The rest of Sean got off more lightly this time. When he got his trousers off, he found only two of the sneaky bloodsucking fuckers clinging to his thigh. They were easily dealt with, once you knew how.

You didn't just yank them off. They got revenge for an interrupted meal by leaving their mouthparts embedded in your skin, ready to go rancid. Leeches attached themselves to you at both ends, but only the front end – the little end – was actively blood-sucking. Both ends were fastened with suckers. Sean pressed his finger against his skin next to the front end of leech number one and slid his fingernail sideways. The gentle pressure detached the slug, and its mouthparts slid smoothly out of him, immediately followed by a gush of red blood. As well as natural anaesthetic, the leeches also injected a decoagulant to keep the blood flowing freely. The wound would have to wash itself out under its own pressure before the blood flow dried up.

With the front end sorted, Sean quickly did the same to the rear of the leech, the fat end, before the front could re-attach itself. He let it fall to the ground and then concentrated on removing its friend. It wasn't going anywhere very quickly – certainly not fast enough to escape the Vengeance of Sean.

Which came as soon as the second leech had fallen to the ground, and a size-eleven army boot could splat down on both of them from above. Sean's blood shot out in thin jets under the tread.

'Two down, only umpteen billion to go,' Mitra said cheerfully.

'Hey, if we don't stop them here, next thing they'll be back home, stealing our jobs, taking our women . . .'

'*Oh, fucking hell!*'

Tommy Penfold was standing in just his shorts and boots, with the front of his shorts pulled out, staring down at what he had found there.

'Oh, sweet Jesus Christ!' He swung towards Sean, still with one hand keeping his shorts firmly away from the rest of his body. 'Stenders! Look!'

Sean held up his hands. 'No offence, Penny – I

know it's been a long time for both of us, but you're just not my type.'

'I . . .' The colour had drained from Penfold's face. 'I just put my hands in there to pull it out and, you know, take a slash . . .'

'Yeah?' Sean couldn't help grinning, and he was not the only lad to crane his neck and peer at what Penfold was trying to show them.

'Shit, Penny, what are you going to call it?'

'Aw, it found a little friend!'

'Identical twin, I'd say . . .'

'Can't blame it for forming an attachment, can you?'

'Guys, what should I do?' Penfold begged. 'You all heard the MO say you shouldn't pull it off.'

'Yeah, but what about the leech?' someone inevitably asked.

But Penfold had a point. If it didn't respond to the method Sean had used – and no one was going to try it apart from Penfold himself – then dousing it in mozzie repellent or touching it up with the tip of a lit cigarette was agreed to be the best way. Cue half the platoon, smokers and non-smokers alike, fighting for the privilege of puffing a fag inches away from the Penfold family jewels.

Sean left them to it. He needed a piss so he pulled his

trousers back on and headed off to the nearest broken-down mud-brick hut, where a pile of rusted empty oil drums gave some privacy without completely blocking off the view. With a happy sigh he let go a stream of urine, aiming at an insect that was crawling up the wall, knocking it down to the ground and harassing it as it scuttled towards the shelter of the drums.

The stream hosed off a camouflaging layer of earth, and Sean was suddenly staring at an electric cable that disappeared into the ground.

The urine came to a stop, and the bug took advantage of the ceasefire to disappear. Sean stood very still, and felt his dick and balls withdraw into his abdomen.

Cables in the ground only meant one thing, in his experience. He'd had the briefings and seen the pictures . . .

An IED – the weapon of choice of insurgents in Afghanistan and Iraq and other places where they'd rather just blow you up at a distance than come out and fight like a gentleman. Somewhere between a bomb and a mine, it could be disguised as any old thing, or just buried out of sight, ready to be triggered by any disturbance or a signal from a nearby operator. They could blow the legs off anyone who walked on them, or send a vehicle flying, or spray red-hot supersonic fragments of metal in a circle around them, cutting down personnel like a lawnmower over grass.

So Sean was very probably standing next to an unknown quantity of explosive. Which could go off at any moment.

Chapter 4

But Sean couldn't stand there for ever. He very cautiously glanced over his shoulder. No one was looking in his direction – no one whose attention he could grab. He didn't want to shout and wave. If the device had an operator in the vicinity who realized they were twigged, they might just set it off.

Was anything he did going to make it go bang? He scanned the ground all around him, swivelling his hips to get the best view of any tripwires or pressure switches covered with leaves or painted to match the colour of the grass.

But there wasn't anything.

So he very slowly walked backwards, stepping – as close as possible – in exactly the same places he had stepped on to reach this spot, careful not to knock anything with his boots.

He kept going backwards for several metres. Then

he turned and hurriedly walked towards Adams, the other NCO and the three officers, who were in conversation. He tried for quick but casual, which meant that he felt like someone had shoved a broom handle up his arse.

That would certainly explain why his butt cheeks were clenching like they were.

Sean didn't bother waiting to be excused. In the field you didn't salute or stand on ceremony; if you had important news, then you didn't wait politely to be noticed. He addressed Franklin directly.

'I think I've found an IED, boss.'

Their easy smiles quickly faded into something harder.

No one said anything like *Are you sure?* because no soldier was going to piss about making up jokes about bombs.

'Whereabouts?' Franklin asked.

Sean indicated with his head, not looking round. 'Pile of cans at two o'clock, sir. Look old and rusty, but one of them has what looks like brand-new cable going . . . somewhere.'

'Shit.' Franklin angled his head slightly to peer past Sean. The other two officers subtly shifted position to look themselves, without making it obvious to any watchers.

'Well, if we were under observation, they'd have set it off by now,' said Kokumo after a moment.

'True,' Franklin said. 'Or they could just be off having a slash, or they could have bugged out weeks ago and just left this for us . . .' He looked at the other Rupert. 'Do you have anyone trained in EOD, Neil?'

Hanson shook his head. 'No one experienced enough yet – though if we're going to start getting these things, we'll have to do something about that.' He looked like he had just chewed down on something bitter. 'I believe it was my lads responsible for checking that area. We will have . . . words. Later.'

But no one was throwing blame about at present.

'Cross that off as an option, then,' said Franklin. 'Captain Kokumo, sir – any recommendations?'

Kokumo spread his hands in a big shrug. 'Your men, your decision, Lieutenant. For what my opinion's worth, calling in for a heli will take time, and maybe alert the insurgents.'

'If it's a typical device, sir,' Adams said, 'it'll be a homemade, low explosive, or an ANFO main charge with a high-explosive primer. Rigged to go off if it's disturbed.'

If it's a typical device. Sean felt it was a big *if.* Because they were improvised, knocked together by whatever the insurgent had to hand, no two IEDs were alike – which made them hard to spot and even harder to dispose of, since there was no standard factory plan for an EOD expert to work with.

But Franklin seemed happy to go with it. 'So let's disturb it.'

He passed on his instructions. The two NCOs nodded, and strolled casually over to their men. Then Franklin gave the signal and the sergeants burst into life.

'*Stand to! Grab your helmet and weapon and get over to the water's edge, right now!*' Adams clapped his hands together and bellowed into the faces of any men who were caught by surprise at the sudden outburst of activity. '*Chop chop! Shift your arses!*'

The other sergeant was doing the same with his men. This being the army, there was even a slight feeling of competition to see which platoon could be in place first. Whatever the risk of being horribly maimed or killed by a terrorist device, honour was honour.

Sean hurled himself down at the edge of the water, just below the bank. For half a second he felt safe. If the thing went off now, thirty metres away, he would be protected by the earth.

But the point wasn't to be safe. He wriggled into position, poking his head above the earth and bringing his rifle to the ready as the other platoon pelted towards him. His heart pounded enough to lift his body slightly off the ground with each beat as he squared the pile of drums in the centre of his ACOG. He had to take some deep breaths to slow it down. He couldn't afford to have his aim put off.

If it went off, he told himself, he would only notice it *after* the bang. And the memory would mean he had survived. If it went off and a piece of red-hot debris skimmed horizontally across the ground, precisely aimed at the small gap between the earth and the rim of his helmet . . .

Well, he wouldn't feel a thing.

One minute later both platoons, still in various states of undress, were lying along the bank. Their feet trailed in the lake, their bodies were shielded by ground and only their heads stuck up above the bank.

'On my command,' Adams ordered in a voice that carried all along the line. 'Target is pile of oil drums next to the house at two o'clock. Platoons will fire continuous three-round bursts until told to stop or until . . . Well, you'll know when to stop.'

Sean set his rifle's fire selector to automatic, and centred the drum he had just been pissing against in the middle of the ACOG.

'Aim . . . *fire!*'

Sean squeezed the trigger.

The rifle bucked in his hands, and the crackle of thirty other weapons roared through the jungle and sent birds shrieking up from the trees. Streams of NATO standard ammunition converged on the drums, and for half a second they began to crumple under the withering fire—

BLAM.

The blow was like a simultaneous slap in the face and a thump with cupped hands over both ears. The drums vanished in a flash of smoke, converted by the explosion into a rain of lethal shrapnel that was meant to cut the soldiers down where they stood. Sean buried his face in the dirt as the metal slashed through the air above his head, though he knew the basic laws of physics meant that if you could hear it, you had already survived it. The mud bricks of the surrounding huts simply disintegrated where they stood, shocked by the explosion into a cloud of dirt.

Sean raised his head, looking at the small crater and the circle of scorched grass. He knew that everyone around him would be thinking, *That could have been me going up in smoke . . .*

Franklin was already on his feet. 'Sergeant Adams. Have the men get their kit on, ready to move in two,' he ordered.

The NCOs rattled off the orders to the men and they started to get ready. No time for self-congratulations or catching up. That could come later.

Sean and Bright shrugged their PLCE back on and checked their rifles. The debrief would come back at base; until then only a few people knew what role Sean had just played in the excitement. No one liked a gobby blowhard. Best to leave the big reveal to the officers.

'After the big bang, back to leech city central,' said Bright. 'And twenty-four hours till Tidworth. Christ, bring it on.'

'What, enema ground zero for Salisbury Plain?' Sean asked, remembering what Bright had said earlier.

'Mate, my opinion of Tidworth hasn't changed,' Bright said. 'But I'll take it over leeches and malaria and IEDs. C'mon.'

He gave his weapon a final check and went to join the others.

But Sean took his own last look back at the lake beyond the village, and thought about his time in Nigeria.

Weird.

He was going to miss it.

OK. Six months of tropical sweltering, and then someone had tried to kill him twice in the space of twenty-four hours – though it hadn't been personal in either case. The country had still expanded his view of the world by about a thousand per cent.

But still, he thought as he held his rifle at the ready and slouched into place with the rest of the platoon, there was no place like home.

Chapter 5

Tuesday 1 August, 23:00 GMT+1

'It's got *music*,' Bright whispered. 'And *light*. And *soft seats*. And – fuck me, Stenders, it's so *beautiful!*' He choked on a sob.

'Piss off,' Sean murmured as they shuffled their way down the aisle of the Boeing 777. They pushed past civvy passengers who were trying to jam bags into the overhead lockers.

It might not have been his smartest move to let the lads know he had never flown on a civilian plane before. They'd been taking the piss ever since.

At least he'd kept quiet about not liking flying in the first place.

The flight out to Nigeria – his first time outside the British Isles, and his first flight anywhere – had been in a giant army C-17 Globemaster. The Globemaster was a cargo plane, the nearest thing real life got to the latest *Call of Duty*, designed to shift tanks and other heavy ordnance around the world. When it carried people, they just bolted rows of seats down the middle of the hold. In-flight entertainment was your iPhone or a book, or a pack of cards.

But Nine Platoon's reward for staying on for the extra handover week was that they could go home by CivvyAir or, to be more precise, the scheduled British Airways flight from Murtala Muhammed International Airport, Lagos, to London Heathrow. It flew through the night, departing 23:00, arriving 06:00, with no jet lag as Nigeria was almost due south of the UK. The platoon were flying home in two halves: Wolston's section today and the rest tomorrow.

Sean intended to make the most of it. A database of movies, comfortable seats, cabin crew who had to be nice to you, and pilots – he hoped – who treated passengers like humans, not hardware, should take his mind off the fact that he was still suspended in a steel tube five miles above the ground.

The lads were scattered around the cabin – Sean wasn't sure if that was a security measure or just how it went down at check-in. Wolston was a few rows down, in the central block of seats between a couple of Africans. Chewie West – so called for his phenomenal porn-star sideburns and moustache – was almost at the very back, and somehow the lucky sod had snagged a couple of hot girls all to himself. Sean was in a window seat near the front.

He wriggled around to get comfortable. Definitely better than the Globemaster flight from Brize. He wondered if civilian planes also rattled and shook like they were a washing machine and the passengers a load of dirty boxers, or did BA do it more smoothly?

Bright settled into his seat in the row behind. 'All right, Stenders? Just remember, if it all gets too exciting you can ask a stewardess to read you a story.'

Sean silently held up a finger for Bright to see, and kept it there until he remembered he was also giving it to the rest of the cabin. So he turned his attention to the flat LCD screen on the back of the seat in front of him, and started to explore the options of the in-flight entertainment system.

'*Salaam*,' said a voice. A young African man in a traditional white agbada robe and round cap was looking down at him. The guy squinted at his boarding pass and the seat numbers above them. 'Nineteen B. This must be me.'

'Reckon it must,' Sean agreed. There wasn't much else to say. The dangling hem of the guy's sleeve brushed annoyingly against Sean's face as he put his bag in the locker. Then he sat down, gathering the many folds of his robe around himself. Sean went back to the screen menu. *Bloody hell. So many movies, so little time to watch them all . . .*

And so Sean and his neighbour didn't exchange any further words until a couple of hours after take-off when the cabin lights had been turned down. It was oh two hundred and he should get some kip, he thought – snatch a few hours to be ready for the rest of the day after they landed. He leaned forward to find the complimentary pillow in the seat pocket in front of him, and became aware that his African neighbour was looking at him.

'*Salaam*,' the guy said again. 'It seems rude to travel next to you and never even greet you. Okwute.' He held out his hand.

'Uh. Sean.' Sean held out his and they shook.

Okwute regarded him with his head slightly cocked, like Sean presented him with an interesting puzzle. His accent was somewhere between London and Lagos.

'You are young for a diplomat or businessman, and I saw you in Departures with a group of similar young men, all your sort of age with very similar short hair-cuts. So I deduce you are a soldier.'

Sean immediately tensed up. It wasn't like he was travelling undercover or anything. It was just drummed into you that you didn't make your affiliation public.

Okwute smiled slightly, maybe sensing his alarm. 'It

is no secret that the British Army are in Nigeria to train our own against Boko Haram.'

'Well.' Sean shrugged. 'You're welcome.'

'As are you, fighting our common enemy. They are an insult to Islam. They murder innocents and force children to join their army. At least you had a choice about joining yours. Do you believe in your cause?'

Sean had his pillow. He wedged it between his head and the aircraft hull, and wriggled himself into position against it. If Okwute had any basic brain, he would take the hint.

'I don't really have a cause,' Sean said, and closed his eyes.

'Then why do you fight?'

Sean kept his eyes shut. Somehow he sensed that Okwute was still looking at him, waiting for an answer, and he was never going to get to sleep until the man looked away.

Eventually he opened his eyes and saw that he was right. 'I try not to,' he said.

Okwute nodded as though Sean had passed some kind of test. 'Were you training our army to try not to fight too?'

'No.' Sean pushed his head more firmly against the pillow. 'I guess we jumped straight to the bit after the trying stops. Look, no offence—'

'It is a worthy cause, trying to end conflict peaceably,' Okwute said. 'But if they are prepared to take a human life, a right that belongs only to Allah, and that is wrong, then how are you different in claiming that right for yourself?'

Sean looked away. 'I was—'

He clamped his jaw shut. Fucking hell, he had to be more careful than that! He had been on the verge of blabbing about something that was still marked top secret. The one and only time he had fired a gun to kill someone. That bastard hard man Malcolm. Back in London.

Sean had had him at gunpoint and had told him to stay down. Any sane person would have obeyed. But then the guy had charged him with a knife, and Sean hadn't even thought about firing. At the age of seventeen, Sean Harker had taken his first life. For a moment it all came back to him . . . *Fuck!*

And Okwute saw it, even though he couldn't know the details. His eyes widened by a millimetre. 'You *have* claimed that right!' He didn't seem shocked.

'Look,' Sean told him, 'I just know that if someone's coming at you, or going to kill you, you're justified in fighting back. No one says you started it. You're just the one who ends it.'

He remembered the shots. The gun going off. The

body falling . . . But it had been pure self-defence, and if he hadn't done it, then many more people would have been killed. That knowledge pushed him to keep talking, though a small voice at the back of his head said it would be best to shut up now.

'And the same goes if they're planning on hurting someone else. I see a guy back home beating up a little kid, I step in and stop him. Same thing here, just on a bigger scale.'

'Ah.' Okwute nodded. 'The Just War Hypothesis.'

'No idea what you're talking about, mate,' Sean snapped. God, he wished he was back on the Globemaster. The conversation there had involved rating the shaggability of various soap actresses. *That* had been about his level.

Okwute went on. 'I have a theory that religion is what scientists would call a force multiplier. The good that is put into it comes out better, the bad comes out worse.'

Sean thought of the imam who had cared for the Muslim inmates at Burnleigh Young Offender Institution where he'd done time. He had walked the talk – a decent, straight-up, honest guy, never pushing his beliefs down people's throats, just living up to his calling by caring for people with company and chat and good advice. Or the Salvation Army couple who had lived on Littern Mills where he grew up. They had always been there for his mum whenever she wanted a shoulder to cry on – usually because of her latest boyfriend, or because Sean had done something to upset her. They weren't out for converts and they didn't try to make you follow the rules in their little book. Even the Guyz – Sean's old gang – had left them alone.

'Yeah,' he said, half expecting a catch. 'I'll go with that.'

'And we can all agree that it is a duty to defend the defenceless.'

Sean wasn't sure if that was a question or a statement. 'S'pose.'

'So, what if the defenceless are your brothers and sisters who are prevented by their own government from living out their faith, when their only crime is to point out how their government fails in Allah's eyes? How, to curry favour with powerful Western allies, that government makes itself more and more Western, and then betrays those very Western values by oppressing its own people? Does not sheer hypocrisy fire your blood? Is it not good to fight against that? And if it is, what would give them the right to fight back?'

No one had ever put it quite like that to Sean before – and he wasn't going to let Okwute start now. Maybe he could see where Okwute was coming from.

Sort of. But he wasn't going to reach any kind of answer in the middle of the night when his brain was sluggish and he just wanted to go to sleep. Why wouldn't Okwute just shut up?

Then, suddenly, he became aware of a close, angry presence hanging over them. Sean looked up into Shitey Bright's angry face.

'Bollocks!' Bright spat. 'Total bollocks!'

Chapter 6

'*Salaam*,' Okwute began.

'Don't you salami me, mate!' Bright was standing up so that he could speak over the back of his seat. 'I've been listening to you gobbing at my mate here. The fuck are you on about? "Just war"? I'll tell you what's just, mate. It's blokes like me and Harker here putting our lives on the line to stop the nasty people getting at you, so you're safe and secure behind us to come up with crap theories about how horrible we all are.'

'I would call that very *un*just,' Okwute said.

'Oi, keep it down!' someone called.

Bright swung round. '*You* keep it down!' Back to Okwute. 'You swan around in your poncy bedsheet' – he had just insulted the culture and dress style of half the cabin, but he seemed past caring – 'bleating about your poor defenceless brothers and sisters—'

'Shitey—' Sean began.

'Stenders, mate, let me handle this . . .'

The arguments began to spread. Electronic pings sounded up and down the cabin as call buttons were pressed.

The core of the argument was still Bright vs Okwute. As Bright grew angrier, Okwute just became calmer. Arguing with Okwute was like wrestling with a pillow. If you got a grip on one bit of him, three or four other bits just bulged out.

And suddenly Wolston was there, standing in the aisle, finger outstretched in Bright's face. 'Shut up and sit down.'

'But this guy—'

Wolston snapped his fingers, loud, half an inch from Bright's nose, and pointed again. 'Live with it. Sit. Down.'

In any civilian situation this would have earned Wolston an immediate decking.

But this wasn't a civilian situation. An order was an order, and that was all there was to it. Bright's eyes burned with fury and his face was red, but he slowly subsided.

Wolston returned to his seat, his gaze sweeping around the cabin from lad to lad to reinforce the point. In seconds the noise level had returned to a background murmur. But Sean suddenly realized that the whole thing had neatly identified all the service personnel on the flight. Had that been Okwute's aim all along?

Sean shot his neighbour a sideways look, but the man was now quietly reading a book under his overhead light like nothing had happened. Sean couldn't bring himself to look back at Bright. He'd been a complete plonker.

The best thing would be to revert to plan A and grab some kip. Sean reluctantly closed his eyes again, feeling the vibration of the plane's engines through the foam padding.

But all his other senses had no intention of shutting down. The sneaking suspicion that they had all just made some kind of carefully orchestrated mistake wouldn't go away. He kept going over it all in his mind. He couldn't get over the way Okwute, without raising his voice or asking one leading question, had managed to establish that Sean was in the army, had a low opinion of religious fundamentalists, had killed in the line of duty, believed violence to be acceptable at the right time . . . and had identified every fucking soldier on the plane. Looking back, Sean felt like he'd somehow been played, and he didn't like that one bit . . .

Sean woke up with a sudden jolt, and the feeling of tumbling. The plane was shaking. He sat up abruptly and clutched his seat. Shit, they were falling out of the sky!

Except that they weren't. But creaks and groans ran the length of the fuselage, and passed through his body en route. He had been woken up by the *ping* of the seat-belt sign. He hadn't realized he'd dropped off.

He checked his watch – he had been out for a couple of hours. It must be close on dawn, but the view out of the windows was pitch black. The plane felt like it was rolling sideways into the dark.

A flight attendant saw him looking around in confusion. 'Just turbulence,' she told him as she went past. 'Nothing to worry about.'

Then a flash of light at the window caught his attention. He stared in disbelief as light rippled across the sky below them. Huge columns and layers of cloud, miles across and miles high, were picked out in a white snapshot blaze. Black claws of cloud reached up for them, then suddenly were swallowed by night as the light died away. And then another flash, from a different angle, showing different shapes.

They were flying above a thunderstorm – and a massive one.

Awesome. And terrifying.

That was the moment the cabin lights came back on.

'*Good morning, ladies and gentlemen.*' The voice over the PA was calm. '*As you can see, we're encountering some turbulence and so I have put the seat-belt sign back on. The plane may experience some rocking, but I can assure you it's built to take it. However, I am also sorry to have to inform you that we are no longer landing at London Heathrow.'*

What the fuck? Suddenly everyone was paying attention.

'I can't give you any details other than to say that there are security alerts at various London airports.'

The tension in the cabin was electric.

'We have, however, been cleared to land at London Southend in approximately two hours' time. The turbulence should pass soon, and once it does the cabin crew will be serving breakfast. I will let you have more information as it comes in. Thank you.'

Sean felt a claw gripping him inside. It was the same claw that twisted the guts just before you leaped out of the back of a Warrior, or as you waited in ambush and the enemy drew near . . . Only this time there was no leaping anywhere. No way of getting out. It occurred to him that here on this plane they were not in any sort of control.

Next to him, Okwute had been listening to the announcement without any visible reaction. He pulled his book out of his seat pocket and glanced at Sean.

'We are all in the hands of Allah,' he said with a smile.

It didn't help at all . . .

Chapter 7

'OK, guys, listen up. Here's the deal,' Wolston said. 'We were all supposed to be going home, and going on leave. Now it looks as if we are flying into a bit of an unknown situation. Either in this aircraft, or on the ground.'

Via a mixture of sweet talking, persuasion and the nicest bullying Sean had ever seen, the corporal had managed to get half a dozen civilian passengers to swap seats. Now the whole section were grouped together in a block of centre seats.

'At the moment there's no point trying to guess what's going on. Guessing won't do anyone any good. Just be grateful that we're not diverting further north – or, for that matter, somewhere in Europe. If this was a 9/11 situation they'd just be dropping planes onto the first flat bit of ground they could find.'

'Yeah, but Southend?' Bright said. 'Where the fuck is that anyway?'

'End of the Thames,' Sean told him.

'Oh, right. Your part of the world.'

Sean stared at him. 'Huh?'

'Well, you're from London and that's on the Thames, isn't it?'

Sean took a breath. 'Mate, there is a world of difference—'

'Cut it out,' Wolston said without raising his voice.

'I didn't even know there was an airport at Southend,' said Mitra.

'Well . . . technically . . .' Lance Corporal Marshall was flicking through the airport maps at the back of the in-flight magazine. He held up a page that showed a very simple outline of a single runway and a few buildings. 'I mean, it's got a runway – but it's half the length of the ones at Heathrow.'

This sank in with everyone for a few seconds. Sean didn't know how much runway a 777 needed, but he knew they didn't land vertically, and presumably the runways at Heathrow were that length for a reason.

'Well' – Mitra put a little too much effort into appearing cheerful – 'I hope they checked the brakes before we took off.'

The plane started to shake again as it began its descent and passed deeper into cloud. Wisps of vapour whipped by, and raindrops smeared against the windows. Everyone had been told to stow their tables away and put their seats up, and it seemed to Sean that the people he could see were all sitting a bit straighter than they had to. Only Okwute was still deep in his book.

'*Cabin crew, prepare for landing.*'

The plane began to make new sounds – whines and whirs as bits of it expanded or contracted. Sean jumped as a particularly loud mechanical drone started up, and kept going.

'Just putting out the flaps,' Mitra said next to him. 'So we can fly slow.'

Sean was no expert, but as the noise went on it felt like they must be sticking a hell of a lot of flap out. Even up in the air, he could feel something tugging his body forward as the plane lost speed. They weren't slowing, they were coming to a fucking standstill! Was that normal?

Why couldn't he be doing something easy and relaxing, like wading through swamps and blowing up IEDs? At least you knew where you were with that.

And then they descended below cloud level, and it was like they were underwater. Sean could see the rain driving against the windows. Distant lights were distorted by the drops on the pane. The captain had said they would be coming in over Canvey Island and the estuary, so that had to be London on the left. He couldn't see any billowing clouds of smoke, any explosions, any obvious signs of emergency . . . but from up here, that meant squat. There had been no further update on the situation on the ground, apart from the captain saying he didn't have any further info.

They had to be within range of a signal now, but no one had got their phones out to check the news. No one wanted to put the airline's no-calls rule to the test at this particular moment.

There was the strange sensation of air whistling inside his head as a slightly blocked ear took longer than usual to equalize pressure. And then a massive *thud* made the entire fuselage shake. Sean gripped the arms of his seat so hard that his knuckles went white.

'That was the wheels,' Mitra said. He seemed to have adopted the role of Sean's official plane nanny, though Sean suspected he was just gobbing out to steady his own nerves. Once again Sean wished he'd kept his mouth shut about never having flown in a civvy plane before.

Lights moved past the windows – and Sean realized they were streetlights. Which meant that the plane was really low—

It hit the runway with the sound of machinery pushed right to its limits. Immediately the engine noise doubled, trebled, as they reversed with all the thrust the captain could give them. The deceleration pushed Sean forward in his seat so that the belt tightened around his hips and he had to brace himself against the forward pressure. Behind him he could hear someone throwing up. The plane shook and shuddered. Some loose object, something like a tin can, went rattling down the length of the cabin. *Shit, I hope that wasn't something important.* Rain crashed against the windows, blocking out what little light there was outside.

Sean told himself that it could have been so much worse: the massive plane hurtling down the titchy runway. Not enough room to stop, even with the pilot standing on the brakes. He saw it smashing into whatever was at the end. The fuselage ripped open, fuel splashing out, the plane and everyone in it gripped by an inferno . . .

Oh shit, no. Not fire. Please, not fire. Just let me die instantly.

Sean's personal Room 101 was fire. Always had been, since he was a kid. The gut-twisting, bladder-loosening terror had first struck him when an old guy had accidentally started a fire in a neighbouring flat, and they had had to evacuate . . .

And then the noise was dropping and Sean could feel his butt sliding back into his seat again. The raindrops on the windows were trickling down vertically, no longer blown back by slipstream. And the captain sounded happier than anyone ever had before in announcing:

'*Welcome to Southend, ladies and gentlemen.*'

Wolston had his phone out the moment they touched down.

'Yes, sir,' Sean heard him say. 'This is Corporal Wolston, just landed at Southend with my section en route back from Lagos . . . Uh, yes, sir, I confirm Southend . . . No, sir, nor did I . . .'

Sean was waiting for his phone to warm up and the bars to appear.

'Fuck,' he heard Mitra mutter, staring at his own screen. The good news slowly crept onto Sean's phone.

Major security alert affects Heathrow, Gatwick, Stansted, Luton.

Thousands of passengers delayed.

Threat 'to be taken seriously' in light of Summit, says Home Secretary.

'What Summit?' he asked.
Mitra tapped a link and squinted at the screen.

'Only every head of every Commonwealth government, all in London for a big circle jerk. So, yeah, OK, they're not going to piss around.'

'Right.' Wolston shut off his phone with a grim flick of the wrist. 'I was hoping they could fast-track us through Immigration, but apparently we're not that much of a priority. The adjutant says the minibus that was going to pick us up at Heathrow is en route to Southend, but that will take at least a couple of hours whichever way round the M25 it goes. Till then, we sit tight and go nowhere. And meanwhile, lads, fill your minds with happy thoughts of Tenerife.' He smiled. 'Because everything you've been looking forward to – beaches, warm sea, soft sand, drinking the Playa de Las Americas dry, dancing till dawn, getting laid by numbers' – he paused – 'isn't going to happen. All leave is cancelled.'

Sheer relief at being on the ground, in one piece and in no danger made the passengers talk just that little bit too loudly as they disembarked. Except for the dark, fuming knot of pissed-off Fusiliers who were now trying to push their way to passport control and get through the airport as quickly as possible.

'Fucking leave fucking cancelled,' Bright grumbled. 'It's giving in to terrorism, that's what it is. And this fucking airport is nothing more than a large fucking shed.'

The main airport building was heaving. Sean could see why. Parked up next to their Boeing was another plane of similar size, and presumably it had kicked off the same number of passengers. Further along were a couple of little EasyJet runarounds parked nose-in to the terminal as well. Southend airport wasn't designed for crowds like this.

Passport control was a wide open space divided into twisty lanes heading down to the passport desks at the end, like the entrance to a theme park. The queue for EU passports was almost out of the door. The lane for non-EU passports was almost empty, and the Nigerian contingent from the plane promptly streamed down it.

'Fuck this,' Wolston said. He headed down the non-EU lane after the Nigerians, and gestured for everyone to follow him.

'Shit, Corporal, that's leadership,' Marshall said.

'Learn from the best, Lance Corporal.'

A few paces ahead of him Sean saw Okwute calmly waiting with his passport already open. Otherwise it seemed like the people in the queue hadn't realized they would actually be expected to produce a passport, and had all taken bets to see how deep down in their hand luggage they could bury theirs.

Sean's eyes lingered on the woman going past the passport desk now. Nice action. He had always been a rear-view man. He followed her as she slipped her passport into her bag and headed for the exit door marked BAGGAGE RECLAIM.

And so he saw the way her body language changed – a split second before he saw why. The casual walk came to a sudden jarring halt – and then she took a reflex step backwards as a black-clad arm appeared and shoved her further back into the hall. Sean tensed himself for action, his instinctive response whenever aggro loomed on the horizon – even though she was on the other side of a whole group of people and he couldn't have reached her.

Sean always remembered the next bit in slo-mo. The owner of the arm appeared. A man in black – black trackies, black gloves, black balaclava mask, black webbing around his top half holding spherical HG85 grenades, a pair of white phosphorous smoke bombs, the size and shape of insect spray, and spare curved black magazines – brandishing a black Heckler & Koch MP5, holding the pistol grip in one hand and pointing it at the ceiling. And then it was back to normal speed. With his free hand the guy pulled back on the cocking handle, took hold of the stock and sprayed a half-second burst into the roof. At the same time two other guys with MP5s burst in behind him. The shots roared in the enclosed space, and the echoes faded away into screams and shouts. A baby howled as the first man grabbed a megaphone dangling from his neck.

'*Down on the ground! Now!*'

Chapter 8

Wednesday 2 August, 07:00 BST

The burnt smell of discharged propellant was sharp in Sean's nostrils as he flung himself flat on his stomach. The rest of the section were half a second behind him. When you're caught in the open without a weapon, it's the only place to be. Above them, the great British public screamed and milled about in confusion.

Sean's first instinct had been to reach for his weapon, but it was back in Nigeria. His second had been to bury his face in the worn lino and wait for it all to go away. Which wouldn't achieve anything. So he lifted his head as far as he dared and kept on looking around, while he felt his heart thud beneath him.

There were still some people who couldn't seem to believe that this was real, or were just plain paralysed by fear and shock. They were still up, or sort of crouching halfway down like they were waiting for confirmation of the original order.

Sean found himself beaming willpower at them.

Get down! He said get down and he meant it!

Because people who had got as far as firing live ammo in public weren't doing it for the lulz.

The guy with the megaphone fired another ceiling burst. '*I said down! Now!*'

It was muffled by the mask but it sounded like a bog-standard Essex accent.

The message sank in and the hold-outs let themselves down onto the floor of the hall to join the rest. Meanwhile the lads' bodies were all complying with the gunman's instructions but their minds were in overdrive.

A second gunman was gesturing with his MP5 for the passport staff to come together on the airside with everyone else. The third ran up the side of the hall and stood poised halfway, where he could cover everyone from the flank.

Sean was no expert tactician but he could still see the basic problem. How the fuck were three guys going to secure an area this size? Even three guys with weapons. They could exert control through fear, but if the worst came to the worst they couldn't shoot everyone.

But no civvy was going to take the chance that it might be them who *did* get shot.

And did the gunmen know that their hostages included a section of Fusiliers? Sean was going to guess that no, they didn't, and that would give the lads an advantage. But they had to take it quick. He had heard tales of hostage taking. Sooner or later the hostage takers generally went through wallets and IDs, clocking people they didn't like, such as Americans, Israelis . . . Members of the British Army would be in the same category, and the lads all had their military IDs in their wallets.

And the thing soldiers did when they came under fire was to bunch together and fight back as a unit. Sean glanced over at Wolston in case the corporal was ready to give any orders, but he couldn't see his face with Bright's butt in the way.

The first gunman stood at the head of the queue for the passport desks. The second made his way along the line of prone bodies.

'*You lot. On your feet.*'

Between them they had cut off the head of the queue. About fifty people were being made to stand: black and white, men and women, and every lad in the section. Somewhere Sean could hear sobbing, and that baby was still crying at top volume.

'*Hands on your heads. Move forward.*'

At gunpoint, the hostages were herded past the desks towards the baggage reclamation area.

'*Keep your hands on your heads.*'

Sean's eyes darted left, right, up, down, taking in the location. Its pluses and minuses. Mostly minuses. The two areas were linked by a short passage; the narrow walls meant that the hostages had to bunch closely together. The lads grouped themselves in a unit, hands still on their heads but poised for action.

'Wolston?' Marshall muttered. Sean guessed he was carefully not saying 'Corporal'. 'Orders?'

'No talking! Keep moving!'

The gunmen could dream. It felt like the lads were the only ones keeping shtum. Otherwise there was a steady background drone of muffled weeping and sobbing.

They were coming out into the baggage reclaim area. It was smaller than passport control. More defensible. There were solid walls on three sides, and the fourth wall was the outside one: a big window that looked out onto a car park.

Shit, we should be able to do something with that!

That window meant that the whole hall was totally exposed. But Sean could also see its advantages to the gunmen. They would spot anyone sneaking up on them.

'Go forward and sit between the luggage belts. Go on!'

The room was dominated by two large conveyor belts that trundled ceaselessly around with the luggage from the plane before theirs. Each one was fed by a smaller belt that came up through the floor in the middle of the carousel. The few passengers in the hall who hadn't already fled at the sound of gunshots stood rooted to the spot. The lead gunman, megaphone man, hit the emergency stop button and leaped up into the centre of the left-hand belt. He gave the ceiling another spray for the benefit of newcomers, and got the expected chorus of shouts and screams in return.

'*Everyone! You lot*' – he waved the weapon at the passengers already there – '*and you*' – that was to the hostages – '*into the middle.*' He aimed at the floor between the two belts. '*Sit down with your hands on your heads. Go!*'

'Orders?' Marshall repeated, a bit more insistently. Sean shot a sideways look at Wolston – and couldn't believe what he saw. The corporal's face had gone blank, his eyes glazed. Suddenly he looked like he had been on an all-night bender, inhaling the kind of thing that could get you cashiered with one whiff of a suspicious Redcap's nose.

Marshall had clocked it too. Sean saw the flash of dismay, and his jaw begin to drop. But then he pulled it together. The look of determination on Marshall's face was almost scary; Sean guessed it meant he was trying to hide the fact that he didn't know what the fuck he was doing, and as Lance Corporal he was second in command.

'Right,' Marshall began – and suddenly Wolston was back in the room and looking ready for action.

'Gobby guy with the megaphone is designated *Clarkson*,' he said. His lips barely moved. 'Bright, Mitra, West, your mark. Guy on the right is *Hammond*. Marshall, Harker, Penfold, you're on him.'

The second gunman – *Hammond* – had jumped up onto the right-hand carousel and was beckoning them on with his MP5. That meant gunman number three was still behind them, bringing up the rear and sealing it off.

Wolston rattled it all off as confidently as if he had been up all night practising. 'Guy behind us is *May*. Burnell, with me.'

Pete Burnell had tried for the SAS. He hadn't passed selection and had been returned to unit – but just the fact that he had trained up to the point where he was prepared to hack it still made him about fifty times harder than Sean felt he would ever be. *May* was an unknown factor and would only be tackled by two lads, so Wolston was keeping the best for himself.

'You go when we go. Each group grab a pew near to your target.'

Sean could feel his own pulse speeding up. Excitement and fear mixed up inside him and he had to fight back a grin. Shit, it was like the old days on the Littern Mills estate had never gone away – setting an ambush, or even being a decoy to lure out another gang. Amble along, look innocent, don't do anything to put their guard up . . . and *pow*.

Of course, the other gang had never been kitted out with MP5s. Still, Sean knew the value of the element of surprise, and he also had confidence in his hand-to-hand training.

But they would have to move bloody fast because they could never outrun a spray of rounds.

'*Move! Move!*'

And then they were between the carousels. Sean, Marshall and Penfold tried to drift naturally to the right and clustered together as they squatted down at the base of the belt, close to *Hammond*'s feet.

'H-hands on heads!'

That was *Hammond*, standing above them, without the benefit of a megaphone. Did his voice wobble a bit? Sean shot a sideways look at the gunman. He clocked the way *Hammond*'s feet shifted from side to side, his finger tapping against the stock of his weapon . . . and that voice had distinctly squeaked. Well, well. So

Hammond was nervous? That had to be a break. He was also the least well armed of the trio – he had the MP5 and that was it. No spare magazines, no grenades.

But if he was scared, wanting to prove something, that could make him the most dangerous of all . . .

Sean bit his lip and turned his attention to *May* and *Clarkson*, straining his eyes across and moving his head as little as he could. They were a different story. *Clarkson* stood on top of his belt with his feet apart and his weapon slung casually in his hands – no effort to it, but ready to bring it to bear at any angle. *May* was trotting round the perimeter of the room with the casual lope Sean had seen in wildlife documentaries showing wolves encircling their prey. He slapped buttons that made metal grilles slide down over the exits – the way they had come, back to passport control, and the exit that led to Customs.

Sean could dimly hear sirens. The outside world would have got the message by now. Seriously hard guys in black clothes and masks pretty similar to the three gunmen would be converging on their position. What was the endgame here? What did these guys want?

The other hostages cowered. Some dared to look up slightly, to see what was occurring. Some kept their eyes fixed on the floor. Some had shoulders shaking as they wept. Even the ever-calm Okwute had his jaw clenched as he gazed blankly into the distance. Only the lads were absolutely silent and still, crackling with tension and ready to move. Fuck, how could the gunmen not see that? Sean wondered.

'*Secure?*' That was *Clarkson*, with the megaphone aimed at *May*. *May* had finished his tour of the perimeter and stood at one end of the space between carousels. Wolston and Burnell were right at his feet, sitting cross-legged, hands on heads as instructed. *May's* poise was like *Clarkson's*, casual and deadly. He flashed an O sign, thumb and forefinger together.

'*Right.*' *Clarkson's* amplified voice echoed around the hall, maybe for the benefit of hidden listeners. The security forces would probably be tapping into CCTV and picking this up before they received any official communication. '*Do as you're told and no one gets hurt. We have demands which we'll be presenting to— SIT DOWN!*'

Every eye was pinned on Wolston as he slowly got to his feet. Sean shifted himself, poised to act as the adrenalin pumping through his system maxed out. Any second now . . .

Wolston held his arms apart, palms facing forward, the most unthreatening stance there was. Which didn't stop *Clarkson* from pointing his weapon slap bang at the centre of his body mass. One squeeze on the trigger would cut him in half.

Forget that momentary blanking just now. Sean wasn't even sure if he'd remembered it properly. He was looking at the bravest man on the planet, who had the undivided attention of every person in the room, including all three gunmen. The guy had balls that Miley Cyrus could write a song about.

'You're making a mistake,' Wolston said clearly.

'*I said SIT DOWN . . .*' *Clarkson* thundered.

Burnell kicked out his feet at *May*'s ankles and the gunman toppled over with a yell. His finger squeezed the trigger as he went down and the shots went wild.

Clarkson and *Hammond* didn't shoot, because *Hammond* was scared and *Clarkson* had to adjust his aim a fraction as Wolston dived to one side, and then each of them had their designated three soldiers piling on top of them, dragging them to the ground. On the way down *Clarkson*'s weapon fired off a couple of rounds that shattered the hall's polished tiles, away from the hostages.

On top of the carousel, Sean, Marshall and Penfold knelt on *Hammond*. The gunman writhed and bucked beneath them until Marshall drove one fist hard against his balaclava'd face. The back of his head cracked into the metal casing of the carousel and he went still. Sean was nearest to his right hand and he scooped up the MP5. Still on the carousel, he quickly stood up and moved away from the still gunman, taking the weapon with him.

Fucking hell, it had worked!

Grasping the gun was like meeting a new friend. Its shape and design made it fall into his arms. Together, they were back in charge, and it felt good.

But Sean would let himself feel all that later. He automatically went through the NSPs, pulling the cocking handle back to check the chamber. The gun was cocked and loaded. The MP5 looked like it had started as a simple automatic pistol and then its Borg implants had activated and sprouted new, extra gun fore and aft, sleek, black and deadly. He took a moment to locate the selector lever on the Heckler & Koch design. There was one on either side above the pistol grip. Instead of words or numbers, it used pretty pictures of bullets to show the number that would be discharged at each setting – none, one, two or lots. He clicked it to 'none' – a picture of a single bullet with a cross through it.

Hammond was out cold with Penfold and Marshall on top of him, and he wasn't going anywhere. Wolston stood a safe distance away from *May*, training his MP5 on the gunman, who was flat on his back on the floor.

On the other carousel *Clarkson* was kneeling, hands behind his head, as Bright stood in front of him, weapon aimed squarely at his chest.

'Report!' Wolston shouted.

'*Hammond* neutralized, weapon acquired,' Marshall shouted back.

'Ditto here, Corporal,' Bright reported, less professionally. The triumph of his wide grin was matched in intensity only by the two cold eyes behind *Clarkson*'s mask; they didn't waver from his face.

'Everyone stay seated!' Wolston shouted. 'The police will be here soon, but let us secure the area.'

They needed telling. The hostages were just twigging that the world had changed again, and one thing that could really bugger this up was a bunch of clueless civvies moping around and getting in the way.

'Wonder what the ugly fucks really look like?' Bright shouted. 'Let's see who was really behind this.'

Penfold rolled his eyes. 'Whatever.' He grabbed *Hammond*'s mask and pulled. Nothing happened except that *Hammond*'s collar rode up a bit. The mask was buttoned down. He started to feel round *Hammond*'s neck to release it.

'Oi, ugly,' Bright ordered across the way. 'Mask off.'

Clarkson shrugged. His hands were already behind his head. He moved them further down—

His arms blurred, metal flashed silver in the lights, and suddenly Bright had let go of his weapon while red liquid spurted from his throat around the embedded blade. He dropped to his knees, both hands on his throat, and a strangled gurgle came out of his mouth. In the same move *Clarkson* had swept up his dropped weapon and leaped down from the carousel, hauling a shrieking woman to her feet.

It all happened in the time it took for Bright to topple flat on his face and lie still while a pool of blood swept across the burnished metal of the carousel.

The image burned into Sean's brain, a never-ceasing, relooping slo-mo video. With a wordless cry he dropped to one knee and brought the MP5 up to his shoulder. *Bright falling over*. Wolston was standing with *May*'s weapon also trained on *Clarkson* – and on the weeping hostage.

Bright falling . . .

'Drop your guns, soldier boys!' *Clarkson* snapped. 'Drop them now! Put them down and step away!'

Bright . . .

Sean didn't move. At that moment he was prepared to shoot through the woman and blow *Clarkson* away. His arms trembled with the clashing desires to squeeze the trigger and protect the woman.

Wolston was also hesitating, but a hostage was a

hostage. The weapon wavered, and then he let it drop. 'Put it down, Harker,' he said, his voice heavy.

Sean felt tears of rage prick his eyes. He would not let them through. He shifted aim slightly, snuggled the butt more firmly into his shoulder, slowed his breathing so as not to make the weapon wobble. *Clarkson*'s face was above the hostage's shoulder, and Sean had the MP5's iron sights square on it. He was sure he could fire, give the woman the fright of her life as a single round zipped past her head at supersonic speed and sprayed *Clarkson*'s brains over the rest of the hall. If Wolston gave the word. By the time the woman clocked what was happening, it would be over.

'Put it down, Stenders,' Marshall said quietly. He and Penfold stood very still on either side of *Hammond*'s slowly moving, groaning body.

'Fusilier Harker! Lower your weapon!' Wolston snapped. He led by example, bending at the knees to lay his MP5 on the floor. Then he straightened and took a step away from it. His hands were back in the palms-out position to show – *Look, no threat.*

Which just meant that Sean was now the sole focus of *Clarkson*'s attention. The gunman kept the MP5 on him, but he could only hold it by its pistol grip. His other arm was locked in a chokehold around the hostage's neck.

In theory, that gave them all a chance. Weapons like that were designed for two hands for a reason – the recoil made them unmanageable with just one. Held like that, any discharge could go anywhere – but at this short range, just between the two baggage carousels, it would probably go into Sean first.

And Sean knew he was beat. His breath came in short spurts as he unpeeled his left hand from the stock. Each finger seemed to require a conscious act of will to move it. He brought the weapon away from his shoulder and began to lower it to the floor.

It was only a tiny shift in *Clarkson's* stance – maybe a fractional movement of the barrel as he tracked Sean properly, a tension in his body. But that was when Sean just *knew*.

Shit, he's going to fire.

And even as he was bringing the weapon back up and raising his left hand, he remembered, *I put it on 'none', didn't I?* And he knew that the half-second taken to flick it to 'one' would be a quarter of a second too long.

Sean surrendered all voluntary control of his muscles. Pure instinct took over. The simple message to his brain was: *Keep me alive.*

Close beside him was a vertical, knee-high steel wall. He didn't even clock what it was there for, just that it was cover, and he flung himself behind it. The ground vanished beneath him and he tumbled down a slope. The wall was the lip of the feeder belt, the entry into the depths of the earth that disgorged unloaded suitcases onto the main belt.

Behind him he heard the screams of the hostage, and the roar of the MP5, and the metallic clang of rounds hitting the steel. But he was already below the level of the carousel. He somersaulted into the depths of the airport in a clumsy tangle of limbs and weapon, and hit the bottom with a blow that knocked the breath out of him.

But he was only still for a moment. His brain was still following its last order, and as he realized, *Shit, I'm exposed*, he was already rolling over to one side, off the belt and onto a hard concrete floor. He was in a low space that was wider than the hall above. Everything was concrete – pillars and floor and ceiling, all bare. This was not a public area. It smelled of diesel and damp, and it was empty. A luggage trolley stood next to the belt, half unloaded but now abandoned. Any civvies around here would have already cleared off.

Sean scrambled to his knees and brought the weapon to bear on the gap in the ceiling above him. A flick of the thumb set the MP5's selector to 'lots'. Any black-clad head showed itself in that gap of light above him, he would blow it apart. His finger on the trigger tingled with anticipation.

There was still shouting and screaming up there, and most of the words he could hear were *Clarkson* and *May* bellowing orders. No head showed.

Instead there was a clank and a rattle, and an HG85 hand grenade – fuse three to four seconds, lethal range of ten metres, and able to take out a man in Kevlar body armour – was bouncing down the belt towards him.

Chapter 9

Wednesday 2 August, 07:15 BST

Shit shit shit shit shit . . .

Sean didn't remember moving. Somehow he was behind one of the concrete pillars, pressed hard against it, making himself as thin and vertical as he could.

The explosion was a *crack*, a snapping sound that spat 1800 fragments of hot metal out in all directions at speeds that would slice through a human body like a knife through butter.

But they couldn't get through the concrete. They clattered against the pillar, and Sean was safe in its shadow.

It was one, very small bright side.

Shit shit shit . . .

He drew several deep breaths to calm his pounding heart, and considered his options. Tried to think strategically.

This was him. On his own, cut off from his unit.

The logical thing now would be to try to escape and make his way to the authorities. He could tell them what he knew, give them int that might help them retake the hall – but fuck that: he had just seen one of his best mates killed.

OK. He blinked away the rage and anger that he wanted to feel whenever he thought of Bright, lying there with a knife in his throat. That would come later. For now he had to be cool. Serve his revenge cold.

Everyone upstairs must think he was dead. The lads *and* the gunmen. They weren't chucking any more grenades down. At least, not yet.

So he had an advantage.

He looked around, and he didn't have to search far. There were two carousels up top, which meant there were two feeder belts down here. His leap behind the pillar had put him nearer the second one. It was a twin of the first, a conveyor belt rising up at a forty-five-degree angle and disappearing into the ceiling.

It was a vulnerability.

Give the gunmen a couple more seconds and they would work it out for themselves, and take precautions. Which meant that Sean had less than a couple of seconds to get there first. He instinctively shook his head to clear the sweat from his eyes, even though he wasn't wearing a helmet, and leaped onto the belt.

He advanced up at a crouch, weapon held before him, ready to open fire on anything that moved. He was prepared for what he intended to do. He had killed someone once before, in instinctive self-defence. This time he would mean it. The objective was to eliminate the threat of the gunmen before the bastards knew what had hit them, and the most effective way of doing that was to put a couple of rounds into each of them. As his instructor had drummed into him the very first day he picked up a rifle, shooting to wound is a convenient Hollywood fiction that doesn't exist in real life. If you open fire with live ammunition, you expect to kill. His only regret was that he couldn't do this *Battlefield* style, savouring the expression of the bad guy who suddenly realizes what's coming and can't do anything to escape it.

He crouched just below the steel lip and reluctantly dialled the selector back to 'one'. This would have to be precise – with innocent warm bodies present, he couldn't just spray rounds about like they were on special offer. He let his ears do the recce for him. He was just a couple of paces from where *Clarkson* had been – which meant that Bright's body was also lying nearby, just out of sight. Sean coldly pushed the image from his mind. Meanwhile, judging by what he could hear, *Clarkson* was no longer on the carousel – in other words, no longer just a few steps away from where Sean was now. It sounded like he was down on the floor among the passengers, maybe four metres to Sean's right.

'*Right!*' Clarkson was shouting. 'All you soldier boys, line up over there. *Move!* I'll count to five, and then your man here loses his head. *Shift! One, two—*'

'And the rest of you, *shut the fuck up!*'

That was *May*, conveniently giving Sean his location. He was moving – pacing slowly down the space between the carousels, over on the other side.

Clarkson had reached three and was beginning on four when Sean moved. He had the butt in his shoulder, hands on pistol grip and stock, and he rose smoothly to his feet, aiming at where *Clarkson*'s voice was coming from.

Shit.

The lads were kneeling in a semicircle around the lead gunman like worshippers before an altar, though their god required his followers to clasp their hands behind their heads. But each carousel had a large display screen on a pillar next to it, giving details of flight arrivals, and the pillar was in the way. Not badly – Sean could plainly see *Clarkson* – but enough to obscure a clean shot, and certainly enough to provide ricochets into the hostages if Sean took a punt anyway. Until he moved, *Clarkson* was off limits.

But plan B was good. *May* was exactly where Sean had expected him to be, standing by the other carousel while *Hammond* sat up, rubbing the back of his drooping head. *May* froze at the sight of Sean emerging, for exactly as long as it took Sean to aim and put two single shots into him. They tore through his body and threw red streamers onto the steel of the carousel behind. He crumpled where he fell. Hostages screamed and the nearest ones scrambled hurriedly away.

The lads didn't need telling. The pillar also stopped *Clarkson* firing immediately back at Sean, and the lads moved while, for half a second, he was torn between options. For the second time *Clarkson* disappeared beneath a crowd of Fusiliers.

Hammond climbed unsteadily to his feet, and immediately Sean had him at gunpoint with his own weapon. The gunman's hands shot into the air. His eyes were wide, his pupils dark with fright behind his balaclava. Now Sean was out on the main belt, he could see Bright's still body. He wanted to go over to him, see if there was the slightest thing he could do – but he had to push that idea away, because keeping tabs on *Hammond* was more important.

Then Sean heard someone shout '*Shit!*' – just before a cloud of black, choking smoke burst out from the knot of lads over *Clarkson*. In half a second it had enveloped them and was billowing out into the rest of the hall, with the background roaring hiss of a smoke grenade, and chokes and shouts from the lads. Sean remembered the ugly little cylinders hanging from *Clarkson*'s webbing.

There was nothing Sean could do to help them – he couldn't open fire on an unseen target without causing a lot of collateral damage in the form of his mates. But he could keep *Hammond* at bay. In fact, he began to ask himself if he shouldn't just do the world a favour and take *Hammond* down anyway – was that what the SAS would do?

He saw *Hammond*'s eyes go even wider – maybe the guy was thinking along the same lines.

Except that a second smoke bomb suddenly flew out of the expanding cloud and landed at *Hammond*'s feet. In a moment the gunman had disappeared like the assistant in a cheap magic act, and then the cloud had filled the space between the carousels.

'*Clarkson*'s got away!' Sean heard Wolston bellow from the depths of the fog. The hostages screamed and shouted twice as loud. 'Harker, if you see him . . .'

The smoke stank and clogged up Sean's nose, and he could see fuck all. Shapes of bodies blundered about in the haze, and he had to squeeze his eyes to slits as what felt like a swarm of bees settled onto them and started to sting. A man clad in the flapping outline of Okwute's robes stumbled towards him.

Something metal fell on the tiled floor with a clank, and Sean recognized the sound even before he saw what it was. A brushed-metal sphere the size of a piece of fruit.

He drew a breath to shout a warning, and fought every instinct of self-preservation to make himself reach down for it. But before he could move, Okwute had scooped it up and flung it as far away as he could with a strong, flowing overarm throw, across the hall and away from the hostages.

'Grenade! Everyone get flat!' Sean shouted, and suited actions to words as he dropped to the tiles.

Okwute landed with a thump next to him. They stared into each other's streaming eyes from a distance of a few inches. A few seconds later Sean heard the *crack* of the explosion. The screams shot up the scale, but his ears told him that it was just good old panic and fear, not the sound of anyone who had just been hit by red-hot shrapnel.

The smoke was clearing. Shapes were becoming more distinct. Sean quickly clambered to his feet.

Okwute leaped up onto the carousel, his face set and determined. He laid a gentle hand on Bright's head and murmured, '*Inna lillaahi wa inna ilayhi Raaji'oon.*'

He glanced up at Sean. 'To Allah we belong and to Him is our return. Our prayer for the dead.'

Sean was barely listening. The adrenalin that had fuelled him ever since he climbed up the ramp was still there, and it wanted a new outlet. Like, point his gun at the ceiling and set it to fully automatic, and just scream and empty the mag.

But he was holding a weapon and he should do something useful with it. Wolston had his weapon back and held it at the ready, legs slightly bent as he circled about, aiming at anything that looked like it might be *Clarkson* or *Hammond*. Sean brought his own weapon up and looked around.

'Where the fuck are they?' Wolston shouted. 'Anyone, report! Do you see them?'

Sean whipped his head around, staring into every corner of the terminal. Dismay settled onto him like a dead weight in his heart.

They couldn't have fucking got away!

But they had. Bright lay dead at Sean's feet, and his killers were nowhere to be seen.

Chapter 10

Wednesday 2 August, 09:30 BST

'Right.' Wolston's face was haggard, his voice dead as he put away his phone. He had lost a man on his watch, and that hurt. 'We will be met back at camp by the adjutant and representatives of the Security Service, and debriefed on arrival.'

For once, no one was in the mood to make jokes about being 'debriefed'. The occupants of the minibus were subdued as it climbed up towards the QE2 bridge and started the slow crawl round the M25 before finally making a break for the M3 and down to Wiltshire. Down in the south-west the sky was bright blue: it was promising to be a great day back home. The black clouds here, and the road spray kicked up by the traffic around them, suited everyone's mood better.

It wasn't the first time they had lost a mate – apart from Wolston and Burnell, they had all been serving together at the time of the Tidworth bombing, which took the life of Fusilier Toni Clark and several others – but it was not something you ever got used to.

Out of habit, Sean had expected the police to be harder work when they finally showed up. He knew cops get touchy about people other than them discharging firearms, even if they are on the same side. And maybe the couple of PCs and sergeants he had spoken to had been gearing up to give him a hard time – but the inspector in charge had known how the world worked. Wolston had checked in with the adjutant immediately the siege was lifted, and been ordered to say nothing. So the inspector had realized that two incompatible forces were clashing, army orders to keep shtum versus the Met's obvious desire to get answers, and this would all be sorted out by people above his paygrade. The lads had been allowed to go, after undertaking to be available for interview at a later, unspecified date. It would all be on CCTV, anyway.

And now they were on the final part of the journey home. For the debriefing. And how would that go? Sean wondered. Praise, or bollocking?

'You all did well.' Lieutenant Colonel Levene looked Sean in the eye. 'Bloody well. There will be inquests, of course – there have to be in the event of any death – both on Fusilier Bright and on the dead gunman – and you may be called as a witness, but the army will back your actions to the hilt, and we'll do everything we can to keep your name out of the media.'

It answered Sean's question very clearly. Praise, apparently.

There were four of them in the colonel's office. Levene, a guy from the Green Slime (aka Military Intelligence), a civilian from Special Branch, and Sean. The colonel was working through the section one by one. Sean sat on a chair across from Levene's desk, and tried not to feel embarrassed appearing before a senior officer like this – unwashed, unshaved, in civvies, while Special Branch wore a jacket and tie, and the other two officers were both in cleanly pressed No. 8 Temperate Combat Dress.

'Thank you, sir.'

He had been braced for it to go either way. The army was big on its members showing initiative. It also crapped from a great height on anyone who showed initiative in the wrong way or at the wrong time. And if it resulted in casualties, then the crap could get piled on top of you – the sky was the limit.

Despite the congratulations, Levene still looked just as morose as the lads. Sean felt a stab of annoyance. What was his problem? He hadn't lost anyone . . .

But then he realized that Levene *had* lost someone.

And not for the first time. He had also been around for the Tidworth bombing, and now he had lost another man. The death of a Fusilier rattled all the way up the chain of command. *Everyone* took it personally.

'You sound surprised, Fusilier . . .' Levene shot Sean a look. 'Let me guess – you thought that with so much military bullshit flying around, you might still end up covered in it? No. You had every reason to believe that your lives, and the lives of others, were in danger. That automatically clears you to take action. From what I hear, you were all a credit to the regiment – and to the taxpayers who have paid so much to get you where you are.'

And this was on the record. One major way the army kicked the civilian world's arse was that when a higher-up said they had your back, they really *did*. Sean felt the pilot light of pride that burns inside every soldier *whoomph* up a little.

But he kept his face still. That same pride meant you didn't show it. You didn't grin all over your face like you'd just got a gold star in class for sucking up to teacher.

Especially as there was still nothing to be glad about. Bright was still dead. That was all.

'Thank you, sir,' he said again.

Levene's face clouded. 'The fact that one of our own

lads lost his life . . . Taking any kind of action is a non-science and always subject to shit happening. How do you feel about Fusilier Bright?'

Sean's first reaction was *Mind your own business*, but you don't say that to superior officers, and they do need to know the capability of the men beneath them. So he took a moment to think.

After Toni Clark got blown to pieces by a bomb hidden in her car, he had very nearly lost everything that counted. The whole point of joining the army had been to get out of the gangs, but the desire to avenge Clark had driven him into the arms of the very people who had killed her. And it had almost destroyed him. He had let his two worlds, army and gang, overlap to a point where you couldn't tell them apart. He had put his mum in danger and he had betrayed his new friends in the army.

This time . . .

It wasn't the same. Maybe it was because Clark had been murdered out of the blue, while Bright went down fighting, in a combat situation, giving as good as he got. And if Sean hadn't got *Clarkson*, who did it, he had still seriously upset his plans.

And there was also the simple fact that he had grown up. He was a year older than when Clark had died; he had spent one year more in the army. He'd seen and understood more. He had a better grip on how the world worked.

'He was a good mate, sir,' he said. 'We were pals from day one.' He shrugged. 'Going to miss him.'

There wasn't much more to say. Bright wasn't coming back. Every day now would be a day Sean woke up in a world without him. On the one hand, he just had to live with that. On the other, it left a hole so big he would have to put a lot of effort into filling it.

'Of course, of course. You do know the chaplain is always available to talk to, and there is counselling . . .'

Sean couldn't help giving a kind of face-wiggle that showed exactly what he thought of talking to the chaplain or getting counselling.

The colonel's lips pursed in a kind of flat smile. 'I understand. Just remember: no one is ever so big and tough that they don't need to talk about it sometimes.' He looked down at his notes and tapped the end of his pen on the table. 'One more thing. How would you rate Corporal Wolston's actions? Frankly?'

Sean hesitated, but the man had asked. So he looked the colonel straight in the eye. 'If he doesn't get a third tape for this, sir, there's no justice.'

Levene's eyebrow went up. 'Go on . . .'

Sean had already thought long and hard about Joe Wolston. It all came out. 'Like you said, sir, shit happens . . . Well, Corporal Wolston saw the shit coming and he got us through it. He gave us the strategy. He gave us the code names for our targets and assigned us. He put his fuc—' Sean remembered just in time who he was talking to. There was permission to speak frankly, and there was pushing your luck. 'He put his life on the line, sir, when he stood up and confronted *Clarkson* to kick things off – and he held things together even when things went south.'

'As plans generally do,' Levene agreed, 'when it turns out the enemy haven't attended the same briefing and haven't been informed of how they're supposed to behave.'

Sean remembered shuffling into the baggage hall at gunpoint: Wolston had seemed to go blank, and for a moment Sean had seriously thought the guy had lost it. He now realized it must have been his mind revving overtime, trying to piece a plan together.

Then a totally unwelcome memory burrowed its way into his head – that abort command back in Lagos, when the scooter kid opened fire. Sean remembered Adams's fury – so he hadn't been the only one to find it weird. But Adams had also accepted Wolston's reasoning. *Your hot seat, your call.* Maybe any position of command was like that. You had a thousand different inputs that no one else had, and you had to make the best of them.

Someone with courage issues might have given the same abort command. Someone with courage issues might have gone blank when faced with masked gunmen. But one thing Sean *did* know was that Wolston had no issues there at all. The guy had come out of Afghanistan with an MC and a glowing record. That was the kind of thing you couldn't fake. He had been through the toughest kind of shit, and lived to tell the tale. And today they had all seen what he was made of.

'Well, yes, sir,' he said. 'We're alive because of him.' He met Levene's appraising gaze, and the colonel nodded.

'You're dismissed, Fusilier. Please send in' – he checked his list – 'Fusilier West.'

'To Shitey!'

Seven pint glasses clanked together in the front saloon of the Monty, the discerning squaddie's pub of choice. Wolston had cemented Sean's opinion of his leadership qualities by buying for the section.

'May his anal emissions for ever be blowing the angels off their clouds,' Mitra added.

'Christ, Kama Sutra, that silver tongue of yours'll

get you into trouble one day,' West said, pretending to wipe away a tear.

The section had all been debriefed, and now they were reunited for a pint and the first decent nosh since hitting UK soil again. The Monty's fish and chips were legendary and had been much missed for six long months in Nigeria . . .

Sean gave himself a mental kick. *Stop thinking like that.* Because the lad who had gone on about the fish and chips most was the one who wasn't here. And never would be again.

He looked around the pub. Red and orange airport-lounge-style carpet, slightly sticky. Flashy jukebox. Taps for five different types of lager. Large flatscreen tuned permanently to sport, with scrolling news headlines which – of course – were all about the airport situation, but saying nothing new.

Nothing had changed and everything seemed different. It felt bizarre that this place had still existed, quietly normal, while he was wading through a Nigerian swamp. Risking his life at the airport. Taking down *May*, and losing Bright.

Over in one corner was a couple – civvies: you could tell at a glance. Their body language said they really wished the lads weren't there – they were obviously trying to ignore the noise. *Sorry, mate – you go into a*

squaddie pub in a garrison town, this is what you get.
They were here to give Bright the send-off he deserved.
Leave might have been cancelled, but they weren't on
duty. As long as they didn't actually do anything like
throw up in the corridors of barracks or assault an
officer, they could get as pissed as they liked.

'There's a little way my old sergeant taught me to
honour a fallen mate,' Wolston said once the pints were
down past the halfway mark. Everyone was all ears.
'You go to the ranges, you get the biggest fucking guns
you can find and you seriously dent the defence budget
by letting them off. Who's with me?'

As a plan of battle it received a classification of
fucking A, which was the highest form of approval
there was for seven male squaddies looking to let off
anger and adrenalin. It meant putting the getting pissed
on hold for a while, because the army tutted when
people rolled up at the ranges reeking of booze and
unable to walk in a straight line, so everyone headed
back to barracks for a clean-up and to get changed
into proper No. 8. They arranged to RV at seventeen
hundred.

Sean lived in Single Living Accommodation, in one of a
collection of en-suite rooms based around a common area.
He kept his eyes firmly ahead as he walked past

Bright's room. Soon that room would be stripped. Bright's family might reclaim stuff, other kit might be auctioned off for charity. And then a new lad would be installed.

And that lad would be just as much part of the platoon as Bright had been. He would be made to feel just as welcome. Because that was how it went.

Sean went on back to his room for the ritual of shit, shower and shave, plus the daily anti-malarial pill that he hadn't got round to taking yet, what with the other distractions. After that it was time to get down to some serious kit maintenance. Everything that had come out of his kitbag, battered and crumpled from its time in the aeroplane hold, needed to be folded or scrubbed or polished until it was up to proper standard. After a year in the army he wasn't going to just turn up in gear that he hadn't personally brought up to scratch.

At sixteen forty-five there was a knock on Sean's door.

'Uh, Stenders?' It was Chewie West's voice. 'Someone here to see you . . .'

So Sean stepped out of his room, straight into the arms of a pair of Redcaps. Military police, immaculate in khaki, and the signature red barnet. West waited just behind them.

'Uh . . . Hi?'

He couldn't believe they were there for him, but there was no one else about and they stood side by side in a way that blocked off the only exit.

'Fusilier Harker?' Redcaps weren't known for their broad smiles and wacky personalities, and these two were a credit to the team. 'Come with us, please.'

Sean shot West a look. He returned it, equally baffled, and shrugged.

So Sean did the only thing he could – and followed them.

It wasn't quite an arrest. He had seen people being arrested and frogmarched to the guardroom at double-quick time. At least these guys let him walk normally through the camp – but with one of them on either side there was still no question that they were the ones in charge.

What the fuck was this?

His mind whirled. Every action of the last few days he could think of, in either Nigeria or England, and in international airspace, got held up under the micro-scope and studied. Nope. His conscience was clear of any recent criminal activity, though this didn't stop him from frantically searching through it.

Was it because he'd taken unauthorized action back at the airport? This seemed an overreaction, and anyway, Levene had assured him he was in the clear.

But the guardroom loomed ahead, and the fact was, he was under arrest.

And when they took him into a back room, and he clocked the two people waiting for him, he knew he was really screwed. He recognized them immediately for what they were – even though he still had no idea what they wanted, and he had never set eyes upon them in his life.

Chapter 11

'Fusilier Harker. Sit down.'

There were two men – one probably in his forties, one quite a bit younger, maybe not even thirty yet, with dark hair. And even though they were in civvies, they gave off a vibe that Sean had encountered only once before in his life. And he had vowed, *Never again*.

The last time Sean had been interviewed by two members of the Security Service – or, as it was generally known to everyone except the spooks, MI5 – it had been a man and a woman. They had looked totally un-remarkable, not people you would ever look at twice – but when they had him in the interrogation room, on the ropes, nowhere to turn, they had been something else. Invulnerable, untouchable. They twitched their little fingers and you went to jail, or you did as you were told.

And that was exactly what Sean got off these two. If they weren't also MI5 spooks, then he was Okwute.

But they were also technically civilians, and they weren't going to get to him that easily. He didn't owe them any respect. So he took his time sitting down, and when he did, he slouched. He wasn't going to treat them like superior officers. He put his hands in his pockets and waited for them to speak.

They looked at him. He looked back. He waited.

The 'waiting' bit didn't come from his past experience with spooks. It came from an earlier, darker time in his life. Nowadays he could draw on all kinds of anti-interrogation training – how to cope with starvation, sleep deprivation, psychological meddling – but his basic education had started when he was just a boy, facing the cops across the table. You said nothing and you let them break the silence.

The older man spoke first. In fact, he did all the talking while the younger one just watched him.

'We've assessed your debriefing reports on the airport action.' The guy placed a folder neatly on the table top and squared it up with his fingertips. 'Very impressive. You showed a lot of initiative.'

They'd read the report already? Sean thought. Quick work. But he said nothing.

The man's tone changed abruptly.

'You didn't get off to the best start in the army, did you, Fusilier? Stealing weapons to equip terrorists.

Basically just continuing the trend you'd already begun as a delinquent minor. Not what you'd call a fresh start, putting the past behind you.'

That stung – enough to jerk Sean out of his natural defensiveness. Because they were exactly right. He'd joined up with the best of intentions, and fucked up most royally.

'I was a prat,' he said. And he meant it. Maybe he should have kept quiet – but it wasn't like he was digging himself into a hole, was it? They already knew it.

'That's one way of looking at it.' The man's tone grew sharper. 'Your actions were borderline treason. Do you have a problem with this country, Fusilier?'

With this country? No. With some of the people who work for this country . . .

But Sean was already regretting saying anything, so he kept quiet.

The man went on. 'It's not as if the country did a lot for you when you were growing up. It's understandable if you felt pissed off with life. If you developed a sense of injustice, and a desire, along with it, to put things right.'

Sean's fists clenched in his pockets, out of sight, as he remembered Bright, and *May*, and the two fuckers who had got away. What part of a year of blameless conduct since his last brush with MI5, and then personally icing a terrorist, did these pricks not understand?

'I did put things right. At the airport.'

'Of *course*.' The man nodded, the way you might if you were agreeing with a small kid. Was he *trying* to get a rise out of Sean? 'Very nicely too. Or perhaps, very nicely planned?'

He cocked an eyebrow at Sean. Sean reverted to just looking back – what he should have done from the start. The man put his hand flat on the folder and abruptly switched to businesslike.

'When did you last see Zara Mann? Or Emma Booth?'

At last, a proper question. Sean gave a proper answer, which was also one hundred per cent truthful.

'I have no idea who you're talking about.'

The man looked sceptical. 'I think you can do better than that, Fusilier.'

Sean hid a smile – of triumph, not of pleasure. He could handle this. Now he had got over the surprise of the spook's line of questioning, he realized that on the scale of the day's general shittiness so far, this inter-rogation barely registered. The guy could rile him, drop heavy hints that Sean was lying through his arse, and it wouldn't make the slightest difference.

'I expect you do.'

'You were at school with them, for a start.'

Sean snorted. That didn't narrow it down. 'Which one?'

'Markwell Secondary.'

'There's your answer, then. I might have seen them for about five minutes, five years ago. I don't remember those names. I don't know who they are.'

He tried to work out why they were dragging up names from his past, but the names still meant fuck all to him. He had no clue where this was going.

Markwell was the second of the three schools Sean had been dumped on between age eleven and getting nicked. He was reasonably sure he had even attended some lessons there, but couldn't for the life of him remember much about it. There was nothing he wanted to remember. He'd never got on with schools. His education, what there was of it back in those days, had happened out on the street with the Guyz. He had learned about cars (maintenance and nicking of), and fighting, and other things that had seemed far more useful for life.

'They also both live on Littern Mills.'

Sean frowned. He had no reason not to believe the man. But then, a lot of people lived on Littern Mills – the Walthamstow estate where he had grown up. And a lot of them came and went. His mum was still there, but there were new families and new gangs moving in all the time.

'In case you missed the bulletin, I joined up nearly two years ago,' he said. 'And I spent the last six months in Nigeria.'

'You've still been back home? Before Nigeria?'

'Sure.' Sean shrugged. 'I keep an eye on my mum.'

Not often, but he had been back every couple of months since all the crap blew up a year ago. Looking out for her had been one of the reasons he got involved in the first place.

'You don't look up old friends when you go?'

'Nope.'

Sean's closest friends from the old days were either in jail or dead. As for the rest, if he never saw them again it would be a million years too soon.

The man finally opened his folder and pulled out two photos. They were both close-ups of faces. From the elevated angle, Sean guessed they were from CCTV.

'We know for a fact that you saw Mann and Booth recently. At the airport.'

'Yeah?'

Now he was interested despite himself. Sean sat forward to study them. Both pictures showed fit-looking white girls. One had dark shoulder-length hair; the other's head was wrapped in a scarf and you couldn't make the hair out. She also wore clear glasses. Now he came to think of it, he *did* recognize them. They had been sitting next to Chewie on the flight, and they had been in the crowd of hostages scooped up by the gunmen.

The girls were looking vaguely frontwards – he guessed the pics were from the passport queue before the gunmen attacked. They couldn't be more than seventeen. And in just over a month he would be nineteen – which meant that, at Markwell, they would have been twelve to his fourteen. And these guys thought he would have known them? Did they think he was into jailbait?

'This is Zara Mann.' The man tapped the dark-haired girl. 'And this' – *tap, tap* – 'is Emma Booth.'

The other spook spoke for the first time. 'Possibly.'

The older spook swung his head round and glared at his colleague. The younger spook just smiled blandly back, and Sean sensed the undercurrent of a much older, longer disagreement that still hadn't been resolved. The older guy turned to face Sean again.

'This is *possibly* Emma Booth. Mann has been positively identified by fingerprints from her seat on the plane – she has a minor record. Provisional identific-ation of Booth is by facial recognition software, and that scarf and the glasses complicate matters. We know for sure that neither of them were travelling under their own names. They were working at the Sacred Cross Hospital in Lagos, using the stolen identities of a pair of genuine charity volunteers. And they are now missing.'

Sean frowned. 'What, they did a bunk from the airport before you guys got to talk to them?'

The spook shook his head, and continued to scowl like it was all Sean's fault. 'They did a bunk from the airport with the surviving gunmen.'

'*What?*'

'Before the smoke bombs went off, they were with all you other hostages. When the smoke had cleared, they had gone. What does that tell you, Fusilier Harker?'

Sean looked at him carefully. No way was he answering a question like that. It was way too leading.

The spook obviously enjoyed the sound of his own voice. 'It tells *me* that everything that happened this morning was a ruse to get them back into the country without any Customs and Immigration control checks. In the time it took us to realize they were missing they could be safely back in Littern Mills or anywhere else – and, of course, because Littern Mills wasn't under surveillance until now, we have no way of showing that they ever left it. What do their time in Nigeria and Littern Mills have in common?'

He steepled his fingers and leaned forward. 'One thing and one thing only, and I'm looking at him. Start talking, Fusilier Harker, because it will go very badly for you if you hold out on us.'

Sean just stared back at him, not even aware that his mouth was hanging open.

What the fuck?

That morning he had only gone and helped foil a terrorist raid on an airport, and lost his closest mate.

And now he was under suspicion?

Chapter 12

Wednesday 2 August, 17:15 BST

The door flew open.

'What the *hell* is going on?'

Sean glanced over his shoulder at the newcomer, clocked him, and immediately shot to his feet. He stood to attention, heels together, eyes forward.

Lieutenant Colonel Levene stormed into the room, not even looking at Sean, his glare fixed on the spooks. 'Dismissed, Fusilier.'

'Sir!' Sean started to salute, remembered he wasn't in uniform, prepared to about-turn.

'Stay where you are, Fusilier Harker,' the older spook snapped. 'Colonel Levene, I presume? We're not finished with your soldier.'

'You should not have even started with my soldier without my knowledge!' But maybe Levene sensed this battle wouldn't be straightforward. He glanced at Sean and modified his earlier order. 'Wait outside, Fusilier.'

'Sir!' Sean about-turned and marched smartly out.

The two Redcaps were still outside, on either side of the door. Both parties looked warily at each other. The Redcaps looked a little less confident than the last time Sean had seen them. They had just seen a senior officer being extremely pissed off. Maybe they had been the first target for his anger, a practice run before he took it out on the spooks. Sean couldn't really find it in his heart to feel sorry for them.

They stood at ease, but Sean had just been told to wait, so he took a chair. He sat upright and made himself look smarter than he had for the spooks.

Raised voices came through the door: 'How dare you . . . without permission . . . completely out of order . . .'

That was Levene. Any replies were just a low buzz through the woodwork.

The colonel reappeared five minutes later, still with a thundercloud hanging over him. Everyone came to attention together.

First Levene snapped a look at the two Redcaps. 'You're dismissed.'

They marched gratefully away like a pair of synchronized robots, still with balls intact.

Then the colonel swung his attention onto Sean.

'Fusilier Harker. Be in briefing room three at seventeen forty-five. Talk to no one about this.'

Sean was in the briefing room at seventeen thirty-five – bang on time.

The army didn't do early or late. You were on time, and that was it.

So to guarantee that you were on time, you told yourself to be there five minutes before the designated time.

Which then meant that you had a new designated time, so you added five minutes to *that*. So now, even if you broke a leg as you stepped out of the front door and had to drag yourself along the ground, or ISIS launched a surprise attack on Andover, or aliens landed out on Salisbury Plain, you had ten minutes to make everything right before anyone could accuse you of not being on time.

The room followed the British Army's usual pattern of providing its men with the best, most up-to-date fighting equipment . . . and the crappiest furniture it could find. The wooden table frame was scarred and chipped, the Formica top was battered and peeling, and there were cork boards on the walls that just smelled old.

The handle rattled, and as the door opened Sean

jumped to attention. And then Wolston was standing there, looking as surprised to see Sean as Sean felt to see him.

'Very kind of you, Stenders, but there's no need,' Wolston said as Sean pointedly came down from attention. He moved further in to let Mitra past. One more surprise.

'What are *you* doing here, Kama Sutra?'

'Beats me.' Mitra shrugged. 'You didn't show for the shootfest, then we two get orders to be here—'

'Excellent,' said a voice. 'Let's get started.'

All three came to attention as Levene entered, followed by the younger of the two spooks that Sean had met earlier. He was carrying the older spook's folder.

The colonel simply gestured for them to sit. Then he and the spook pulled out their own chairs.

Levene spoke. 'Gentlemen. As Fusilier Harker will be able to tell you in his own time, there has been a breakdown in communication between this battalion and the Security Service.'

Sean felt his cheeks burning. He knew Mitra and Wolston would be interested to hear all the details about this later.

'I am pleased to report that this has been ironed out with the removal of one individual and the involvement of the proper chain of command. That is, me. It's a very short chain. What you are about to hear is top secret and not to be divulged to anyone not already in this room. Finally any plans you have for the next forty-eight hours have just been cancelled. I will now hand over to' – he scowled at the spook – 'this gentleman, whose orders you will follow as though they were my own.'

'Call me Dave,' the spook said, with a smart Home Counties accent and a friendly smile that still left his eyes sharp. 'From now on we're all on first-name terms. Dave, Sean, Ravi, Joe. No ranks, no nicknames. We're all civilians. Everything you hear in this room comes under the Official Secrets Act, which already binds you as serving soldiers, and the Military Aid to the Civil Power Act, with which you might be less familiar. An operation under the MACP needs to be signed off by the Home Secretary, which this will be by the time it becomes relevant. Essentially it allows the armed forces to provide assistance to the civil power in keeping law and order, when the armed forces have specialist capabilities or equipment that the civil power doesn't. And what the military currently has that the civil power doesn't is manpower with local knowledge for a very specific operation. Now. What follows is exactly as explained to COBRA. You're in exalted company, gentlemen . . .'

He leaned forward to open the folder, and began the briefing.

'The TLDR version is: we suspect a terrorist plot with an imminent payoff, we don't know what's going on and we are invoking the MACP to find out.' He let that sink in – Sean guessed he was giving them just enough time to think, *So what the fuck does that have to do with* me?

'In more detail . . .'

At first Dave explained what Sean already knew, only without the accusations. At least he seemed to take the view that getting people's cooperation involved treating them decently, which made a pleasant change from the other spook, who had obviously just wanted to scare or bully Sean into helping.

So. Two girls from Littern Mills – Zara Mann and *possibly* Emma Booth – had been in Nigeria under fake identities, they had returned on the same flight as Sean, and they had slipped back into the country under the cover of the airport siege and subsequently gone missing. The girl who was *possibly* Emma was to be referred to as Girl X.

Then came the new stuff, and it riveted Sean to his seat.

'Yesterday, just as your flight was taking off, two masked gunmen burst into the home of one Joanna

Harford of Fareham in Hampshire. They held her husband and two small children hostage, and ordered her to go to work as normal and follow a precise set of instructions.' A beat. 'Mrs Harford is an air traffic controller at the London Area Control Centre in Swanwick. Her instructions were to see that your flight from Lagos was specifically diverted to Southend. Not Manchester, not Edinburgh – Southend. She followed her instructions to the letter, and I'm pleased to report the Harfords have all been safely reunited.

'Meanwhile the gunman taken down by Fusilier Harker' – above the friendly smile Dave's eyes were cold; Sean felt his face burning again – 'has been identified.' He held up another photo – a police mugshot of a white guy in his twenties. 'Michael Joseph of Haringey, already a person of interest to us because of his involvement with certain extreme organizations. His face will be all over tomorrow's front pages and is already trending on social media.'

The smile had gone.

'Put all that together, with some precisely delivered security threats that led us to close some London airports but not others – and you find that someone went to a great deal of trouble to get those girls into the country, at Southend, without their having to go through passport control. You see, when the girls left the country, a new biometric security system was being installed at all UK airports. Fingerprint and retina scanning – almost foolproof. When the girls left, it was still in beta testing, but it became operational while they were away, and on her return Zara would have immediately been flagged, despite her false passport. She has previous for possession with intent to supply, so she's on the system, and it's quite possible that no one had thought this might be a problem in terms of her returning to the UK until she was out there. Hence, to get her back in, they had to lay this on. Yes, Sean?'

The informal atmosphere had encouraged Sean to put a hand up. He had clocked this point earlier, just not been able to put it into words.

'Sir—' He caught Dave's frown. 'Dave. If they're trying to keep it quiet so no one notices, it's kind of backfired. All they've done is run up a big red flag saying, *Look, we're secretly smuggling these girls in*. We wouldn't be talking about this now if they'd done it different.'

'Exactly.' Dave's mouth flattened as he tensed his jaw. 'But the fact is, they *did* do it this way, which suggests there is some pressing need. Something time sensitive. And they probably didn't have other options.

If it weren't for the whole security diversion thing, we might just assume that the girls are drug mules – smuggling white powder in condoms they previously swallowed abroad. It's amazing how many glam celebrity users gloss over the fact that the stuff they put up their nose has been crapped out of the arse of a slightly dim girl. No, you don't go to these lengths for drug smugglers – but you do if you're radicalized jihadis planning a terrorist strike to a specific deadline, and you need key personnel on the ground to make it happen. So it has to be assumed that Zara Mann and Girl X are highly dangerous and might be with people who are even more so. Yes, Joe?'

It was Wolston's turn to interrupt.

'No easy way to say this. You say *jihadis*, but aren't all the people we've talked about a little bit . . . white?' He glanced sideways at Mitra. 'No offence.'

'None taken, but you're coming back as a cockroach.'

Dave gave his flat smile again. 'You've lived a sheltered life in Afghanistan, Joe. If you'd served in the Balkans you'd have encountered whole populations of white Muslims. The 9th Muslim Liberation Brigade during the Bosnian War were mostly white guys, ethnic Bosnians. And radicalization is colour blind. It suits certain sections of society, not to mention the media, to think that the only threat comes from people with *al* and *abu* in their names – it makes everyone feel better if they can just put a problem into a different pigeon-hole to their own. Wrong. Michael Joseph converted to Islam last year, and as for the girls – have any of you heard of Samantha Lewthwaite?'

The name rang a bell. Sean frowned as he tried to remember.

'Aka the White Widow,' Dave continued. 'Nice Protestant Ulster girl who married one of the London bombers – Germaine Lindsay, who blew up a train on the Piccadilly line on seventh July 2005. After that she went on the run – and is now thought to be behind over four hundred deaths, including attacks in Mombasa and Nairobi in which she personally took part, and the training of suicide bombers in Syria and Yemen. As white as they come, and her father was in the Lancers. So don't be fooled by colour or background. In fact, don't be fooled by anything you currently believe because it's probably wrong.'

He held his arms out as far as they would go. 'There is a huge gap between where someone like Lewthwaite starts out and where they are now. So you think something major must have happened to get them from *here* to *there*. Wrong. It's small steps all the way.' Dave made little chopping motions in the air with his left hand, bringing it closer bit by bit to his right. 'Never big ones, because that might be too much to swallow. But every single little one makes perfect sense in the context of what's gone before.'

They looked at him in silence.

'It's not brainwashing – that's changing someone's belief against their will. It's more a problem of impaired decision-making. It begins with preconditioning through factors that are outside anyone's control. Poverty, perhaps – feelings of helplessness or disassociation, which may be grounded in reality or may just be psychological. It's often a simple background situation that is so massive, so crap, that there's no way you can fix it on your own. With Lewthwaite, it's thought to have begun when her parents split up. She was eleven. It gutted her and she found comfort with Muslim friends whose strong family network gave her strength. So far, so reasonable, right? This led to her formal conversion to Islam as a teenager. Still perfectly normal.

'Then, if you fall in with the wrong people, the more you go in, the easier it gets. More and more you're surrounded by like minds who identify as having the same belief but have a very different outlook to the one that first attracted you. Or, to be really clever – and the people who drive the radicalization *are* really clever – you get what *appears* to be debate, a carefully staged way of showing both sides of the argument. But they make sure you come to the conclusion they want. And because you're surrounded by them, you get no disagreement, no argument. In social media and in real life, you just get approval, no criticism. You end up as they want you to: a long way from where you began. And, as I said, all in small steps . . . Sean has something to say.'

Sean hadn't realized his feelings were showing so plainly on his face. Maybe it was the sceptical way he was twisting his mouth.

'Still sounds too easy, Dave. The way you say it, this Lewthwaite girl could have been *me*. *We* were stone broke, *my* childhood was pretty shitty. I didn't get radicalized.'

'Didn't you? As I recall from your record, you loved your gang so much that you took one for the team so that your mates could escape, and ended up getting nicked. There's a file the size of the Yellow Pages containing all the conversations you had with social workers, every time you got into trouble with the police, but you clearly just blew them off because someone else was filling your head with the rubbish you *wanted* to hear. If that doesn't sound familiar, then you haven't been paying attention.'

Sean's face blazed, but he let it go. He couldn't argue.

'But you're also right, Sean, that it's not a universal

rule. Not everyone takes such a course. The huge majority never will. In 2003 over a million people marched against UK involvement in the Iraq War, but no way did the war produce a million home-grown radicals. But you don't need a million. Just a few, with a gun or a bomb, to make a real impact.' Dave spread his hands like he had just performed a clever magic trick and was waiting for the applause. 'And there you have it. Jihad.'

'So much for "Thou shalt not kill",' Wolston muttered. Now he got the benefit of Dave's bland, 9mm gaze.

'"Thou shalt not *kill*", or "Thou shalt not *murder*"? Not *quite* the same thing, are they?' He waggled his hand. 'Just enough of a difference to produce some really radical changes in behaviour.'

Sean thought of the deaths at the airport that morning. *Clarkson* had *murdered* Bright. He, Sean, had *killed May*. So, OK, yes, he thought, there was a difference.

Dave was still talking.

'Yes, religion has rules – and where you have rules, because human beings are awkward sods who just love to be contrary, you get loopholes. Once someone is committed to jihad, they're exposed to a whole framework of religious argument that can tie knots in any holy book you care to name. For instance, many radicals today follow the concept of "defensive jihad" – which basically lets them off the normal rules so that they can do things that might seem profoundly unIslamic with a clear conscience. Radicalization is not the same as finding religion – that's just a convenient shortcut for the headline writers. It's a perversion of what the religion has to offer – structure, stability, empowerment.

'And that's probably where we are now. Gentlemen, whatever the full story behind it all, those girls came in as they did for a purpose that involves them, and their target. The most obvious candidate for a target is the Commonwealth Summit starting in London the day after tomorrow. Naturally all the obvious parts of London have been swept to within an inch of their lives with all the resources we can throw at them. And then this happens. But did anyone ever sneak a peek at Littern Mills? I'll give you a clue. No, of course not. Why should they?

'And so suddenly the Security Service is scrabbling around for the most basic int – which, when you work for an organization that's meant to know what you had for dinner or when you last had sex, is kind of embarrassing. If we suddenly spray personnel at the estate, having previously left it alone until now, the terrorists will know that we suspect something and they might slip through the net again. Whereas all we know for sure so far is that Zara and Emma, who is *possibly* Girl X, live in Wolsey Tower on Littern Mills.'

He instantly clocked Sean's surprised reaction. 'Correct, Sean. Right opposite Gladstone Tower, where your mother lives. Zara lives with dad Jamie and brother Ste. Emma lives on her own, though officially it's her mum's place. So Littern Mills is where we begin. It may be where whatever they're planning goes down; it may just be their base for an operation elsewhere – but we have to start somewhere, so it starts there. Yes, Sean?'

Sean had no fondness for Littern Mills, but fuck that, it was *home*. The thought that it might also be base camp for a terrorist operation severely pissed him off.

'You said an operation elsewhere, si— Dave . . . What kind of operation?'

Dave sighed. 'So many possibilities. There could be a weapons cache on the estate. A bomb-making factory for suicide vests or backpack IEDs. It could be a command location that is sending information to other cells on where, when and how to attack.'

'So . . .' Sean frowned. 'How does that tie in with the girls being in Nigeria?'

'*Exactly!* We need to *know*. The command location

is actually the easiest option for us to explore. We have an army of smart bots and humans analysing every phone call made on the estate, and every byte of data passing in and out. But for the rest we need covert eyes on the ground. And therefore, under the MACP, we are sending in an undercover unit. The unit will be based in an OP on the estate and its prime objective will be to identify the nature of the threat, especially if it is to the Summit. Secondary objectives are: to establish the whereabouts of Girl X and Zara; to establish Girl X's identity; to identify any other cell members; and to identify whatever might have been trafficked between Nigeria and here. And – although I cannot order; I can only ask for volunteers – it is my very strong desire that the unit will consist of' – he flashed the three of them a dour smile – 'you.'

Sean, Mitra and Wolston stared at him, and then at each other.

Dave waved with a broad palm at Sean. 'Sean – born and bred on the estate. You will have an instinctive knowledge of the place that even the best-trained under-cover operator could never match. Ravi – you will be pleased to know that there will be an element of house-breaking involved, which will also be signed off by the Home Secretary. This supersedes your undertaking to the judge not to indulge in that particular habit again.'

Now it was Mitra's turn to come under the very interested stare of his two mates. Sean had had no idea that Mitra had previous. Usually unflappable, Mitra looked like he might actually blush.

'And, Joe, Colonel Levene quite rightly insists on using the existing military chain of command where possible, and your accent will not be out of place on Littern Mills.'

'I'm from Dartford,' Wolston said.

'Close enough.' The smile switched off and Dave was suddenly serious. 'So. Volunteers. Can I count on you?'

Sean's heart thudded.

Whenever he thought he was putting Littern Mills behind him, it had a habit of reappearing. The last time that happened, it had almost dragged him back down again, and his mum's life had been in more danger than she would ever know. Two good reasons to stay well away this time.

But it was a chance to get back at Bright's killers. Just the thought of his mate on the carousel, choking on his own blood, was enough to make him want to take on the world.

So he nodded.

On either side of him, Wolston and Mitra nodded as well.

'Only,' Wolston added, 'you do know we have zero training in undercover work . . .'

'I know. And that is why the fourth member of the team will be – me. I know my accent will make me as out of place as a condom salesman in the Vatican, but I have done this kind of thing before. I'll spend my time in the OP. But I'll be there to support you . . . And Sean has another question.'

Adams always said you couldn't ask too many questions, even if you felt like the class moron for not getting it. It was better to be clear than to make assumptions. So Sean pressed on with yet another.

'One thing I'll tell you about the estate straight off,' he said, 'is we notice outsiders pretty darn quick. Where's this OP going to be based so no one notices?'

Dave's sudden grin wasn't amused. 'Well done, Sean. I am *so pleased* you asked that question.'

And Sean knew the answer before the words were even out of his mouth.

Chapter 13

Simmering with anger, Sean hesitated in front of the scuffed wooden door. He shot a final, resentful look at Wolston, Mitra and Dave, queuing behind him. He got three tense, nervous stares back at him. Dave nodded in a way that said, *Get on with it.*

So Sean rapped out his accustomed *one-two, three, four* knock on the door of flat 403, Gladstone Tower, West Square, Littern Mills, and stood back.

The door opened and he put on his biggest, cheesiest grin.

'Hi, Mum!'

Janice Harker squealed. '*Sean!*'

The lads had asked Sean to describe his mother; he had said, 'Short and fat.' He assumed he got his tall, muscular build from his father. Judging by her boy-friends, it did seem to be her preferred male body type.

He hadn't been completely fair. A year ago, what with bad boyfriend trouble and no money to spend on food, she had been down to skin and bone. But if she hadn't quite replaced all the lost pounds, she had made a serious effort – enough to knock him back a step when she flung her arms around his neck and kissed him.

'Oh, Sean! It's so good to *see* you! Weren't you off to Tenerife?'

The sheer delight on her face made him feel a bastard. Not just for letting her down, like he was about to, but for putting her in danger *again*. Last summer she hadn't known that she was being used as leverage to get him to perform an act of treason. And now her home was going to be used as the base for an anti-terrorist operation that could bring down all kinds of retaliation on her if it ever got out.

Though Sean did feel pleased with himself in one way: she could now be truly glad to see him. She was coming back from rock bottom. When he came home a year ago, she had been clinging to the hope that her son wouldn't notice the missing furniture, and that he and the loan shark who was stiffing her for every penny wouldn't cross paths. She had lost out on both counts.

Now she noticed that behind Sean were three more young men, all in jeans and leather jackets like her son (on Sean's advice), and all with duffel bags slung over their shoulders.

'Oh.' She let go of Sean, and unconsciously dusted her dress down while she tried a nervous, hopeful, welcoming smile. 'Hello.'

Then it was back to Sean. She tugged him to lower his head, speaking quickly and urgently. 'Sean, you were coming back today, and they said a Fusilier was killed at the airport, and you're a Fusilier . . .'

He had expected her to put two and two together and he had to hit that one right on the head. They didn't want his mum telling her friends about her son's airport-hostage nightmare.

'Nah. Completely different unit, Mum.' Denying Bright like that, he felt a little bit of him die inside, but it had to be done. 'We were in the plane behind. Can we . . . ?'

She stepped back, and the others followed Sean into the flat, nodding to Janice as they trooped into the living room. There was the sofa and a table and a couple of chairs that Sean had bought for her off Gumtree. They slung their bags on the floor, and stretched and flopped down like they had already moved in.

Mitra pulled a four-pack out of his bag and passed around the cans. 'Want a beer, Mrs Harker?'

She silently shook her head while her puzzled

expression begged an answer from Sean. OK, here it came. Time to lie out of his arse with a smile on his face.

'Tenerife's off, Mum. You heard about the airport thing? Well' – he shrugged – 'they're not letting us out of the country. So we're kind of having a . . . What's that word, Joe?'

'Staycation,' Wolston called as he cracked open his can.

'That's it. So we're staycating. Catering. Cationing. Whatever.'

He pretended not to notice her slight look of horror as he put his arm through hers and turned to the others. 'This is Dave . . . Joe . . . Ravi. We were all going to hit the nightclubs together in Tenerife, but now that's off, so instead we thought we'd come up to town – and, guess what? I said I knew this little place we could all stay rent free . . .'

As Sean had predicted, they had been pinged the moment they set foot on the estate. He had seen the glances – sideways looks from the older locals and full-on curiosity from the groups of teenagers who hung around doing nothing except look hard. Sean had paid the closest attention to the second group because he knew from experience that if they were going to have a problem, it would be from them. They would have given themselves a hard-sounding name (Killaz, as far as he could tell from the graffiti), they would have their own obscure rules for who was in and who was out, and their primary objective would be to claim their territory as their own. So any incursion from outside could be viewed as enemy action.

But either the Killaz didn't view the unit as a threat – or, Sean liked to think, they recognized that a superior predator was on the scene, and decided that mutual non-aggression was the best course for everyone. Whichever it was, they didn't interfere.

Since everyone knew they were here, they had taken care to hide in plain sight. Before heading up to the flat they had grabbed a KFC, then stopped off at the pub and bought a round, with one for the bargirl, all the time bitching loudly about cancelled plans and reduced pulling possibilities. Mitra had showed signs of sub-merging himself in the role – he'd had to be dragged away before he made body-language promises to the bargirl that he couldn't keep. Sean had clocked some familiar faces, even nodded at a few of them.

Then Wolston had produced his *Game of Thrones* boxset, saying that he had been waiting ages to have a really good catch-up session, and the others had split between sharing his enthusiasm and groaning loudly.

So by now the word would be well out that Sean

Harker and three soldiers were here on leave. If any of them were seen out on the estate, then it wouldn't raise eyebrows – and thanks to *Game of Thrones*, no one would be surprised if some of them spent all their time together back in his mum's flat.

Nowhere on the estate was exactly *safe* – nothing you'd give a good rating on TripAdvisor – but their cover story made them about as secure as they were going to get.

Janice's smile at the lads was distinctly forced. 'Oh, Sean, it's so nice to meet your friends, but' – she seemed torn between the pleasure of their company and the practicalities of the arrangement – 'I've got nothing in for four hungry lads, and there's only the two beds . . .' She looked at their bulging bags.

Sean swooped in before she made the mental calculation of how much each of them was bringing in for 'just a day or two'.

'Thought of that, Mum. We had a whip-round.'

Her eyes went saucer-round as he pulled a wad out of his jacket. He pressed it into her hand and folded her fingers over it.

'You deserve a treat, Mum. There's over a grand there.' Dave had made sure it was a non-round figure, in mixed notes, as it would be if they really *had* dug into their own wallets to pile the money together.

Though in that case it would have been a lot less than a grand. The plan was to keep her off balance enough to get her out of the door before she thought too deeply about anything and spotted the bits that didn't fit. For example, that they wanted somewhere to stay rent free, and were paying her over a grand to provide it.

'And . . .' With a flourish, Sean produced a folded sheet of A4. She opened it up cautiously and frowned her incomprehension up at him.

'That is only confirmation of your paid-up booking for one room, two nights starting tonight, at the London Marriott, Marble Arch!'

The Commonwealth Summit began the day after tomorrow. If they didn't find anything within the next twenty-four hours, they would be redundant and with-drawn, and Janice could safely come home. Two nights was all they needed.

Her jaw dropped. 'Oh, Sean, sweetheart! I' – her eyes darted from the booking slip to the wad of cash – 'can't . . .'

'Oh, g'wan! You're always talking about the friends up west that you never see. This is your chance. Invite them up to the hotel! Treat them to a spa session. It's all paid for.'

Sean had always suspected that at least some of the

up-west friends were imaginary, but hopefully there was someone she could meet.

She gave it one last try. 'I . . . I suppose I could pull a sickie with Lakhani, but you know he'd dock me a day's pay . . .'

The money that didn't come from Sean, Janice earned by stacking shelves at the mini supermarket on the ground level. Sean simply squeezed her fingers more tightly around the cash. They both knew it would cover a lot of docked days from Lakhani. It was one of those rare occasions when mother and son were on the same wavelength.

'I'll have a word with him, Mum. I'll make sure you have a good cover story.'

Though now he saw a different kind of doubt flickering in her eyes, and he didn't have an answer for it. She was so happy to have him drop in without warning, but she was confused and hurt that he was in such a hurry to get rid of her. He wished he didn't have to lie. He wished he didn't have to be such a shit. And why did he always have to feel guilty when he was with her?

He hugged her and gave her a big kiss on both cheeks. 'Just treat yourself, Mum, because you're the best mum in the world and you deserve it.'

A grand in the hand and two nights at the London Marriott made up for a lot of lying . . .

'Fucking hell, Sean,' Mitra said as Sean let himself back into the flat. He had escorted his mum off the estate, carrying her bag for her, and put her into a taxi, and slipped the cabbie the fare in advance. She hadn't stopped looking confused, but at least she had started to look like she was going to enjoy her treat. 'Are you that convincing when you want to get them into bed?'

'So this is Harker Towers.' Wolston paused for a moment from setting up the tripod on the kitchen draining board and looked around admiringly. 'How many centuries has it been in the family?'

'Ever since Mum got knocked up with me and went on the council waiting list,' Sean said dourly. He knew the joking was just a way of releasing the tension, now that the operation was officially go. But he didn't feel like joining in.

'Shit. Just one thing after another for her, then, wasn't it?'

Sean scowled. 'I still say this is out of order.'

'Noted.' Dave pulled a long, thin box out of his bag and opened it to show a gleaming black telescope that looked like it belonged in a sci-fi thriller. 'Now give us a hand.'

Slowly but surely, the flat was transformed into the OP. Anger still smouldered in Sean's heart as he helped out. It had been burning there ever since the briefing in Tidworth.

He accepted the danger for himself. He had very quickly clocked that he could be a security risk on this mission. Supposing one of their targets pinged him? Remembered him from the airport? They could be blown the moment it happened. He got the feeling that Dave was kind of hoping it *would* happen. He could be bait to lure them out. And Sean would be more than happy to take on Bright's killers in the open.

But involving his mum was out of order. He'd been doing everything he could to keep his army and his home life separate, and then the bastards went and chained them together. There were people out there prepared to bring the UK air traffic system to a halt, hold hostages at gunpoint, use lethal force. Bright's killer was still at liberty – and Sean could be bringing him into his mum's life.

But Dave had spoken, Levene had backed him up: this was how it was.

And it cut both ways. Those people wouldn't have done all that if they weren't planning a lot of hurt and harm. Sean already lived with enough regret in his life. He wasn't going to risk knowing that he could have helped save tens, hundreds, thousands of lives – and hadn't.

Sean and Dave set the telescope on top of the tripod on the draining board, next to the other telescope that was already there. They cut small holes in the kitchen blind and covered them with a fabric that the telescopes could see through from this side, but which from the other side would just look like patches. The telescopes focused on the front doors of the flats of Zara Mann and Emma Booth, possibly Girl X, both in Wolsey Tower on the other side of the square.

Meanwhile there were three laptops warming up on the kitchen table. Dave took charge of calibrating them. One showed the views from each telescope in separate windows. The others would be put into use the next day, when the unit broke into the girls' flats and installed hidden cameras and mikes.

'Now,' Dave ordered, 'each of you select the shirt you'll be wearing tomorrow, and we'll fix the mikes into the collars. And then you're all going for a last visit to the pub so we can shake the system down and get you comfortable with using them in public. You don't want to be seen wandering around in broad daylight having an argument with thin air. And Ravi, Sean – get used to carrying these . . . We'll put them on to charge when we get back.'

On the table he had set down two devices that looked like smartphones with a rugged black rubber casing. Sean picked one up and looked at it with interest. The moment you checked the screen you ceased to mistake it for a smartphone. The names of different types of explosive scrolled slowly past the bottom of a flickering graph.

If there were weapons or explosives on the estate, these two gadgets should let them know.

'We're going to do a test run under cover of darkness,' Dave said. His voice and face were flat and cold. 'Twenty-four hours until the Summit, gents. That's all we have.'

Chapter 14

The anger was still there the following morning. Snatching a few hours in his own bed didn't do much for it – and not just because he'd slept top-to-toe with Ravi Mitra. Opening his eyes and staring at Mitra's feet had just brought it all back. *Fuck, this is really happening.*

Now Sean, wearing overalls borrowed from the council's maintenance department, stretched his hands out along the parapet of the sixth floor of Wolsey and gazed around at the familiar sights.

Home sweet fucking home.

The edges of Littern Mills were a maze of low-rise houses and maisonettes. It was the three squares at the centre – West, East and South, surrounding a triangle of common 'park land' which the locals called 'the jungle' – that were where it was all at, as far as Sean was concerned. Each square was surrounded by four towers. So, twelve towers in all. Wolsey was on West

Square with Gladstone opposite, Cottingham on the left and Coopersale on the right. Each tower had shopping units on the ground-floor level and flats above.

Sixth wasn't quite high enough to escape the smells of concrete, piss and petrol. The square might have been washed clean in yesterday's thunderstorm, but today promised to be bone dry and the odours were already kicking off in the summer heat.

'*Sean, stop looking like you're enjoying the view.*' Dave's voice spoke in his ear. '*You're at work.*'

They had gear that Sean had only previously seen in the movies. Microscopic, flesh-coloured earpieces that would have been invisible to anyone not deliberately staring down their lugholes. Tiny mikes hidden in their collars – the one drawback was that it meant they couldn't wear T-shirts – couldn't be clocked by anyone who wasn't actively feeling for them, and were set to transmit or receive by a concealed pressel switch on their belts. And the pocket-sized, smartphone-like explosive detectors.

So, that bit was cool. It was everything else that pissed him off.

Sean shot a glance across West Square at Gladstone. The towers were all built the same way. Every level had an open shared balcony giving access to the flats, with stairs and lifts at either end. So, from here, Sean could look straight over, and a little bit down, at the fourth-floor balcony of Gladstone and the door to his flat.

'Whatever,' he said under his breath, and turned to where Ravi Mitra, also in maintenance overalls, was busy breaking into Zara Mann's flat. 'Still can't believe you're a fucking tealeaf. You kept that quiet.'

'Well, sorry it wasn't quite as glamorous as grand theft auto . . .' Mitra never took his gaze from the keyhole, where he had inserted two slim bits of metal – a pick and a rake. The pick looked like a long, thin metal spike with a hook at the end. The rake was one of several that Mitra had gone through to select for this task: a thin metal shaft with ridges on the end that engaged with the pins inside the lock. He moved it gently back and forth until something clicked, and then twisted the pick to release the lock. The door opened when he tugged on the handle. 'On the plus side, I never did time in a YOI.'

'No, I bet you just burst into tears and begged to be let off.'

'Got it in one.' Mitra grinned and pushed the door further open. 'Suspended sentence and an appointment at the recruiting office. Shall we?'

He called into the hallway. 'Hello! Maintenance!'

They had rung the bell before Mitra went to work. But there could always be someone who was so wasted or out of it they hadn't responded. Priority One was establishing that the flat really *was* empty, so he pushed the door shut behind him and they split up.

Somehow Sean could already tell it was empty. There was a certain deadness in the air. It was a silence that set his teeth on edge. In the past, whenever he wired a car, he had been able to put his mind into neutral, just concentrating on the task at hand. He had always checked around, or posted a lookout, to ensure that he wasn't interrupted – but if he was, well, he had long legs and he could move them fast. But being in a flat – that was another matter. You couldn't see who was coming, and there was only one way out. The silence just helped him to picture imaginary owners on the balcony outside, getting closer and closer . . .

At least he knew the layout of flats like this. The two doors on the left would be the master bedroom and the living room. Mitra took those. Sean took the two on the right, after the kitchen. Both were obviously young people's rooms, with single beds and the same kind of decoration – sports photos, school certificates, movie posters. He had to look at the names on the certificates to see which room belonged to who – Zara or her brother Ste.

One of the unit's objectives was to establish whether Zara was actually on the estate, or had ever left it. Now they were in the flat, it still wasn't obvious. All the windows were cracked open as far as the security locks would allow for ventilation in the summer heat, so there was no musty smell of disuse. Zara's neatly made bed could have been slept in the night before, or last month.

It was no different from her brother Ste's or her dad Jamie's, and it had been confirmed that they *were* around. Ste was a medical student, placed at Whipps Cross University Hospital. Dad was a long-distance driver. Zara didn't have a job, wasn't a student and wasn't signed on, so there was nowhere to check up on her.

Sean didn't remember any of the Manns from when he had lived here. They would have been a bit too respectable for him. A family that could produce a medical student would have steered well clear of the Littern Guyz.

A bellow of laughter just outside the window made Sean jump about a metre into the room. It was only someone walking along outside, past the kitchen window, chatting into their phone. The voice and laughter receded.

They had confirmed that the flat really was empty.

'That's Ravi and Sean complete,' Mitra reported for Dave's benefit as he came out of the bathroom at the end of the hall.

'Complete' meant they were inside. Dave had drilled

them all on surveillance-speak but it still sounded weird. Like listening to a bunch of three-year-olds talk about themselves, using their names instead of saying 'I'. *Sean wants a wee-wee.* But it was important. It was a way of speaking that always exactly identified who was saying what about where. And it was impossible to mistake for normal talk, so you knew you weren't accidentally overhearing someone else's conversation.

Mitra went on. 'Flat is empty, and Sean is acting like the cat waiting for its owner to discover it's crapped in his slippers.'

'*Roger, and get on with it. You need to start patrolling.*'

'Breaking and entering was never my thing,' Sean said in self-defence.

'Learn from the best, my friend.'

Mitra got a chair from the kitchen and stood on it under the hallway smoke detector. The detector was a white plastic box with a grille and a red test button in the centre. The cover dropped open on its hinge and Mitra went to work.

'You can't have been that good if you got nicked.'

'True.' Concentration made Mitra poke his tongue out of the corner of his mouth as he wired the miniature camera and microphone into place, as per Dave's demonstration back at the OP. 'Probably shouldn't have kept on robbing the block where I lived.'

Sean snorted. 'That's just lame. You don't shit in your own bed – rule number one.'

'Says the man going undercover on the estate he grew up on.'

Sean rolled his eyes and got to work.

They had already done this in Emma's flat on the fifth level, so Sean knew it would take Mitra a couple of minutes to do his thing, first in the hallway and then with the other smoke detector in the living room. He used the time to begin his really close search.

You move nothing without noting where it is, and then putting it back exactly. Dave had drummed the procedure into them. Mitra would make sure he left no footprints on the chair and he would replace it exactly where he found it. They had been told to look for telltales on the doors – small bits of paper, maybe even hairs or bristles positioned so that they would drop down if the door was opened. If they found them, they would put them back.

All the doors were open, but Sean still clocked their exact angle so he could return them to it when he was done. There would be nothing to tweak the sixth sense of anyone in the Mann family – nothing to make them think, *Hang on – someone's been here.*

'*That's Dave getting sound and vision.*' The OP was picking up the signals from the bugs.

Emma's flat hadn't produced anything except confirmation that she was around – somewhere. No clue as to whether she had ever been away; nothing to say whether she was Girl X.

Zara's flat was more helpful. In the dirty clothes basket in the bathroom – Sean took a snap of the top layer of clothes so that he could put them back in the exact same position – he found a lightweight, flowery T-shirt and linen trousers. He felt his heart begin to thump louder as he laid them out on the floor and checked them against the CCTV images of Zara on his phone.

It was an exact match.

'That's Sean with the outfit Zara was wearing at the airport,' he reported. Slowly he let himself grin.

Until then, he suddenly realized, this had all been theory. It still *could* have all been one big misunderstanding. This was the first confirmation that there was a grain of truth in MI5's suspicions.

He simultaneously heard Mitra in the next room and over the radio. His mate's voice was also biting back on excitement.

'And that's Ravi with her passport. Not in her name. Exit stamp from Murtala Muhammed Airport, dated two days ago.'

Grain number two.

'*Roger and excellent!*' They could hear Dave's satisfaction. '*So she's back. Take photos, replace and keep looking.*'

There wasn't anything else – and as Sean was positioning the bathroom door exactly as it had been, it suddenly struck him that there was a significant absence. He went back to the bathroom cabinet and looked more closely at the contents. Hair gel. Deodorant. Two electric razors and two kinds of aftershave – presumably for Dad and Ste. *Three* toothbrushes and *three* different kinds of toothpaste, and considerably more than three kinds of what he would basically describe as 'girly stuff'. Also three towels, but they were all bone dry on a heated towel rail. It was impossible to tell if any had or hadn't been used that day. Ditto the three toothbrushes, which would have dried out in the warm air.

But . . .

'There's no sign of anti-malarials here,' he reported. 'Headache, Strepsils, blood pressure, Wellman – no anti-malarials.'

'None in her room, either,' Mitra reported. 'Suppose she could have them on her, though?'

'*What's the big deal with anti-malarials?*' Dave asked.

Wolston answered. '*Dave, if she'd come back from tropical regions, she'd have them. Like we do.*'

'But we know she's been back,' Sean stressed,

thinking of the clothes. He closed the bathroom cabinet and went back into the hall. Mitra stepped out of Zara's room and they looked at each other. It was weird. Why leave evidence that you've been there and then moved on, instead of just moving on and making like you've never been there at all?

'Roger. We have a result. Well done. Complete your search and get—'

But Sean didn't hear the rest of the sentence – because then a shadow moved behind the frosted glass of the front door and a key scraped in the lock.

Chapter 15

Training took over. Only boyos and civilians stood rooted to the spot when things went south. Trained lads reacted. The enemy appeared, you went for the nearest cover.

Which in this case was the bathroom. While the newcomer was still fighting with the lock – Sean wondered if Mitra had broken it – the two lads had got themselves behind the bathroom door. They stood looking at each other, chest to chest, ears cocked for sounds outside.

Whoever it was had won the battle with the door. It opened and footsteps came down the hall.

Mitra frowned in thought, then turned abruptly and flushed the toilet. 'Dunno what the old bat was on about,' he said loudly as he stepped out into the hallway. 'There's no blockage here— Oh, hello!'

Sean pulled the peak of his cap down as far as it would go without actually blinding him – he didn't remember any of the Mann family, but he couldn't guarantee the same would apply in reverse – and followed his mate. Out in the hall, below the dark half-circle of his brim, he could just see a young white man in his mid-twenties staring in astonishment at the two of them.

'Who the fuck are you?'

'Maintenance?' Mitra said. Sean was happy to let him do the talking. His mate turned round for a moment so that the man could read the council logo on his back. 'Got a report of a blockage. And you are . . .'

'I fucking live here and there's no fucking blockage.'

'Yeah, well, we'd worked that out.' Mitra pulled out his phone and pretended to check it. 'So, uh . . .' He jabbed at the screen with a hint of desperation. 'Uh-h . . .'

Shit, he's forgotten!

They had worked out the details of the cover story in advance. Just in case they got caught like this. But it meant remembering a particular name . . .

'Mrs Patel,' Sean said, not looking up.

Mitra seized on it. 'Mrs Patel . . .'

'Do I look like my name's Patel? My name's Mann. This is 614. Mrs Patel's in 514. One level down.'

Which had been the whole point of the cover story. *Oops, sorry, wrong level. Won't bother you any longer.*

So this was Ste – though Sean had kind of guessed that already. While Mitra kept him talking, Sean studied him, still not giving the guy the benefit of a clear look at his own face. Medium height, skinny, dark hair already matted with sweat on a warm summer morning that was still not as hot as it was going to get. He was wearing a limp, damp T-shirt and baggy cargo pants, and a bag was slung over his shoulder. And someone had given him a nice shiner recently. Sean narrowed his eyes. The dark swelling over his cheekbone meant that Ste's right eye was pushed a little more closed than the left.

'. . . look,' Ste was saying, 'I just pulled an all-nighter and I'm only here to change my shirt, then I'm due back on shift. And there's no blockage. Right?' He ducked into his room.

'Shit,' Mitra called. He glanced at Sean. 'They work you hard. What sorta job's that, then? Bar work?'

Ste came out again, tugging a fresh T-shirt down over his torso. 'Trainee doctor,' he said. He glared down at Mitra. 'You still here?'

'Just leaving, Mr, uh, Mann. Sorry to have bothered you.' Mitra grimaced at Sean and jerked his thumb at the door with a commanding *Let's go* gesture. They exited with as much grace as they could.

They headed for the lifts and stairs in tight silence. Sean would have liked nothing more than to bellow into the mike something along the lines of *Why the fuck didn't you tell us he was coming?* But people tended to notice guys shouting at the air, even on Littern Mills.

So they said nothing until they reached the lifts. Mitra pressed the call button but Sean took his elbow and guided him to the stairs.

'See,' he murmured, 'this is why you kept getting nicked.'

They walked one flight down, and along to 514. Sean pressed the bell.

'Supposing she's in?' Mitra asked.

'Bluff.'

They waited, and Sean rang again. When he sensed someone in his peripheral vision, he glanced to his right.

Ste Mann was peering at them suspiciously from the stairwell.

'Awright?' Sean called. Mitra gave a friendly wave and Ste withdrew without saying anything.

'OP,' Sean said, 'give us confirmation when he leaves the building.'

They stayed where they were until Wolston reported that Ste was crossing the square. Then and only then did Sean and Mitra set off for the lifts.

Sean's furious question still bubbled inside him, but he also had an important observation to report.

Ste had that shiner. Nice one.

It was right where Lance Corporal Marshall had thumped *Hammond* the day before.

Chapter 16

'Because I was watching Emma's flat,' Wolston said through his teeth.

Sean had put his question to him. They stood nose to nose in Sean's mum's kitchen, where the cameras and telescopes were set up behind the blind. Sean's admiration for the man – for his courage, his leadership, his handling of the airport job – had been put on the back burner.

'Dave called the hospital and they confirmed Ste was at work,' Wolston added.

This neatly passed the buck to Dave, who was sitting at the kitchen table tapping away at one of the laptops.

He glanced up. 'And he slipped home,' he said. 'Whipps Cross University Hospital is a fifteen-minute walk from here. He could be here and back in a regular break and no one would notice. Guys, glitches happen in the best operations – like operatives forgetting key names in cover stories, Mitra. Fact is, we've accomplished phase one, bugs in place in both flats, and we've already achieved useful int. Confirmation that Zara has returned home, and I've sent off images of Ste for pattern matching with *Hammond*. Now, brew up and kit up because phase two's going to be a lot harder.'

'Here. Let me.' Wolston took the kettle and started to fill it from the tap. It was a cosy, domestic gesture that Sean also recognized as a way of saying sorry.

'Cheers.'

He still couldn't get Ste's black eye out of his mind. *Hammond* hadn't killed Bright himself, but he had been one of the party. If Ste was *Hammond*, then they were getting somewhere close.

The feeling that he might have been within a few feet of one of the gunmen, and the guy hadn't suspected, was a real kick.

In his pocket his phone buzzed with a text.

Jst wok up.

He shot a resentful look at the time. He had been up for four hours already, with not much sleep before that. And he wasn't exactly well rested from his short nap on the flight home. In fact, he hadn't had a decent lie-in for the last six months, and he wasn't expecting

one any time soon. Recently it had been thoughts of
Tenerife that kept him going. Now he was just flying
on fumes.

> Gng 2 treet mself to a spa now.
> Have a luvly time wiv ur m8s.

'No probs, Mum,' he muttered.

Ten minutes later Sean and Mitra were back outside.
Like Dave said, this would be the hard bit.

Wolston and Dave would maintain constant surveillance from the OP, with telescopic lenses trained on
the flats of Emma and Zara, and with the feed from the
bugs. Sean and Mitra were back in their normal mufti.
They had an estate to patrol and an unknown target to
identify.

MI5 still thought the best bet was a weapons factory,
though Sean couldn't tie that in with whatever Girl X
and Zara had been doing in Nigeria, and he knew Dave
couldn't, either. But MI5 had to start with some kind of
assumption, so it went with the most likely explanation
and hoped that the facts would help it make sense.

Dave had shown them pictures of the kind of thing
they were looking for. Plastic tubs full of powder you
wouldn't associate with explosives, like pepper or

chapatti flour. And more obvious chemical contents like hydrogen peroxide. Any kind of powder, Dave said, was an explosive accelerant – the millions of small particles meant that it had many times more surface area than a solid lump of material the same size. Which gave it millions of times more exposure to the oxygen in the air – the stuff that actually caught fire and burned.

Or it might not be explosives. They could be laying up firearms for a strike on the Summit, or on one of the leaders. But firearms also use explosives – the propellant in each cartridge that goes *bang* as it pushes the pointy bit out of the barrel.

And you fight science with science. The detectors in their pockets were constantly sniffing the atmosphere and comparing what they picked up against a database of substances that was held on a card plugged into the gadget. Which probably didn't include chapatti flour, but did include a lot of other stuff with chemical markers linked to drugs or explosives. At the moment the cards were for picking up explosives only – somewhere like Littern Mills, Dave reckoned (and Sean agreed), they would pick up drugs left, right and centre, and MI5 had more important things to worry about. Readouts were synced by Bluetooth to their real phones, so they could check for readings while apparently updating their Facebook status. And any matches would generate a text, so it would look like Sean's mum was sending another happy little message, when in fact it was telling him: Potassium chlorate within 50 metres.

But that fifty-metre thing was the key. You had to be near the location, and the only way to do that was to walk there. The cool gear – the digital sniffer, the earpieces, the hidden mikes – had a James Bond feel to it, until you remembered you never saw James Bond wearing his soles down doing legwork: 007 would head for the nearest nightclub, pick up a beautiful woman, shag the answers out of her, and go off and get the bad guys. Sean and Mitra had to do it the hard way, by patrolling.

Dave had been full of advice on how to do that too:

'You walk like you belong here. So you're going down this alleyway – well, why the fuck shouldn't you? It's *your* alleyway. You've got a purpose. Anyone eyeballs you, you eyeball them back – like, *What the fuck are you looking at?* Or, *All right?* Whichever works best in the context. But the key thing is, *you engage.* You'll be noticed if you're trying hard not to be there, but if you obviously don't give a toss about being noticed, that disarms suspicion.

'And never explain, never justify, never apologize. Whatever you're doing, you follow it through. It's continuity of action. I had a team mate who found himself accidentally turning down a dead end in the backstreets of Belfast that was overlooked by several apartments, and just to make it really interesting there were a lot of people watching him. Players on the ground, and nosy old biddies in the flats above. If he just went, *Oh, whoops*, and came out again, they'd know he wasn't local. But if he *was* local, he'd know it was a dead end and he wouldn't go down there in the first place. So what did he do?'

'Developed spider powers and climbed out?' Mitra had suggested, and got a sharp glare in response.

'He went down to the end, whipped out his willy and pretended to take a slash in the corner. Then he gave it a shake and zipped up and walked back out again. Believe it or not, he couldn't actually take a leak under the circumstances, but no one was close enough to see that, and he went through every motion of it. His body language was one hundred per cent consistent. And for the icing on the cake, just in case there was any doubt, as he left he put on this kind of sheepish, apologetic grin for the fan club in the apartments up top. Because no one's going to feel their heart warming for a stranger who just took a piss outside their window, but big eyes and a shy grin will get you a long way.

'Now, take plenty of water because it's going to be

hot out there. And you never know when you might need to take an emergency leak.'

'That's Sean needing a code,' Sean said. 'Gate number CT53.'

'*Roger*,' said Wolston's voice in his ear. '*Stand by.*'

Sean stood in front of a grilled gate. On the other side, concrete stairs led down into welcome, cool darkness. The gate didn't use to be there but he was expecting it. He had already checked out the sublevels of Gladstone, and that had been the same. Now he had moved on to Cottingham, between Gladstone and Wolsey.

They had divided their duties, so as to cover the estate as quickly as possible. Their basic task was to get one of the detectors into every single nook and cranny available. Mitra took the balconies and the shopping units. And because he knew them like the back of his hand, Sean descended into the under-levels of the estate – the maze of corridors and damp concrete chambers that ran beneath the squares and linked up the basements of the towers.

After that, if there was no luck, they would transfer their attention to the low-rise apartments that encircled the three squares and their towers.

Now Sean leaned casually against the wall, in the

shade of the overhang, and waited for Wolston to pull the code from the database on the laptop. Dave's briefing about acting like you belonged hadn't really been necessary. Sean knew exactly how to act around Littern Mills.

And there weren't many folks around to take offence at his presence. Heat lay over the estate like a blanket. The air above the concrete square shimmered. They were in the middle of a busy city, but somehow everything felt still. Even the steady background noise of traffic and planes seemed tired and worn out. The estate had always been especially shit in a hot summer, he thought.

'*Sean – double four, double seven.*'

Sean thumbed the figures into the keypad and the gate swung open under his fingertips.

'Roger. That's Sean, going underground.'

Cool air breathed against his face as he stepped forward. At that exact moment his phone buzzed. He whipped it out as his heart pounded.

But it was just his mum telling him that she was at a booth in Charing Cross Road for last-minute show tickets and couldn't decide between matinees for *Les Mis* and *Phantom*, and what did he think?

'Fuck's sake, Mum,' he muttered as he walked down the steps. The bars on his phone went dead and he put it back in his pocket. Reception down below had always been non-existent. MI5's hidden mikes had the same problem – as long as he was down here, he was cut off from the OP. What mattered was that the detector and his phone were only inches apart and could still talk to each other via their short-range Bluetooth signal.

Ceiling lights in thick plastic casings lit the corridor at the bottom with a yellow murk. The smells of piss and ganja were still soaked into the concrete. The walls had once been thick with Guyz graffiti. Now the tags and patterns of other gangs had been slapped down on top of them – most recently the Killaz. But even they were looking old now that the gates had come and only approved people could get down here. There had been some half-hearted efforts to clean it all off. Littern Mills must be on the way up, or trying.

On Sean's left, a couple of dark openings led deeper into the sublevels. On his right, solid, burglar-proof fire doors led into the basements of the shops. Some of them were jammed open to get a bit of airflow going. But even the closed ones weren't airtight, so the detector would still notice if anything was behind them. All he had to do was walk from one end to the other and let technology do the rest.

So he walked with the Guyz swagger, arms slightly bent, held away from his waist, hips swinging. He could hear voices, radios playing, and he had his patter already rehearsed in his head if anyone challenged him. He would be straight about what he was doing.

All right, mate? Yeah – Sean Harker. Used to live here. How you doing? He would make sure to shake – most people will automatically take an outstretched hand. *Nah, I was just checking out me old hangouts. Used to have some real times down here. It's good to see someone's actually looking after the old place now . . .*

The detector stayed silent, so Sean turned his attention to the side tunnels. At the entrance to the first one a sudden pang hit him right in the heart. He had been wondering if that would happen, but he hadn't expected it to be so strong.

It was a wide concrete cavern. A grille at the far end led to a vehicle ramp up to the surface. He breathed in through his nose. Yup, still there – a whiff of petrol and grease above the usual background pongs.

He moved slowly into the space.

Everything had been stripped out – the partitions, the workbenches, the gear. There was nothing to say that this had once been the best chopshop in the E17 postal area – the vehicle workshop of his mate Gaz Dobson's dad. Five years older, Gaz had been like Sean's big brother, and for most of his first sixteen years this place had been Sean's second home. Everything Sean had ever known about cars he had learned down here. How to fix them. How to do them up. How to take them.

And then it all went tits. First Gaz and his dad had got nicked on the same evening. Then Sean after them. Then Gaz had topped himself because his bail conditions said he could never work with motors again, and Mr Dobson had died of a broken heart, and Sean . . .

He was surprised to find that he was blinking back tears.

Sean had got out – into a world that actually offered hope and prospects.

An official-looking notice in a plastic wallet was stuck to one of the pillars. Sean stuck his face up close to read the small print. *London Borough of Waltham Forest . . . planning permission granted . . . conversion into a gym.*

He screwed his face up into a twisted smile. 'Good thing they cremated you, Gaz, 'cos if you had a grave, you'd be spinning in it.'

He took a final look around. The detector wasn't detecting – he had no reason to be here and no reason ever to come back. There was a weapons factory to find, Bright's killers to hunt down. He turned on his heel and walked back up the tunnel.

It took the length of a staircase, bottom to top, for reception to come back to full strength, and Wolston was already there in his ear, urgent and impatient.

'*Sean, come in, Sean – for Christ's sake answer, you moron . . .*'

It was the feeling you get on patrol when the leader suddenly holds up a hand. Sean was instantly alert, poised on his toes, not bridling at being called a moron. He'd had worse from NCOs.

'That's Sean back in touch.'

'*Get over to the park. Ravi is in a situation.*'

'The park . . .' Sean blanked for a moment, then realized, *Oh shit*. He broke into a run. 'That's Sean, foxtrot at the double to, uh, the park.'

'Foxtrot' meant 'walk'. Sean improvised his own 'at the double'. And the park . . .

The area at the centre of Littern Mills wasn't called the jungle for nothing. It was meant to be a recreation area – a mixture of open spaces, and raised flowerbeds planted with overgrown bushes, and a children's playground. But there were bits where even the children knew not to go on their own. It could be as deadly as any jungle in the wild.

Sean's heart sank as he followed the sound of raised voices. *Oh shit oh shit oh shit . . .*

He recognized at once what had happened. He had done it to newcomers himself. Mitra had upset someone, or been pinged somehow, and this was the result.

If the estate had actually had someone to look after the bushes, they would have been kept trim and probably about waist height – in other words, you could have looked over them. But they were taller than an average man, and you couldn't see from one side of the flowerbeds to the other – just in front and behind, if you were wise enough to glance back. They turned the paths between them into a maze of trails. Trails where you could shake off pursuit or set ambushes: lure your prey in, corner them, box them in like the platoon had boxed in those Nigerian kids three days earlier. No way out, nowhere to run.

But as he approached the voices – East London accents, sharp and accusing – Sean deliberately slowed down. He no longer ran. He strode. He braced himself, shoulders back, fists clenched, face like thunder as he swung round a corner into a brick and concrete garden.

He clocked the scene immediately. Mitra in the middle, hands raised, trying hard to stay calm, surrounded by a group of skinny teenage kids whose body language was poised for imminent violence. About ten of them – which meant that he and Mitra, even with their combat skills, stood to lose if it went wrong.

But things were halfway there anyway and Sean didn't have a choice. Engage, take control of the situation. No handshaking here. *Right.*

'That's Sean going in,' he said quietly.

Then every face swung towards him as he bellowed: 'The fuck is all this, then?'

Sean pinged the leader as the one with his face in Mitra's and an angry, accusing finger jabbing into Mitra's chest. A zitty white kid, with arms and legs like four strands of spaghetti tied together, bulking himself out with a big hat and a sleeveless padded coat, despite the heat.

The kid shot him a surprised look. 'Who the fuck are you?'

Sean marched up to him without breaking step, and spoke in a way that made it clear he had an absolute right to an answer to his question. 'I'm the fucker who's asking who the fuck you are.'

So far the opening pleasantries had gone pretty much as Sean expected. The rest of the gang held back, waiting to see what their leader would do.

Sean and the kid stood chest to chest, though the top of the kid's head barely made it to Sean's chin. The kid didn't back off as Sean loomed over him. He reminded Sean of a bristling little terrier, all yap. But even a terrier could deliver a nasty nip.

The kid grinned. 'And I'm the one who's got backup, and who's getting pretty fucking tired of fucking *snoopers*—'

And as he said *snoopers*, a knife flashed in his hand, the point aimed straight at Sean's ribs.

Chapter 17

The knife was in the kid's right hand. Sean waited half a second longer – until the kid's right foot was also forward, so he had no more thrust to give.

Then Sean cross-blocked, putting his forearms one over the other and driving them down on top of the kid's knife arm. It redirected the stab downwards and away from Sean's body. The kid's momentum kept him going and he stumbled forward. His arm ran between Sean's forearms. Sean grabbed him with both hands, just below his wrist, and simultaneously twisted and pushed. He stepped to one side and the kid's arm rotated up behind him. The only way for him to move without having his shoulder dislocated was down. The kid howled and sank to his knees.

The rest of the pack were frozen. They didn't quite know whether to defend their alpha male, or watch him get his arm torn off while they sucked up to the new one. If Sean wanted to take over the gang – humiliate the leader and install himself as the new pack alpha – this would have been the moment. It was only a small step from where he was to going down on his own knees, which would have driven the kid flat on his face on the ground.

But Sean didn't want to take over, and he wanted to leave the guy some dignity. The knife fell out of the kid's grip, so Sean simultaneously let him go and grabbed the knife by the hilt. He stepped back smartly, to let the kid get up in his own time.

'Nice move,' he said, though it hadn't been – it had been about as obvious as you can get. 'Your mistake was getting too over-committed with the thrust. Once you're out like that, you've nowhere else to go and you give the other guy an opening.'

He held the blade between thumb and forefinger, and offered it back to the kid hilt first. It was a typical civilian blade – it could kill if the point went through your skin, but the cutting edge was a joke. It looked way cooler than it was. And Sean had no qualms about handing out free self-defence tips. If he got on the wrong end of the kid's knife again, he knew plenty more that he wouldn't be sharing.

The kid scowled up at him, furiously blinking away tears of pain before anyone could notice them. His cap had come off in the tussle, to show a mop of sweaty, mousy hair that covered his ears. He groped for it and jammed it back on his head while he slowly got to his feet. He and Sean stood chest to chest again. Clashing whiffs of BO and Lynx came off the padded jacket.

Meanwhile Sean's brain had finally subtracted a few years and a lot of zits, and made the ID. The kid's suspicious eyes in the shadow of the cap's large brim took on a thoughtful squint: he was doing his own recognizing in return.

'I know you,' Sean said. 'You're Spence Pearce's kid brother.'

'Yeah, Kieran,' the kid said. 'And you're Sean fucking Harker. Army boy.' His eyes darted sideways at Mitra, and Sean sensed the uncertainty. 'He another of your lot?'

'He's my mate. Ravi, what the fuck have you been doing to upset these guys?'

'Fucker was snooping,' one of the others said. It sounded like his confidence was coming back, now it looked like no one was losing body parts.

Inside, Sean felt his guts clench up. *Oh. Shit.* Outside, Sean put his head on one side and looked sceptical. He had to get this lot on his side before they did the sums in their heads and worked out that ten guys with knives could take on two unarmed ones, however much hand-to-hand stuff the two knew.

'Who, me?' Mitra said. 'Oh, golly, no. I did keep trying to tell you.' He could put on the exaggerated Indian accent if he wanted, and he did so now. 'I was lost, that is all.'

'You – were – fucking – snooping.' Kieran spoke with absolute certainty, but he backed away from Sean, just in case. 'We saw you go down three dead ends, one after the other.'

Sean and Mitra's eyes met. Sean could picture it: Mitra just trying to be thorough in covering all the ground with the detector, while suspicious eyes watched. He remembered Dave's tale about the guy who went down one dead end by accident, and got out of it by pretending to take a piss under the watching eyes of the mums of the Provisional IRA. But three dead ends? No. The cover story was a bust. They would get nowhere by pretending to act innocent.

Shit. He was going to have to bluff this on the fly.

'Hang on,' one of the others interrupted. It looked like two random brain cells had just collided in his head as he looked from Sean to Mitra and back. '*He* knows all this unarmed shit' – he pointed at Sean, then at Mitra – 'so how come *he*—'

There was a blur of movement, and then he was on his front on the ground, arm bent up behind him by

Mitra, who also had his boot planted on the kid's neck. The kid's face was twisted as he tried not to scream.

'I was trying to do it the nice way,' Mitra said in his normal voice.

'Let him up, Ravi,' Sean said. 'We're among friends. Right?' He looked at Kieran. He knew that if strangers came up to the Guyz and acted tough but friendly, then the Guyz would go along with them – at least out of curiosity – for the time being. But the decision had to be theirs. He had to give it to Kieran so that Kieran could be seen to be in charge.

'Friends don't snoop,' Kieran spat. But he didn't give a signal to attack, and he snorted at the kid on the ground. 'Christ you're lame, Errol.'

'So maybe we've got our own business here,' Sean said, getting back to the matter in hand.

Kieran swung back at him. 'Yeah?' There was triumph mixed with the caution, now that Sean had as good as admitted . . . something. 'Well, hear it from me: you *don't* have business *nowhere*. Not without going through the Killaz.'

'So what happened to the Guyz?' Sean asked, playing for time, though he could guess the answer.

The snorts and laughs from the other kids, and the way Kieran's face twisted, confirmed it.

'The Guyz are history. Total losers. Maybe you missed it in the army.' Kieran's eyes burned with fury as he almost spat it out. 'Only went on a fucking bombing campaign, didn't they? Can you believe it? Our own people! Well out of order.'

'Yeah,' Sean admitted. 'I did hear about that.'

Not even Mitra knew about Sean's own involvement in the Guyz' downfall, so there was no way these kids ever would. The two survivors of the bombing campaign, Sean's ex-Guyz mate Matt Turner and Corporal Josh Heaton, had both had the facts of life made very plain to them before their trials. *You want to be out in fifteen, or serve the full thirty? Then you do not mention Sean Harker – not to the cops, not to your briefs, not to your cellmates.* Every little helps, and they had kept shtum.

'So what happened to Spence?' Sean asked.

Spence was the same age as him. They had hung out and done a few jobs together, but Spence had never been part of the same car-busting fraternity as Sean.

Immediately it was like the shutters came down on Kieran's face. 'Moved out with his girlfriend and kid, didn't he.'

Sean filled in the blanks. *And he left you here*, he thought. No family, no gang – it was like Kieran had been robbed twice. He could sense the bitterness.

And he could sense a way forward. He felt his guts unclench. Just a tiny bit. He was feeling his way here.

'Looks like you're doing OK, bro. Respect.'

'Yeah. We are. So what's this business of yours, soldier boy?'

Sean only took half a second to make his decision. The Killaz might be a bunch of immature tossers that the Guyz could have eaten for lunch, but they were here and the Guyz weren't. They could help, or they could be seriously disruptive. There was no in-between.

He jerked his head away from the gang, beckoning Kieran to follow. Then he ducked his head low, close to Kieran's. The other lads would still be able to hear them just fine, but he was giving respect to Kieran by treating him as the leader.

As well as lying to him through his teeth.

'Look, just 'cos I'm a respectable citizen now don't mean I'm out of the game.' He rubbed the tips of his fingers with his thumb in the universal gesture for *money*. 'Still got my eye on the opportunity.'

Kieran's mouth twisted. 'There's no opportunities on Littern Mills.'

'Not what I heard.' Sean looked him square in the eye. 'Hate to break it to you, mate, but you're being played.'

He was falling into the role. Something in the Littern Mills air was working on him. He sensed his thought patterns falling into step with Kieran's. They were talking the same language.

Kieran immediately started to bridle, and Sean pressed grimly on.

'Word gets about, bro. Other gangs are storing their hooky gear on Littern Mills. Cunning, right? You use someone else's space, you've got deniability.'

It had happened once before that he knew of, which was why he could say it so plausibly now. A gang of jewel thieves had been storing their takings on Littern Mills, safely outside their usual territory, to avoid suspicion. Matt and Copper had made sure it never happened again. It was the first serious gang fight Sean had got caught up in.

'The *fuck*!' Kieran spat. The idea of foreigners free-loading on the estate obviously incensed him – which had been the idea. 'There is *no* fucking way!'

Sean shrugged. 'Whatever. We took it seriously enough to come and check it out. Just the two of us. So, yeah, we were snooping.'

He took a breath. 'Ravi, show the gents what you've got in your right pocket.'

Mitra threw him a surprised look, but now he couldn't deny there was anything there. He reluctantly drew out the pick and his collection of rakes, which all dangled together from one ring.

'*Shee-yit!*'

The admiring murmurs went out from the lads as they clocked the class-A housebreaking equipment. Mitra snapped his hand closed around them and pushed them quickly back into his pocket before anyone tried to lay hands on them.

'We thought, with the Guyz gone, we'd have sole possession,' Sean said casually. 'But of course, with you lot now – well, this is your manor. So, how's this . . . You've got your ears to the ground. You must have the feel of the place. You must have picked up vibes that made you think, *Hold on* – but then you just went, *Nah* – but now you know what I've just told you, so you're thinking, *Maybe* . . . That's the kind of place we're after. You give us the address, we investigate, anything we find gets split fifty-fifty.'

Kieran cocked his head. 'You straight?'

Sean knew exactly what would give him the cred he needed. 'You ever hear how I got nicked?'

Kieran slowly grinned. 'Yeah. Fucking legend.' He turned to the others. 'Spence told me. Sean put himself in harm's way, let the cops nick him so his mates could escape. Fucking ace.' He swung back to Sean. 'OK, you're on. We're going to bust these joints together.'

Which was the last thing Sean wanted.

He crossed his arms and stared down at the kid. 'Nice move, Einstein. You any idea how many outfits could be involved? And you're going to barge in and start a gang war with all of them? Go ahead. Me and Ravi, we'll just stand aside and pick up the pieces once you've been wiped out. Everyone's a winner except the Killaz, but – meh.'

Kieran snarled. 'So how's your version any fucking better?'

'Because you're right, the Guyz are history, I'm old news around here, Ravi's a complete outsider. If we bust anyone's joint, no one will trace it back to you. Whereas the Killaz go snooping, that's like sounding a red alert all over town. So, how about it?'

Kieran's eyes narrowed. 'Fifty-fifty?'

'Like I said.'

'Sixty-forty.'

'Fifty-fifty or nothing. Look, this is just one of the leads we have up our sleeve. We have plenty more – you don't have any. You get fifty per cent or you get zero. No middle ground.'

And he meant it – a fifty-fifty split for anything hot they found that was non-terrorist related.

Kieran subsided. He stepped back and regarded Sean, then jerked his thumb at the other Killaz to summon them into a huddle . . .

'Deal,' Kieran said a moment later.

Sean gave a thin smile. He didn't want it to look like relief, which would immediately put Kieran on alert again.

But he couldn't relax just yet. He could keep pressing.

'You know it makes sense,' he said. 'Oh yeah, and Ravi here left his stash back at camp.'

Mitra gave Sean a glare that could have sliced through a Warrior's hull. He had no stash back at camp. No one Sean knew did. If any serving soldier was found to be using, the army showed no mercy.

'I used to get mine off Zara Mann,' Sean went on. 'She still around? Or her mate – whatsername – Emma? Emma Booth.'

At the briefing, Dave had told them that Zara had previous for possession with intent to supply. So Sean gambled that the question wouldn't raise eyebrows.

'Maybe.' Kieran narrowed his eyes again, but he didn't seem too surprised by the claims of drug dealing. 'Think they've been away. We'll keep our eyes out for them.'

Well, his question had been worth a try, Sean thought, even though it hadn't produced useful int. They already knew that Zara had been away, and since she had only got back yesterday, maybe the Killaz hadn't yet clocked her return. And even if Emma *had* been away, that didn't mean she was Girl X.

'Uh – now we are all such good friends' – Mitra put up a hand like a kid in class, then pointed it at one of the gang – 'this gentleman here has taken my phone.'

A-a-a-nd there was still the possibility that everything could go completely tits up right now. Sean had been about to let himself feel pleased with the outcome.

Nothing in his expression gave any clue that Mitra had managed to let a teenage wannabe gangster get hold of a piece of equipment that was tuned in to one of MI5's bomb detectors. Sean simply fixed the lad in question with a glare and snapped his fingers. After a moment Mitra's phone was dropped into his waiting hand. Sean passed it back to its owner, and kept his arse clenched because of the very real risk that if he didn't, then he might crap himself out of relief.

'OK,' he said to Kieran, 'let's talk business . . .'

Ten minutes later Sean and Mitra and Kieran's Killaz were going their separate ways, with phone numbers exchanged and a list of possible locations noted down.

'So, that's Sean and Ravi out of earshot of the natives, reporting in . . .' Sean said. He gave a brief description of what had happened, and braced himself. 'Now standing by for bollocking.'

'*O-kay. Roger.*' It was like an explosion of relief in their ears from Dave. Sean wondered if he had been holding his breath for the entire encounter with the Killaz. '*Bollocking is deferred for now. You got out of that blown cover pretty well – just a shame you got into it in the first place. I have their suggestions listed. Nearest to your position is Fairlight Tower in South Square . . .*'

'Already on it,' Sean said, rolling his eyes. Shit, he knew the geography.

'*Roger, but after that I have a revised route for you . . .*'

Sean could picture Dave poring over the map of the estate, planning the optimum route between Kieran's leads that would still give them plenty of time to patrol the rest of Littern Mills, as planned, if they had to.

'Your own hearts-and-minds campaign,' Mitra said as they walked into the shadow of Fairlight. 'Shit, you should do this for a living.'

Neither of them had ever been part of an occupying force in another country, but Sergeant Adams had, and 'hearts and minds' was one of his mantras. After securing their position, the first priority of an occupier had to be earning the trust of the locals through straight dealing and positive reinforcement. A happy population was a helpful population. Less inclined to take up arms against you, more inclined to aid you instead.

Sean was saved from having to think of a witty comeback because his phone buzzed.

'Oh, piss off, Mum . . .' he began – just as Mitra's phone buzzed too.

Their eyes met.

Then they casually glanced at their phones, like they were just checking an update from a mate.

It was another of those instant alert moments, going invisibly from casual civvy to soldier on standby in the blink of an eye.

'You want to tell them?' Sean said.

'Nah, you're the golden boy du jour.'

Sean touched his belt. 'That's Sean,' he said, 'with a seventy-eight-per-cent nitroaromatic compound in detected sample.'

In English, within fifty metres of where they stood there was something that could make a very big bang indeed.

Chapter 18

'You keep yours out,' Sean said. He palmed his own phone as they headed over to the base of Fairlight, remembering his old Guyz swagger. Two phones out between them would look like they were hunting Pokémon.

A couple of locals were coming towards them. Sean clocked them with his *The fuck you looking at?* scowl, and they passed by without comment. Sean let himself feel pleased. *Oh yeah. Still got it.*

'It's pleased to see me,' Mitra murmured, and he gave Sean a shot of the screen. The bar had shot up to almost maximum size: ninety-eight per cent and rising. So they were heading in the right direction. The gate was ahead of them.

'That's Sean and Ravi needing access code for maintenance passage western end of Fairlight.'

If there was a weapons factory here, then there

would probably be security of some kind. Maybe cameras but, more importantly, the human variety – nasty suspicious bastards, their attention caught by two guys walking up to the gate and stopping, waiting for the code. Anyone and everyone was a suspect. Someone leaning against a wall checking his own phone. A couple lying on the grass. A window-seat customer nursing a cup of everlasting coffee in the café. So they had to walk up like they already had the number lodged in their brains and going through it was the most natural thing ever.

'Sean and Ravi – zero eight two nine. Ravi investigate, Sean keep watch.'

Mitra went through the gate without a pause while Sean lounged on a bench under a withered tree, casually scanning his phone and occasionally smiling like he was reading chat from his mates. The bar was at ninety-nine per cent.

Then Mitra was back, a few metres away, not looking at him. He propped his back against the concrete base of the tower and went through the motions of making a phone call. His voice was clear in Sean's earpiece.

'That's Ravi reporting storeroom for third shop down has padlocked door and reading goes off the scale. No other sign of security.'

Sean stretched, casually looking around. Still no sign of anyone obviously on guard.

'*Roger.*' Dave was decisive. '*Joe is on his way to your location for backup if needed.*'

And so they stayed where they were for the next five minutes – Mitra conducting his phantom conversation, Sean casually texting, and both doing their best to clock any opposition.

It would have been quite cool, Sean thought, to watch a SWAT raid called in on his old home ground at his report. This time he'd be one of the good guys. See how the Met did it, maybe pick up some useful pointers, or offer his own, depending. But the big guns weren't going to be called in without eyeball verification.

'*That's Joe entering South Square.*'

Dave was back on the air.

'*The storeroom belongs to the key-cutting business. Sean to head down to the other end of the maintenance passage and approach from that end. Code that end is one zero seven four. Enter when Joe is in place. Ravi, once Sean is in, to go and join him from your end. Approach target from both directions at once. You are cleared to pick the lock and gain access. If it's live, then we can have armed backup here in five minutes.*'

The passage ran the entire length of the shops, so it

had an entrance at both ends. Sean casually got up and sauntered the length of the units, then wheeled about at the far end to get to the other gate. As he did so, he saw Wolston taking the place he had just vacated on the bench.

He tapped the code into the far gate and pushed it open. Inside was the familiar smell of all the other towers: cool concrete and other substances. On one side, the back entrances to the shops. On the other, the storerooms that were also part of the businesses. Up ahead he saw Mitra's silhouette approaching from the other direction. They met outside the third door from Mitra's end. It was solid and wooden, fireproof, secured with a chain and a powerful-looking padlock.

'Can you get in?' Sean asked casually, still looking up and down the passage.

'The bigger they come, the easier they fall. But first things first. That's Ravi, sweeping for sensors.'

There was only static and a very faint voice which immediately died away. The tower was doing its signal-blocking thing. Mitra tapped a cigarette packet open and pulled out the foil wrapper. He folded it in two and then in two again, to give it some rigidity, and slid it into the thin crack between door and frame. Slowly he worked his way all the way round, from ground to top corner to other top corner to ground again, then last of all along the floor.

'Didn't feel anything. OK, let's do it.'

He hunched over the padlock as his pick and rake worked inside it. His eyes were half closed as he visualized the tumblers inside from the feel transmitted back through the rake's metal shaft, probing and clicking them open one by one.

The padlock fell open. Sean caught it before it fell off the chain onto the floor. Immediately Mitra was at work on the door's fitted lock, the one beneath the handle.

'Christ, I can see why they used a padlock. My baby nephew could get through this . . .'

It clicked open in seconds.

'OK, here goes nothing.'

They looked at each other, and Mitra slowly took hold of the handle.

'Count of three. One, two . . .'

He twisted the handle and pulled.

They were all outside in the square again, a safe distance apart, not obviously hanging together, looking in different directions like they were posing on the cover of an indie album.

But the silence in the earpiece made Sean start to wonder if the signal was still being blocked somehow.

He wanted to kick the nearest concrete wall, hard. Maybe punch it. Do something to cause himself pain and take his mind off the disappointment. He had been so geared up that they might be about to crack this thing.

Finally Dave spoke. '*A drug farm.*'

'Stone cold, not used for months,' Sean confirmed. 'Maybe longer.'

His nose had told him the truth as soon as the door opened, a few seconds before the evidence of his own eyes. Quite apart from what it did to your brain, the distinct, sickly smell of weed was a key reason why he had never got into it beyond the obligatory experimental joints as a kid. The ammonium nitrate that the detectors had correctly reported came from some split-open, mouldering fertilizer bags. It was nothing to do with any bomb factory.

'*Roger.*' Dave said it heavily. '*This does not repeat not get shared with your Killaz friends. We will report it to the Met . . . once the operation is over. Joe to return to OP. Ravi and Sean to move on to the next tip-off location. This has put us off schedule . . .*'

None of them looked at each other as they returned to business as usual. Sean stretched a couple of times to get his body back into the rhythm of moving, and headed off with Mitra to the next of Kieran's possibles.

He checked his watch. Fifteen hundred hours. He had been doing this since they bugged Zara's flat at ten hundred. He had been up since oh six hundred, and Dave's patrol schedule went up to twenty hundred, or later if necessary. At least five more hours of slogging around in thirty-degree heat.

Shit, he could murder a cup of tea.

Sean was the last back into the OP, a bit after twenty-one thirty, when the absolute last dregs of sunlight had disappeared from the sky. He could hear the sound of Mitra drenching himself in a cold shower. He pushed the door closed and propped his back against it, closing his eyes for a moment. Only a moment. His feet were killing him and he was as shagged out as it's possible to be, but he was still on duty.

Wolston had the long-awaited cuppa ready to thrust into his hands. A cold beer or several would have been better for this time of the evening – they had bought a crate from the offy as part of their cover story – but Dave had told them that the operation would be dry until they pulled out.

'So how was it for you?' Sean asked between the two mouthfuls it took to drain the mug.

'Ste Mann has returned home and gone out again; still no sign of Zara or Emma.'

Wolston stood aside so that Sean could see for himself. Dave was sitting at the kitchen table, where two of the laptops showed almost identical views – the hallway and living room of two different flats built to the same design. In one of them, the Manns' living room, a laptop was open on the table. Its screen was a white blur, but the outline of the image prompted Sean to lean forward, squinting to make it out . . .

Wolston pulled a face. 'We learned the hard way that Ste likes to relax after work with a good dose of online porn.'

'Unfortunately, what we could see was all legal,' Dave said. 'Live humans, over sixteen. Otherwise we'd have cause to pick him up and go through his online presence with a fine-tooth comb.'

'But he's obviously not expecting Zara back,' Wolston added, 'because if you thought your kid sister was coming home, you wouldn't leave porn up on your screen, would you?'

'So the day's been a bust,' Sean said flatly. The desire to hit something was back. Life put on hold for twenty-four wasted hours. No weapons factory. No leads of any kind. Bright's killers still out there.

Dave shrugged. 'We've done the best we could with the int we had, and it's not over. You can grab a shower if you like, but after that you and Ravi are taking over with flat surveillance. We're going square-eyed here. I'll send out for a takeaway.'

'Anything but a fucking Indian.' Mitra had emerged from the bathroom, cool and refreshed with a towel around his waist. 'I can't stand curry.'

'As long as it's dead, I'll eat it,' Sean said. 'And if we get to sit down, that'll do me just fine.' He was already peeling off his sweat-soaked shirt as he pushed Mitra aside on his way to the bathroom. 'This is going to be good— Oh, fucking hell – what is it now?'

His phone was buzzing. So far that day, apart from false explosive alerts, it had all been texts from his mum. The last one was an update on the show she had finally picked. *Mamma Mia!* Afterwards she was getting together with some girlfriends in Soho . . .

This wasn't his mum. It took a moment for the message to sink into his tired, overheated brain.

From Kieran.

emmas in affys.

He read it out loud.
'Translation?' Dave said after a moment.

'Affy's is the chippy, and Emma's in there now.'

Sean said it half a second ahead of the realization of what it meant for him, personally. His tired body wanted to groan, but his mind tingled with a fresh zap of energy. They were back in the game.

Dave showed no pity.

'Then what the fuck are you waiting for? Get down there now.'

Chapter 19

At least they'd let him stick his head in some cold water and change his shirt.

It was evening, but West Square was still hot. No more direct sunlight, just acres of sun-warmed concrete giving up its heat, which made the square even more humid after dark.

But the Brits love any weather when it isn't actually raining, and people were coming out to play, hang, chat. Sean took a quick look around for Kieran or any of the Killaz but couldn't see them. Probably lurking in shadows somewhere. What was more important was he had acquired his target. The whole front of the Aphrodite Fish and Chip Bar, aka Affy's, was one big window – so he could see the customers waiting for their orders, and he could see her. She was just paying.

'*Get down there, engage, establish if she's Girl X.*' Those had been Dave's orders.

Take it one bit at a time, Sean thought. *She's a girl – check.*

Emma had blonde, shoulder-length hair, T-shirt, tight jeans moulded round a fantastic bum. He stepped up his pace, timing it so that he would be pushing in through the door just as she was coming out. It wouldn't be the first time he had worked a meeting with a girl matching that description. He would glance at her briefly, do a double take and recognize her. Even if she had no idea who he was, she would notice the attention.

Except that she got there first. She stopped in her tracks and stared through the door at him just as he was putting his hand out. Then she pulled it open. 'Shit!' She was wide-eyed. 'You're Sean Harker!'

'Uh – yeah.' It wasn't hard to fake surprise – it covered up the sound of alarm bells going off all around his head. *She knows me. Does she recognize me from the airport?*

He recovered quickly and moved his hand in a slow circle in the air. 'And you're . . .' He jabbed a finger at her with a big, cheeky grin. 'Emma.'

She bit her lip and a shy grin of her own spread slowly across a classy face. 'I can't believe you remember me.' She stepped out of the way of other customers, and they leaned against the window together. She offered him her bag and he took a chip. 'I was just a kid when I last saw you.'

So far this was going exactly as things would if an off-duty Sean really *did* bump into a fit-looking blonde. It was easy to keep up the pretence. He let his eyes linger on her face – not just to avoid the *Hey, I'm up here* line but to see if he could match her with the airport photo. Girl X's head had been wrapped in a scarf and she'd worn glasses. Emma didn't wear glasses, and her make-up was slapped on a bit thicker than he thought was necessary. Fifty-fifty, he decided. He couldn't be more definite.

'Yeah, I didn't exactly hang around at Markwell.' He nibbled on another chip.

'It was long enough for—' She laughed. 'I shouldn't say. It's embarrassing.'

'No, go on. I'm a gent.'

'Well . . .' She looked from side to side. 'Me and my best friend got this *huge* crush on you.' She leaned forward and whispered, 'You were a *bad* boy! Everyone knew that.'

'Yeah?' He couldn't help feeling flattered. It might even be true. He had been fourteen when Markwell threw him out, but he and the cops were already old friends. He gave a mock-modest shrug. 'Maybe I still am.' She laughed. 'So who was this mate of yours?'

'Oh, you wouldn't remember . . . OK. Zara? Zara Mann?'

He narrowed his eyes so he could pretend to remember. It also gave him time to think. What was going on here? Was this Emma Booth, having a normal catch-up conversation about her best mate? Or was this Girl X, dangling Zara's name to see if he took the bait?

It could have been either. All he could do right now was go with it and see what happened.

'Dark-haired girl? From where I was standing, you two were joined at the hip.'

A shadow seemed to flit across her face. 'Yeah. *Were.*'

He frowned. 'Something wrong?'

'Maybe. So what are you doing here? Didn't you go into the army?'

He nodded. 'I'm just back for a couple of days with some mates. We're staying at my mum's.' He nodded at Affy's. 'I was just getting a food order in.'

'Haven't noticed a group of new fit blokes around.'

'Nah.' He shook his head. '*Game of Thrones* marathon – can't tear themselves away. Antisocial fuckers.'

'Well.' She made as if to leave, a little regretfully. 'Don't let me keep you.'

'Hey, hey.' Whether she was bona or fake, he couldn't afford to lose her now. He slowed her down by taking another chip. 'You're better company than those ugly tossers. So, what's this problem, then?' He put on a look of concern, eyes wide, mouth slightly open. He felt like the world's worst actor.

And if she was faking it, she was the world's best. She leaned back against the window of Affy's with a heavy sigh. 'Long story. How long have you got?'

He glanced down at the chips. 'You on your own?'

'Yeah?'

He grinned, and thought of his mates back at the OP. He pulled out his phone. There hadn't been time to wire him up again – the priority had been to catch Emma while she was pinged – so they wouldn't have heard any of this. He had to text them to let them know he was on his way up to her flat.

'Let me get my own portion, and then you can tell me all about it. And I'll tell the *Thrones* geeks to get their own fucking chips.'

'So, yeah, Zara . . .' Emma pushed another beer into his hand and he mentally toasted the bug in the smoke detector. *I've got a drink, suckers!* Now that he was in her flat – for the second time that day – the others would be listening in.

She had wanted to sit down in the kitchen, but he had gone into the living room like it was the most natural thing, so that the OP could listen in. They sat in comfy chairs with a small table between them and the chips spread out on the top, and chatted about this and that. The table was small and their heads were close together. It was a scenario with plenty of possibilities and Sean enjoyed being part of it. But he could also imagine the frustration back at the OP as they talked about everything *except* Zara – the one subject he couldn't raise without sounding too pushy. At last Emma got round to it on her own.

'I'm worried about her. Apart from the fact I don't even know where she is . . .'

She pushed her sleeve back to show a tanned arm. 'I spent a month strawberry picking in Kent. Caught the sun. Didn't hear from her all the time I was away, and when I got back she'd just vanished.'

Sean pictured the thought processes going on back at the OP as they listened in. Tan – could have been acquired in Africa, or Kent. Strawberry picking – probably cash-only gig, impossible to verify. She had an answer for everything that might or might not show she was Girl X.

'Maybe she's got a bloke . . .'

'Maybe. She's been so . . . withdrawn. If she had a guy, you'd expect her to be happy about it, wouldn't you? And I know she's been cutting her family out too.

Ste – that's her brother – he's worried like me, but he's a student and he doesn't really have time to look out for her too.'

'Shit.' Sean pulled a sympathetic face. 'Wish I could help.'

'You're a sweet guy, Sean Harker.' Emma pushed her chair back. 'Only be a moment.'

He smiled and stayed seated as she headed for the bathroom. He could see one more unexplored opportunity – something they hadn't been able to check out when they bugged her flat that morning.

The moment he heard the door click shut, the smile vanished and he grabbed her handbag, which dangled by its strap from the back of her chair.

What he found – or didn't find – made the corners of his mouth turn up. *Bingo. She's in the clear.*

When she came back, the bag was back as it had been, apparently undisturbed. She leaned against the door frame and smiled. Then she pushed herself away, but she didn't sit down on her side of the table. She perched on the arm of Sean's chair so that he had to sit back and look up at her. Thumb and forefinger plucked the fabric of his shirt.

'So how many DVDs have your mates got to get through?'

'Every fucking series,' he said with a smile. 'Take them hours.'

It was officially the Next Stage, and why not? So far this had exactly matched the scenario an off-duty Sean really would go through, and an off-duty Sean who had got this far into a girl's flat wouldn't be leaving until the next morning. The last time had been before Nigeria, and catching up had been a mission objective for Tenerife for most of the lads, Sean included. But it wasn't going to happen this time, even though he was now as sure as he could be that she wasn't Girl X . . .

It wasn't that he had no intention of giving his mates a free viewing – there wasn't a smoke detector in Emma's bedroom. Or that he hadn't had time to restock his wallet since getting back from Nigeria (and he knew for a fact that there weren't any condoms in the flat).

It wasn't even that he was pretty sure the penalty for shagging while on duty was more than just a slapped wrist. Did it count as misconduct on operations, obstructing operations, or just conduct prejudicial to good order and discipline? He wasn't going to find out.

No – what he really wanted more than anything else was about ten hours of solid sleep.

But finding an excuse to turn down a fit girl who was up for it was a whole new experience. He let the smile slip as he took her hand gently in both of his. 'OK. This is kind of embarrassing . . .'

She looked at him questioningly. He didn't have to

fake his face turning red: this *was* fucking embarrassing, even if it wasn't true. But he had to come up with an excuse that would work. Choices were: make out that he physically couldn't, or . . . or this.

'There was this girl, and . . . Just say that the one time I really *should* have used a condom . . . I didn't. And now the doctors say I shouldn't at all. Not until I've finished the course of antibiotics.'

He could picture the ghost of Shitey Bright pissing himself laughing at that point. Probably the OP all were too.

Her face fell – a little. 'Oh, shit. Bad luck.' She smiled. 'I was right, though – you *are* a bad boy.'

He summoned up the old cocky grin again. 'Not as bad as she was.'

She moved away to let him stand up.

He gently brushed his finger against her face. 'Shit, you're hot! I mean . . .'

He meant, she felt like she was burning up. And now he looked more closely, she looked tired under the make-up.

'Yeah.' She laughed a little. 'I think I got a touch of sunstroke in Kent. So maybe it wouldn't have been the best idea for either of us.'

They held hands as far as the front door, but that was all their physical contact, and she stayed leaning against the doorpost and watched him head along to the end. He gave her a last regretful wave as he disappeared into the stairwell.

But the moment he was out of sight he stepped up the pace to something that was as cheerful as his aching feet would allow. Considerably more cheerful than he would normally be if he had just missed out on spending the night with a fit girl. Even a one-nighter deserved honesty on both sides, and you couldn't have that if one of you was an undercover operative.

But there could be other nights. He had liked her, her story seemed straight, and while they chatted he realized that he *wanted* her to be innocent. And then he had looked in her bag.

As far as he was concerned, Emma Booth was off the hook.

Chapter 20

Dave scowled. 'What is it with you guys and anti-malarials?'

It was reassuring to find a chink in Dave's armour of knowledge. Their leader hadn't made the connection from earlier, when Sean had reported their absence in Zara's flat.

'The malaria parasite can survive in your blood for up to four weeks,' Wolston told him, 'so you have to keep taking them for four weeks after you return. That way you kill off anything that's still in your system.'

'We got it well drummed into us by the MO,' Sean added. 'But Emma didn't have anti-malarials anywhere in the flat this morning, she didn't have them in her handbag now – so she doesn't have them. Period.'

Dave still scowled. 'So on that basis you conclude that Emma Booth is not Girl X?'

'It's the only thing I can think of that she'd do

different if she'd just come back from Nigeria as opposed to Kent. You got any better ideas?'

'But Zara didn't have anti-malarials in her flat, either,' Dave said, 'and we know for a fact that she *was* in Nigeria. Explanation?'

Sean didn't have one, and he bit his lip in frustration. 'Maybe she *does* have them with her. Like Emma doesn't.'

'Of course . . .' Mitra ventured. Sean and Wolston both swung their gazes round on him. 'We're soldiers and we're used to following orders. Emma's just a civvy. What do they know? Maybe it wasn't explained properly to her.' Then he grinned. 'Anyway, she was gagging to shag Sean, so it's not like she's overflowing with good ideas.'

'Ha fucking ha,' Sean said with feeling. 'Zara and Girl X worked in a hospital out in Lagos, so you'd think they really would know.'

'All right!' Dave made them feel like a pair of slapped-down kids as he pinched the bridge of his nose. 'I can see both sides. As for her just being too dim to take the right pills, the Sacred Cross Hospital in Lagos specializes in tropical diseases – so Sean's right, we can assume that the girls would have been briefed and that they'd know about these things. OK. I'm reporting this line of reasoning back to the office to see what they say – and meanwhile we continue surveillance. What's she doing now?'

'She's online.' Wolston didn't look up from the monitors. 'Looks like . . . a ticket-buying site?'

'What sort of tickets?'

Wolston shrugged. 'What you got? Shows, events . . . I can't read the text, I can just see the pictures when her body's not in the way. I recognize the site logo.'

Sean, Mitra and Dave crowded round behind the seated Wolston to look at the laptop. Halfway to clicking on something on screen, Emma was suddenly gripped by a bout of coughing. She convulsed almost double and the small series of explosions came over the speakers.

Mitra nudged Sean. 'If you were shagging to schedule, that would have gone right in your face.'

'But not yours, 'cos you'd have got your zip back up and be out the door by now.'

'Swiftly and with style, my friend.'

'God, it's like having teenagers around,' Dave muttered.

Mitra and Sean glanced at each other. 'We *are* teenagers,' they said together.

He glared at them, then looked back at the screen. 'Is coughing a symptom of malaria?'

'Uh – no,' Wolston said. 'Chills, fever, vomiting, diarrhoea – no coughing.'

'And none of this proves anything. We're going round in circles.' Dave drummed his fingers on the table. 'Maybe there *is* a weapons factory we haven't found, and she keeps the pills there. Did that cross your mind? No. We need leads. Badly.'

'If there was something for the detectors to pick up, we'd have got it,' Sean said, with the sinking feeling that they were about to be sent out again. 'We were fucking everywhere today—'

The sound of the doorbell made his head whip round, before he realized it had come over the speakers.

'Which one was that?' Dave demanded, but Emma had already answered the question for him on screen by pushing her chair back.

'Switch to hallway camera! And get onto the telescope. Can we identify?'

Sean was nearest the left-hand laptop, which showed the view from the two telescopes set up on tripods by the sink, peeking out of the window and across West Square to Wolsey.

'It's a man. Uh – youngish.'

That was all he could tell. The image was slightly foreshortened because Sean was looking up from the fourth floor of Gladstone to the fifth of Wolsey. The guy was medium height, slender build, which didn't narrow it down. His top half was silhouetted against the frosted glass of the front door. He was wearing a coat with the collar up, and a cap.

Sean saw Emma come up to the door, open it. She didn't let the man in. They just stood there, talking. Their voices via the hidden microphone were the only sound in the OP. It was like listening to people in the next flat through a thin wall. They could pick up sounds and emotions, but the two of them kept their voices low, just below the threshold of the microphone, and no words came through clearly.

Then the man glanced briefly to one side, apparently thinking of an answer to something Emma had said. Sean immediately clocked his profile. The shiner hadn't gone down much.

'It's Ste,' he reported.

Ste sounded calm and level – more than when he'd confronted them that morning, now over twelve hours ago. Emma sounded less chatty than just now – maybe tired? More withdrawn?

'Right.' Dave clapped his hands as he came to a decision. 'He lives one floor above her. Who in this day and age walks down a floor to have a private conversation when they can just text? Sean, Joe – get to the bottom of the stairs and hold position for further orders. Sean, you got a mike? No? Take one. He might just go back to his flat – or he might head off somewhere else, and I want him followed if he does. Ravi, you're on the laptops, and I'm squirting that sound file up the line to see if they can make any sense of it. Let's move.'

Sean and Wolston were already on the move, but it didn't stop Wolston asking a question.

'So, what exactly makes this a lead?'

Dave glared at the screen like he could scare the answers out of it. 'This is an anomaly. It's outlying data. It lies beyond the expected range of behaviour and so it gets investigated. And it's all we have.'

Sean and Wolston didn't run. Ste was right over on the other side of West Square, but if they moved too quickly along Gladstone's balcony, then he still might snag them. Just for half a second, just long enough to bust them.

So they walked. Along the balcony towards the stairwell.

Mitra came online in their ears.

'*That's Ste foxtrot, parallel to Joe and Sean.*'

So Ste was walking along the balcony on Wolsey towards his own stairs. Sean glanced sideways, straining his eyes over and turning his head as little as possible. People notice when they're being looked at. Even from a distance.

Sean and Wolston had a slight head start. The moment they were in the stairwell, out of sight of Wolsey, they sped up and took the stairs down two at a time, gripping the rails as they hurled themselves round the corners.

If Ste just went back to his flat, then they had wasted time and got a bit of extra exercise. If Ste went into any other flat in Wolsey, they would find an excuse to get close up and see what was happening. And if he left the building, he would be followed.

Once they reached ground level they slowed down again, strolling out into the square, two mates having a chat. Or maybe, given the five or six years between them, big brother and kid brother. Before leaving they had each grabbed a can from the fridge, and now they joined the groups of lads still lounging against the dry fountain in the centre of West Square, even though it was pushing midnight; they took careful sips while making it look like they were knocking it back. Wolston pulled the names of a couple of imaginary girls from thin air, and he and Sean had a conversation about which one had the best imaginary tits. Meanwhile they kept an eye on the exit from Wolsey's stairwell.

And they kept on keeping an eye.

And kept on. No Ste.

'So, what do you think?' Wolston asked after a couple of minutes. To an onlooker it could have been a slightly out-of-sync comment in the tits debate.

'*Ste hasn't exited the stairwell on any level,*' Mitra reported. '*He's still in there.*'

'*So he's gone into the sublevels,*' Dave said. '*Unless he's just sitting on the stairs and waiting, it's the only thing he could do.*'

Wolston and Sean glanced at each other, and Sean felt his heart begin to thump in its pre-action warm-up routine. They knew what was coming and, sure enough, it came.

'*Joe, Sean, get down there,*' Dave ordered. '*I want Ste pinned down.*'

Chapter 21

Thursday 3 August, 23:45 BST

Mitra had the code for the gate ready, so they could go straight on in.

The sounds of the square vanished in seconds, cut off by the concrete bulk of the tower. No sound of movement, no conversation, no music playing.

They moved cautiously, though there was no cover, nowhere to hide if anyone saw them. All the doors – storage units, and the back doors of the shops – were shut and locked for the night, though they studied them closely for a sign that anything had been opened lately.

No Ste.

The real bummer was that Sean had been here earlier that day – and the detector had drawn a blank. He took it out again, checked the screen. Still nothing read higher than trace levels. He held it up so that Wolston could have a shufti for himself. The corporal just nodded to acknowledge the point. Whatever Ste was down here for, it didn't involve explosives.

They came to an opening that led down a flight of concrete stairs into the depths beneath the square. Here, there was noise. The ventilation and heating systems of all the buildings were down there and they made a steady drone.

Wolston pointed at Sean, then at the floor where he stood – a basic signal for *Stay here*. Sean nodded as Wolston crept down the stairs. If there was a chance of anyone being spotted, then better if it was just one of them.

Wolston reached the bottom and peeked round the corner, then beckoned. Sean padded silently down to join him.

The passage at the bottom ran parallel to the one they had just been in. There were more locked doors down one side; the other was a jumbled mess of nooks and crannies buried in miles of pipework.

The doors down here were just for privacy and basic security. They weren't solid and fireproof like the shop doors – in fact, there were wire meshes in the wall above each one: ventilation for the room behind. All the meshes were black squares, except for one which had a light behind it. The fifth one along.

Target acquired. Sean fixed his eyes on it, then looked at Wolston for orders. Wolston waggled his beer can in Sean's face, and crossed his eyes and stuck his tongue out of the corner of his mouth. Sean got the message. If they were spotted, they were a pair of drunks who'd got lost. *Fuck me, Sean mate, there's people down here!* Maybe this would be the moment to pretend to take a slash.

They moved silently along the passage, taking extra extra care where their feet went, to avoid kicking or scuffing anything. Even over the background drone, the sound of Sean's rubber-soled shoes parting company with the concrete floor sounded like a route march over gravel.

They waited by the fifth door, ears straining, pressed to the crack on either side. Then their eyes met and they allowed themselves grim, triumphant smiles. Over the mechanical rumble they could hear voices in there.

Wolston raised his eyes to the mesh. He jerked his head up at it, and then crouched down, hands locked together, fingers twined into a stirrup resting on his knee.

Sean had often wondered what it would be like to put his head above the rim of a trench during a firefight. This had to be similar. He nodded, and took a breath, and put his foot into the stirrup so that Wolston could hoist him up into the air. He rested his hands against the wall as gently as he could, and put his face to the edge of the mesh.

The room was a bare concrete box, and the angle from up here was wrong for looking down. But he could see the top of a man's head. It was Ste. He seemed to be bent at the waist, like he was maybe studying something on a table. Or someone lying down.

'OK, you know the drill,' Ste said. 'Flex your fingers . . .'

A woman's voice spoke – slowly, sounding weak and drained, like Sean's mum when she had one of her heads. Similar accent to Ste.

'Yeah, yeah, I know, not too fast, get a rhythm going. This is so *boring*. Think you could get me some more DVDs?'

'Yeah, well, sorry you're bored, sis,' Ste said irritably.

Sis! Sean felt his guts tingle with satisfaction. He lowered his hand to the level of Wolston's face and gave an emphatic thumbs up. They had found Zara, and now they knew that Ste was involved in whatever it was too. What that actually was – still no idea. Yet. So Sean kept listening.

'You know, we could both have been doing this up in the flat,' Ste went on, '*if* you'd come clean about your conviction. And Fayez wouldn't have had to come up with the airport thing at the last minute . . .'

Sean remembered making the exact same observation to Dave: that the whole airport drama had only gone and drawn attention to what was meant to be a secret. Dave had said that new security measures had been put in place since the girls left the country that would have stopped them getting back in.

Another man spoke, right below Sean, out of sight, and Sean froze. He must have been leaning against the door just below the grille. He would have heard if Sean and Wolston had made more than the absolute minimum sound.

'Have more faith, Ste. Arranging the airport diversion was, yes, a challenge – but we all came through it.'

He had an accent which Sean couldn't quite place. Middle Eastern? Asian? The top of his head came into view. He was bulkier than Ste, and balding.

'Is that not proof of the rightness of our cause?' he added.

'And I wanted to be part of the mission.' Zara sounded sulky, like she had been threatened with a treat being taken away.

'Yeah, and I almost got killed!' Ste snapped. 'That wasn't in the plan.'

'All of us are on jihad!' said the other man. 'Any one of us who dies is assured of Paradise. And for a man with no guerrilla training, Ste, you did very well. We told you to follow the leads of Omar and Mike, and it worked.'

Sean made a note of the names in his head. Mike – that would be *May*, the gunman identified as Michael Joseph who he had shot. Omar was a new one. He must have been *Clarkson*. And he had confirmation that Ste had been one of the gunmen – so he had been *Hammond* – and that the whole operation had been a lash-up job. The names were adding up – Zara plus Girl X plus Ste plus Omar plus Mike plus Fayez – and, on the journey up from Tidworth, Dave had said that the bigger conspiracies got, the easier they were to locate.

After a day of utter bollocks, Sean still felt like he had stumbled on a treasure trove. Until he thought of Emma.

Arse.

Not so long ago he had convinced himself that she was in the clear; he'd been thinking of ways to get together with her when this was over . . . Well, there was still nothing to prove or disprove that Emma was Girl X, but he had to admit it seemed a hell of a coincidence that Ste had talked to her, then come straight down here. But, Sean told himself, that still didn't *prove* anything. Maybe it was just *Guess who I just saw?*

'So how come Mike ends up dead, Fayez?' Ste demanded.

'Mike is waiting now for us to join him in Paradise,' Fayez said, with total, calm conviction.

Sean had heard bad and good motivational speakers in his time. Social workers trying to persuade him to go straight. Officers laying out a plan of battle. The bad ones sounded like actors delivering corny lines with a hidden smirk because they didn't quite believe it themselves.

But the good ones could deliver exactly the same lines with one hundred per cent conviction, so that you were swept up in it without realizing. Some clever shift in their voice, something in the rhythm of the words? This guy had it down pat. Even Sean could almost believe him.

Fayez went on. 'And the infidel who martyred him . . .'

'Is here in Littern Mills right now.'

There was a freezing pause on either side of the grille.

'Explain?' Fayez's voice was almost a purr.

'That's what I was going to tell you. I just learned that a man called Sean Harker is here on the estate . . .'

Sean flinched at the sound of his own name. *Shit.* So, yes, Emma had told Ste. Sean willed Ste to give more details. Had his name just come up in conversation? Or had it been a deliberate warning?

But Ste went on in his own way. 'He grew up here, he lived here until he joined the army a year or so ago, and I'm *almost* sure he was the man who shot Mike, and . . .'

Suddenly Ste was pacing around the room on the other side of the grille, from side to side and from one end to the other. It meant that he briefly came into Sean's field of vision. His eyes were round with anger and shock. But Sean couldn't make out the rest of his face – bizarrely it was covered with a surgical mask.

'This morning!' Ste shouted. 'It was him! Why didn't I *see* it . . .'

'Explain . . . ?' Even more purring, like a cat that is about to pounce on the mouse.

'When I came back from Whipps this morning, there were a pair of maintenance men in the flat. I took them for the usual incompetent— But one of them, the tall one, had his hat down over his face, and now I think about it, I'm sure . . . I'm *almost* sure it was Harker. He's meant to be on leave with his friends, but if he's snooping . . . Don't you see? They're on to us! Do you think he was planting bugs?'

The shock socked Sean in the guts. Busted! Like the

time he'd been on lookout while Gaz wired a car: he'd glanced away for just a second to follow a fit girl with his eyes, and when he turned back, there was a cop coming from one direction, a traffic warden from another and the car's owner from a third, and there was no good way out of it except to run for it *now*. Shit fuck arse wank – *busted* . . .

'This morning? At what time?'

'Whenever I came home. Tennish?'

A pause, and then Fayez had reverted to his previous tone of calm, convincing reassurance. 'And over twelve hours later, here we are. The estate is not crawling with special forces. They may suspect, but they have found nothing—'

Everything happened at once. Wolston head-butted Sean's knees as a half-second warning that he was about to be dropped, and a voice shouted, 'Who are you?'

By the time he got to 'are' Sean was falling, and he hit the ground on 'you?' He dropped into a crouch to absorb the impact, and halfway to straightening up he finally clocked the shape of a man hurrying towards them down the passage, and realized what the out-stretched arm meant. Wolston grabbed Sean by the collar and hauled him sideways just as the crack of a pistol shot echoed down the tunnel.

Chapter 22

There was only one possible place affording cover and Wolston headed for it – a doorless concrete alcove in the wall directly opposite the room.

The walls of the alcove recessed to each side, away from the entrance, which meant that Sean and Wolston could press themselves into it on either side. It was the one thing in their favour, because otherwise they were sitting ducks. If anyone wanted to take them out, they would have to burst in and take a fifty-fifty guess as to which side of the doorway the target was. And with Sean and Wolston on either side, one of them would always be lucky.

Unless there were *two* guys with guns.

How many times had Sean practised something like this? Being in a situation where, in real life, a round could hit him at any moment. He had been taught not to think about that. Your job was to take down the opposition. You didn't look any further ahead than that. Every breath you took was a small victory over the guys who wanted to kill you. As Adams liked to say, 'If you are still breathing, you are still winning.'

So, even though his heart was pounding fit to bust, he forced his fears into a small ball and pushed them to the back of his mind. *Concentrate on the mission.* He gazed across the short distance of a couple of metres at Wolston, flat against the wall on the far side of the doorway. He could only make out his outline and the whites of his eyes. Wolston's teeth were bared, probably not a big cheesy grin. Something else glinted as he held up his hand. He had a knife. Shit, where had that come from? But Sean was very glad of it. It didn't exactly level the playing field but it made it a shade less vertical.

They heard the door to the room open, and Fayez speaking.

'Jaz? What is—'

'Stay there!' It was impossible to guess the new-comer's ethnicity from his name or accent. 'Intruders. Two of them.'

Sean could picture them communicating by gesture. Jaz pointing with his gun at the entrance to the alcove. Fayez, his eyes going wide. Maybe he was retreating into the room. Or pulling out his own gun.

'Armed?'

'Unknown.'

Sean heard Ste's voice:

'Was one of them white, tall, fair-haired, well-built?'

'Looked like it.'

'Sean Harker?' Fayez asked it quietly and must have got a nod, because he raised his voice. 'Sean Harker? Is that you?'

The purr was back. The more Sean heard it, the deadlier it sounded. He kept quiet, not taking his eyes off Wolston. The corporal silently shook his head.

'You must know there is no escape in there. Come out now and we can talk about this. Otherwise you know what is inevitable.'

A pause.

'We know where you live, Sean Harker, and we know you have no way of warning anyone. There is no reception down here, as you have doubtless worked out. We can hold you at bay in there and send a party to investigate your flat.'

Where everyone was as unarmed as he was. The thought sent a shiver through Sean's body. Someone with a gun, kicking their way in through the door – or why even go that far? They could just shoot through the kitchen window, taking Mitra and Dave out before they could react.

But that only *might* happen. Sean knew what *would* happen if he broke cover now. So he stayed silent.

Fayez gave a loud, theatrical sigh. 'I can see you are not prepared to be reasonable—'

Jaz burst in. He fired a shot as he approached the alcove, just to make a loud noise and disorientate Sean and Wolston. It whanged into the concrete wall, and he leaped in after it.

He could have gone left or right. He went right, towards Sean. Sean was already braced for the move. A rookie mistake was to fight the *man*. The important thing was the *gun* – the thing he was holding that could kill people. So Sean went for that. He knew the move to disarm a guy waving a handgun around – grab the barrel with one hand, hook your other hand under the hammer and pull.

But Jaz had had training of his own. Somehow there was a fluid blur, and then the gun was in his other hand, not the one Sean was aiming for. He fired again. In the confined space the shot crashed against Sean's eardrums and he felt the round pluck at his shirt, missing the skin of his ribs by millimetres. No time for finessing now – with a clenched fist he lashed out at the centre of Jaz's face.

They were now too close together for Jaz to bring his gun to bear, but again he seemed to blur and Sean's punch missed its target. Next thing a pair of hammer blows from Jaz's free hand thudded into Sean's ribs, making him gasp, and then his knee pounded into Sean's balls like an RPG. Sean bellowed and dropped to his knees, bent over double as his guts exploded in agony.

Dimly, through his pain, he clocked a couple of things:

Jaz had stepped back and was lifting the gun to point at his head.

Shapes behind him – Fayez and the rest of them, unarmed, urging their pet killer on.

And Wolston was still stuck in the same place, just looking at them, his knife in his hand.

With all the will in the world, and with only a second left before his brains were blown into jelly, Sean still couldn't make his body straighten up to lunge at Jaz. But he could sort of topple over, rolling the bulk of his body against Jaz's legs and making him stumble backwards.

And bump into Wolston – which seemed to jolt the corporal out of whatever daze he had gone into. Wolston flung his arms around Jaz to pin his gun hand to his side. Jaz raked his foot down the inside of Wolston's leg – provoking a cry of pain. Then Jaz had wriggled free, and he and Wolston were grappling face to face.

Another shot, and this one sounded different: muffled, not echoing. The round had ploughed into Wolston's chest. Blood sprayed against the wall behind him and he crumpled like *May* had done at the airport.

But he wasn't dead yet. As he fell, he lashed out with the knife – it sliced into Jaz's gun hand. Jaz screamed and let the pistol drop. Sean, still lying in an agonized knot on the floor, scrabbled for it with one hand while the other still clutched at the nuclear explosion going on between his legs.

But there was no one to aim it at. Jaz had gone, and the door of the room opposite stood open. Dimly, over Wolston's groans and ragged breathing, Sean heard the sound of running footsteps. He summoned every atom of willpower, mind over matter, to force his aching body to stagger up and out into the passage. He raised the gun, single handed, still unable to prise his other hand off his balls. The barrel wavered like he was a kid with a potato gun at the funfair. He couldn't make himself fire without being able to aim it properly. Through blurred vision he just had time to make out the fleeing figures before they disappeared. Four of them, different shapes and sizes. Ste and Fayez both had surgical masks. Fayez was helping Zara. She was in jeans and a hoodie with rolled-up sleeves, and she had a bandage around her upper arm. From the way she staggered along, she was as weak as her voice had sounded. Jaz was light on his feet, but he stumbled as he clutched at his injured hand, and Ste was bizarrely lugging what looked like a picnic cooler.

Then they were gone.

Sean stuffed the weapon into his waistband and limped back to Wolston. The details of what he had just seen were put to one side for the moment. The corporal was the priority. He collapsed onto his knees and put his first two fingers lightly against Wolston's neck, desperately feeling for a pulse.

Don't you dare go and die on me fuck it don't you dare don't you dare die we're not going to lose another one don't you die . . .

And there it was – a beat. And another. Just about regular, but not strong.

Meanwhile he assessed the injury, eyes darting over the corporal's still form, hands poised for whatever turned out to be the first priority. The round had hit Wolston's right pecs and gone all the way through. Blood soaked the front of his shirt and pooled beneath him.

Sean put his ear to Wolston's chest and listened. He already had the heartbeat but he needed to hear the breathing. If Wolston had a punctured lung, then he would have a sucking chest wound that slurped as he breathed. The lung would have collapsed and air would be sucked into the cavity through the hole.

There was no slurping, just ragged but regular gasps. Lungs intact.

But he still wasn't in the clear. A shot in the same place on Wolston's left would have grazed his heart and he would probably be dead by now. But the shock wave as the round passed through any part of the chest area was bad news – a massive jolt to the central nervous system; maybe enough to send him into fibrillation.

And it could still be enough to top him. Just a little more mistreatment could make his body say, *Fuck this, I'm switching off*.

Wolston's face was grey, even in the dim light. His eyes were wide as dinner plates.

'Hold on, mate. Don't let go.'

Basic first-aid procedure took over. Even though he still felt like someone had ripped his balls off with a pair of rusty pliers, Sean prepared to tend to his friend.

First thing – gain access to the wound. Sean found Wolston's dropped knife and slit his shirt open. The entry hole was a dark circle in the middle of his shoulder, with red blood surging in pulses out onto his white skin. Sean drew a breath, thinking ahead. He'd had basic field medical training – everyone had. He knew how to handle a gunshot wound with his eyes shut. But that assumed he had the usual field medical kit on him. Sterile gauze, bandages, lactate solution to make up the volume of lost blood.

'Hang on, Joe. Eyes on the prize, right? We're going to improvise.'

Keep him talking – that was one thing Sean could do. Wolston nodded weakly.

Priority had to be to stop the bleeding. You stop the flow by applying pressure and replacing the fluids that have already leaked out. Nothing else would work if there wasn't enough blood inside Wolston to keep his body going. So Sean needed bandages. He could have used Wolston's shirt, but it was already soaked to capacity, and Sean needed something that was still absorbent. So he pulled off his own shirt, and used the knife to cut it roughly in two, stuffing the collar mike into his pocket.

'OK. Gonna roll you onto your left side. You with me?' Sean braced his hands behind Wolston's back. 'Two, six, *heave*.'

He pulled the corporal over onto his side, and Wolston groaned loudly through clenched teeth as his body moved. But the wound was on his right and everyone's heart is on the left, so just by turning Wolston over, Sean had elevated the wound above the heart. The heart wanted to pump blood out of the holes, but simple gravity would help keep it in.

Sean cut the rest of Wolston's shirt away so he could peek at the exit wound. It was larger than the entry one, as he had known it would be. The round would have slowed down and spread out inside Wolston's body, even if it hadn't hit anything solid. It would carve out a tunnel that was wider than the entry wound, and push out all the flesh and blood and muscle ahead of it, compressed by the shock wave, making the wound even bigger.

Sean folded one half of his shirt into a square and clamped it against the entry wound. He took Wolston's left hand and used it to keep it in place. 'Hold that there, right?'

He took the other half of the shirt, balled it up and forced it as hard as he could into the exit wound. Wolston bit back a scream, but Sean held it there. It had to be as far in as possible.

Sean cocked a look across the passage at the open door. Ste and Fayez had had surgical masks. Maybe there would be other medical gear in there. Antiseptic fluid and decent bandages. But if he moved now, the improvised exit-wound bandage would fall off.

With clumsy tugs, Sean single-handedly unbuckled his belt.

'You're just . . . determined . . . to get your kit off . . .' Wolston breathed.

'You've already got further than Emma did.' Sean whipped the belt around Wolston's neck and shoulder and over the bandage, securing it as best he could. 'I'm going to see if they've got anything across the way . . .'

Wolston's breath rattled, but he nodded as Sean forced himself to his feet, still not quite able to stand up straight. He staggered over to the entrance of the alcove and took a look back – just in time to see Wolston's hand slide limply to the floor.

Chapter 23

'*Shit!*'

Wolston had passed out. Sean wavered for half a second, turning back, turning forward, then hurried on into the room. The corporal was still breathing, and Sean couldn't do anything more for him without the proper gear.

There were sterile bandages in there, more than you could shake a stick at, in packages marked PROPERTY OF WHIPPS CROSS UNIVERSITY HOSPITAL. And other stuff too – some that he could use, some that he had no idea about. Sean clocked it all in a second, the way he used to sum up a row of parked cars and decide which one to come back and lift. Dave was going to want to know about all this.

But his first priority was to stabilize Wolston. He ran back to the unconscious corporal, breaking the seal on a bottle of antiseptic fluid as he went. He knelt and poured half of it out onto the bloodstained piece of shirt on Wolston's back. If he just pulled the shirt off, then it might break any clots that had started to form in the wound, and blood would start to flow again. He needed to let it soak in and leave the clots intact.

He peeled the makeshift pad away when he judged it was safe, and poured the rest of the bottle straight on. Finally he pushed sterile gauze into the wound and tore open one of the bandage packs to wrap around Wolston's upper half and hold the gauze in place.

Then, with another bottle and more gauze and bandages, he repeated the procedure on the entry wound. Last of all he tugged and pushed Wolston into the recovery position, mouth down and chin up so that his tongue wouldn't fall back down his throat and choke him.

He stepped back to assess his work. This was as good as he could make it. He had nothing to replace the lost blood with. Unless he got help now, it would only be sheer willpower keeping Wolston alive. And pretty soon the platoon would have two fatalities. Unless he shifted.

'Just going up top to make my report, mate,' Sean said. Even passed out, the sound of a human voice might make a difference – give Wolston's mind something to hold onto.

Sean ran back into the room to snap pictures of

everything he could find, then turned and threw himself down the passage again.

Halfway along he realized that Ste and his buddies might not have gone very far. They could be waiting . . . He grimly pulled the pistol out of his trousers and racked back the topslide to push a round into the chamber, ready for firing.

Bright lights shone in his eyes and he staggered to a halt, squinting, hands shading his eyes. *Oh, fucking hell, more of them?* He braced in case he had to throw himself into another alcove.

'*Put your hands in the air!*'

The voice was amplified and crackly. Spoken through a gas mask. So, not a terrorist. Sean's hands shot up, still clutching the pistol. Behind the lights he could make out black-clad forms. Black overalls, black helmets, black gas masks, black Heckler & Kochs shining red laser beams right at him. Armed cops, he guessed. For the second time in two days, the good guys were treating him like a suspect. And he was waving a gun about. Shit, he couldn't afford this delay.

'Listen, I'm—'

'*Lie down on the ground! Move!*'

Sean ground his teeth together, but obeyed. The concrete was cold and rough and gritty against his bare chest. Black legs and boots moved past his eyes.

'There's a gunshot wound back down the passage,' he called over his shoulder. 'He needs an ambulance . . .'

Someone kicked the gun away from him so that it slid across the concrete floor. Someone else grabbed his arms and pulled them behind his back. *Oh, fucking hell!* He was gripped by a sudden terror that the cops would just haul him away, and do that thing where they just blank out everything you say that doesn't fit the arrest pattern. *Guy waving a gun, obviously guilty, so nod calmly and make out you're noting it all down while he protests his innocence.* And meanwhile Wolston would quietly bleed out . . .

'I've got ID!' Sean bellowed. 'Wallet, left trouser pocket. I'm a British soldier. Fusilier Sean Harker, Royal Regiment of Fusiliers. The GSW is Corporal Joe Wolston. We were staking out—'

One of the men delved into the pocket and pulled out Sean's wallet, where his ID nestled next to his driving licence. Then he abruptly rolled Sean over and held the card next to his face. 'That's Harker, ID confirmed.'

He folded the wallet and handed it back as Sean slowly picked himself up. The man's face was invisible behind the gas mask, but he cocked his head the way Sean would if he was listening to his PRR. Then he looked directly at Sean. It was like being addressed by an Imperial Stormtrooper.

'They've found Corporal Wolston. You patched him up?'

Sean nodded. PRR made its own signals – they would be able to use it down here.

And then he realized he had made a wrong assumption about these guys. Cops didn't use PRR.

'You'll be, uh . . .'

The man looked at him, eyes so neutral behind the gas mask they were like blazing warnings.

So Sean didn't say *SAS*. Not out loud.

Dave came pushing through down the steps, ID in his outstretched hand, which he waved in front of SAS guy's mask. 'I'll take responsibility for Harker.'

SAS guy studied the ID, then just nodded and stepped back. Sean watched him go. The realization that Wolston was now in the best possible hands, that actually a proper ambulance would be turning up, was like a cold shower at the end of a long day.

'So how did they get here so quick?' he asked.

'I've had them on standby since the operation began. I called them in the moment I heard shots.'

'You didn't say anything about them.'

'You didn't ask.' Dave took in Sean's half-naked

appearance and pulled off the light jacket he was wearing. 'Report, Fusilier,' he said as he handed it over.

Sean clocked that the first-names thing was history now. It was strangely reassuring. As he pushed his arms into the borrowed jacket, he felt he was back where he belonged. He was broader across the shoulders than its owner, but he felt more comfortable with it on.

'Down there.' He waved a hand. 'Four of them in a room. No, three. One of 'em was Zara. The fourth guy, Jaz, he came up and . . .'

Now that stage of things was over, it was hard to come back to the present. The priorities of making his report, and getting help for Wolston, and catching the conspirators – they were all banging together in his head. After midnight at the end of a long and tiring day, he barely had the resources to put them all in order.

'From the beginning, soldier.' Dave took him by the shoulders and stared into his eyes, the way Sean would with a mate who was completely out of it on booze, trying to get him to focus. 'Step by step. What happened after the two of you went underground?'

The attention helped Sean to pin his thoughts together. He took a couple of breaths. 'Best if I show you . . .'

He led Dave down the passage to the room, briefly describing what had gone down. In the alcove, a pair of SAS guys were bent over Wolston's still form, giving first aid with kit of their own. When Sean reported that Ste had identified him by name, Dave broke off to tell one of the SAS to put an armed guard on the OP in flat 403, Gladstone Tower, *now*.

'And I found all this,' Sean finished as he turned to try and enter the room.

Dave put up an arm to block him, and an SAS guy appeared at his elbow.

'We need to secure this area—' the man said.

'Or even better,' Dave interrupted, 'leave it completely alone. Why were they wearing surgical masks?'

From the doorway, his gaze darted quickly around the room, taking in everything Sean had already seen. The concrete walls were painted grey. Thick pipes ran across the ceiling. The lighting came from a bare fluorescent strip. It was all as Sean had left it, kitted out with everything needed to put Zara up for a few days. A camp bed, a chemical toilet, a laptop, a couple of DVD boxsets, bottles of water, the remains of food.

And some serious-looking medical stuff. White plastic machinery that Sean didn't recognize, even from his own stay in hospital the previous summer. A waist-high cabinet on a metal trolley with a flatscreen monitor and various poles and pipes attached. Tubes, needles, clear plastic bags.

'Did you touch anything?' Dave asked.

'Just the stuff I took for Wolston.'

Dave drummed his fingers on the door jamb. 'Right.' He turned to SAS guy. 'I'm calling in experts to assess the scene and the civilian authorities to take over the management, but until they get here, post a guard by the exit doors either end of this passage. No one to come down without authorization. And we will all withdraw now. Provisionally I'm declaring this a biohazard zone.'

Sean recoiled. 'Biohazard?'

'They were wearing those masks for a reason. And what was in that cooler box? You use coolers to keep biological material fresh – usually food, but it would work for any other kind too. We need to know what they were doing – and where the hell they've now gone. And what they've taken with them. But I think it's fair to say we're blown, so we can stop hiding. I'm now in a position to fling resources at the estate: we'll start with the locations you got off the local boy. No more detectors – I'm having those doors properly kicked in by professionals, and I'm having Zara and Emma's flats secured. Meanwhile, Fusilier Harker, get back to the OP. You and Fusilier Mitra are to dismantle everything and await evacuation. I'll call transport in to escort you back to base.'

'We could just stay in the OP and leave in the morning,' Sean said. He had been running on adrenalin for God knows how long. Now it was draining away, and his body was realizing it had been on its feet for most of the last eighteen hours. He felt exhausted.

'You can kip on the way back to Tidworth – apart from anything else, the SAS will want your armed guard back. You've done your part and I want you out of the way—'

They both heard the sound at the same time. Police sirens, up above. Multiple ones. Powerful engines roaring into silence and doors slamming.

'Oh, great.' Dave set off up the steps, Sean following close behind. They emerged into the warm night air.

Sean didn't know how the SAS had got into the basement of Wolsey, but he was prepared to bet that no one in any of the towers had even noticed.

The police did it differently. They put on a show. Vans were pulled up at the base of the tower block, grilles down over the windscreens and splashing pulses of blue light around the square. A couple of smaller saloon cars with more blue lights pulled up behind them.

And their arrival had been noted. Lights were coming on in the flats, and the balconies were soon lined with onlookers. So, a sudden police incursion into Littern Mills, Sean thought with a sinking heart: this was not going to end well.

'You didn't have them on standby?' he shouted over the noise as more black-clad figures burst out of the vans. After seeing the SAS in all their battle kit, he thought, the Met's finest looked like kid brothers trying to be as hard as their elder sibs. But the Heckler & Kochs all looked pretty similar, and just as effective.

Dave shook his head. He stood still with his arm out, ID dangling open in his hand, waiting for someone to notice him. 'It's the Summit. There'll be an SCO19 unit on every street corner. Someone must have reported the gunshots. *Shit!*'

He drew a breath as a pair of cops sidled up, weapons to their shoulders. One of them squinted suspiciously at his ID. Sean didn't move, apart from holding his hands out at his side to show that he was no threat.

'Identify yourself!' the SCO19 guy snapped.

'Security Service.'

The man came closer and peered at the ID. Then his face seemed to turn inside out with disgust, like he was sucking on a lemon. 'Oh, fucking hell. What are you guys doing here? We weren't told there was an operation in progress.'

'No doubt.' Dave sounded tired. 'Who am I speaking to?'

'Sergeant Toby Wilson, Specialist Firearms Command . . .'

'Well, Sergeant Wilson, I was going to send for you people anyway, so as you're here, you can make yourselves useful. This is a Security Service operation.' He waved the ID again. 'Please confirm that you recognize my authority to assume command.'

Wilson wasn't going to give in so easily. He turned away pointedly as he spoke urgent words into the radio on his shoulder.

When he turned back, he looked like he'd added a few cups of vinegar to the lemon. 'I'm ordered to follow your instructions.'

'First of all, send men up to flats 614 and 508 in Wolsey Tower to secure the premises and detain anyone found there for questioning. As of five minutes ago, 614 was empty and 508, we believe, contained a single teenage female, unarmed, but take no chances with either. And you, Fusilier' – Dave looked at Sean – 'get going. Send the armed guard back down. They won't try anything now the cat's out of the bag.'

*

Sean found Ravi Mitra almost wetting himself with impatience. Dave had ordered him to help Sean take down the OP, and not to waste time with queries unless there was a new development.

Sean peeled off Dave's jacket and pulled on a fresh shirt of his own while Mitra demanded details. Apart from the fact that Wolston was down, but still alive, Sean could only tell his mate what little he had seen. It all took time to tell, because they had to concentrate on the main job of putting the equipment away. The telescopes, the computers, the wires, the detectors – everything had its place in foam compartments inside the containers it had arrived in. It was pushing oh two hundred and Sean's brain had lost the ability to do two things, like think *and* talk, at the same time.

He glossed over the details of the fight because you didn't grass on a mate. Especially not a mate who was now fighting for his life. But at the back of his mind he still had a clear image of Wolston freezing, even as he brandished the knife that would tip the balance. One day he would come back to that.

Mitra, still shaken about Wolston, eyed Sean warily at the mention of biohazard. 'And you're safe?'

'Dave must have thought so. I didn't get a cut or

anything. And stop looking at me like that. As long as we don't have unprotected sex, you'll be fine.'

'My mate the plague zone,' Mitra muttered.

Sean gave a tired grin and made to close the last of the laptops. Then he remembered there were still pictures on his phone that should be uploaded – the ones he had taken in the room below Wolsey. Which meant digging out the USB cable to join the two items together. Once they were connected, he called up the phone's picture gallery and dragged the icon over to the mission folder on the screen. The empty box began to populate itself with thumbnails.

'Hold on!' Mitra put out a hand to stop him, and squinted at the images. Then he clicked on one to enlarge it. It was the white plastic gizmo. 'You ever given blood, Stenders?'

'Nope.'

'I have. My parents do it like it's a competition. We've got drawers full of golden hearts back home. It drives them both mad that they have to wait six months to donate again every time they come back from visiting Nana-ji. But this thing that looks like R2D2's little brother – it's what hospitals use. It sucks it out and bags it up for you.' He looked sideways at Sean. 'And that's what they were doing to Zara.'

'Right . . .' Ideas started to gather in Sean's head. And then . . .

'*Oh shit!*'

He stared down at his hands as if expecting them to start sprouting some weird fungus. He gaped at Mitra, who was looking back at him, torn between amusement and alarm.

'Yeah?'

'Got to report this,' Sean gasped. 'Dave will want to know.' He scrabbled for the pressel on his belt, remembered the mike was no longer on his collar, and pulled it out of his pocket to speak into it. 'That's Harker with something to report.'

'*Roger. Go on.*'

'At the briefing you said if it wasn't for the airport diversion, you might think that Zara was just a drugs mule. Well, she *is* a mule, but it's not drugs she's smuggling. I think it's germs. Diseases.'

Images swam in front of his eyes. The bandage on Zara's arm, and the cooler box being lugged by Ste. You could transport blood under refrigeration . . . couldn't you? But for how long?

He could see Mitra's eyes go wide as the realization sank in.

'They put something into her blood in Lagos and now they're taking it out again. Here. In London.'

Dave must have got it by now, but Sean couldn't stop talking. All he was getting was silence. Fucking hell – didn't the man realize?

'So you were right,' he pressed on. 'It *is* a biohazard zone, and that's why they had masks . . .'

'*A bio-mule scenario,*' Dave said calmly at the other end. '*Yes, that is now the most likely hypothesis we're working to. I guessed the moment I saw the blood-transfusion machinery.*'

'Bio-mule . . .' Sean rolled the word around in his mouth. It felt odd. It wasn't a term he had heard before but he immediately knew what it meant. He tried to picture how it might work. If a bio-mule wasn't obviously ill, then airport security wouldn't pick them up. Once they were in the country, they somehow had to get the bugs out of that blood and into people. How?

It wouldn't be something like malaria, which needed a specific insect to bite you and then someone else. It had to be simpler than that. How simple? He imagined Zara coughing her way down somewhere like Oxford Street on a Saturday afternoon, spraying out . . . whatever the fuck it was in all directions. She might drop dead by the time she got to Tottenham Court Road, but how many hundreds – make that thousands – of shoppers would have breathed her germs in the meantime? And then gone home and repeated the process themselves, coughing on the train or the Tube . . . before someone finally clocked what was happening?

But then, why were they taking blood *out* of Zara?

Mitra must have been thinking along similar lines. He looked dazed. 'So that's why Zara didn't bother with anti-malarials,' he said. 'What's the point when you know you've deliberately got infected with something way worse?'

Sean stared at him. 'Kind of missing the fucking point, Kama Sutra? *I was in that room!* I could have it . . .' His mind spun. Should he grab a shower? Douse himself with TCP, burn all his clothes? 'I was in that *fucking room* that is now a biohazard zone!'

'Hey, hey, hey!' Mitra waved his hands in a calm-down motion. 'If you were in danger, if you were infectious, Dave would have said something – and he'd have had you out of here by now. Not wandering around Littern Mills. You're not thinking, Stenders.'

Sean let the logic sink in, and his racing heart slowed down. 'Yeah. Whatever . . .'

Even so. First thing in the morning he was going to get on to Mum and tell her to get out of town. Find a hotel somewhere else. Andover, maybe, where he could keep an eye on her. But *get out*.

'*Harker.*' Dave was abruptly back on the air.

Mitra and Sean shot each other wary looks.

'Harker, roger?' Sean said.

'*Get yourself down to the square. A situation is developing with your little friends from the estate and I need to know their intentions.*'

Chapter 24

Friday 4 August, 02:00 BST

Jeers and insults floated up in the warm night air as Sean stepped out onto the balcony. The Killaz were making their presence felt. He craned his neck down at the square, but could only see the tops of a few heads. They must have been gathered in the overhang in front of the Gladstone shops, where they would just be outlines to the cops across the way in front of Wolsey.

He groaned. How the fuck had this come as a surprise to anyone? A hot night when no one would be going back to their airless flat. Bored kids out for entertainment. And cops whose idea of winning hearts and minds was to come down hard and expect the people they were sitting on to be grateful for the protection.

The police had set up their own forward operating base at the bottom of Wolsey. They had arranged their vans in a semicircle round the entrance to the sublevels.

It gave them a secure area behind and hid what was going on from prying eyes. Meanwhile a line of cops had moved out from the semicircle, standing shoulder to shoulder with their backs to the vans.

Every now and then someone from below would run out into the light and make graphic wanking gestures or moon his arse before retreating into the shadows again. That and the shouts of 'Pig!' were all pretty much what Sean had expected the moment the first set of cops gatecrashed the party.

So what the fuck am I supposed to do about it? But Dave obviously expected something.

He took the stairs two at a time, but as he got to ground level, he made himself slow down. He didn't want to burst into the midst of the Killaz looking like he gave any kind of shit. He stuffed his hands into his pockets and swaggered out.

The first thing Sean did was clock their faces. He could see them all – excellent. It was the best scenario for the time being. Caps and hoodies, yes, but they didn't have scarves pulled up. When faces got hidden, that was when you knew a riot was about to happen. At the moment this was just a break in the usual dull routine, a chance to let off steam.

How this turned out depended on the attitudes of both sides. If either of them was spoiling for a fight, then a fight would happen, no doubt about it. The cops weren't there to bust heads, just to secure a crime scene, so they should have a high tolerance level for any crap the Killaz put out – but many of them might also be pissed off to find that an MI5 operation had been going on under their noses, and want to take their frustration out on someone. And the Killaz were definitely pissed off by the uninvited police presence.

'Yo, Sean!' Kieran had clocked his presence and he waved him over with a big grin.

'What the fuck's happening?' Sean demanded. 'I was trying to get some kip and you dickheads let off.'

'What's happening? The pigs are happening!' Kieran looked at him like he was a moron. 'It's a fucking liberty, but hey, make the most of it, right?' He gazed over Sean's shoulder, and his expression changed to delighted wonder. 'All *right*! Dead pig! *Dead pig!*'

The others took up the cry. 'Dead pig! Dead pig!'

An ambulance had pulled up outside the semicircle, and stretcher-bearers came out from between the vans to load Wolston up. He was under a thermal blanket, with an oxygen mask over his face. A paramedic held up a bag of clear liquid attached to a tube that disappeared beneath his blankets.

'*Dead pig!*'

Sean clenched his fists and consciously fought the

urge to strangle the little git. He kept quiet while everyone else celebrated what they thought was a fallen policeman. But he couldn't help feeling a gush of relief that washed away fears he hadn't allowed himself to think about, because *Wolston was still alive.* The platoon wasn't about to lose its second member in two days.

'One down, several hundred thousand fuckers to go!' Kieran shouted.

Sean drew a breath to calm himself down. 'You're well spoiling?' Even though he just wanted to walk away in disgust, he still needed to know their plans. Was Kieran going to start a fight? Or was it all just dick waving?

'Too fucking right! But we're not stupid. Some of them have got guns.'

'Do you know what set them off? What got them here?'

'Not a clue, mate.' Kieran looked sideways at him. 'Thought maybe you might know . . . That stuff you was looking out for – you reckon they found it?'

'Could be.' Sean had to agree, to keep up the pretence. 'Something upset them. Expect it'll be on the news.'

'Mate, we *guarantee* we're going to be on the fucking news! Too good a chance to miss.'

'Well, take care,' Sean said. 'I'd hate to hear they

found the body of a zitty white kid with a mag full of warning shots in the back.'

Kieran grinned. 'I can look after myself. Take care, mate.'

They bumped knuckles and parted on what looked like good terms.

Now it was time to duck round the sides of the square without Kieran seeing and deliver his report to Dave.

Chapter 25

'So you think it's just high spirits?' Dave asked when Sean had finished. They were back behind the cordon at the base of Wolsey.

'I reckon so. As long as no one does anything stupid.' Sean looked meaningfully at the nearest cop, who either didn't hear him or chose not to.

'I expect to have this lot withdrawn shortly,' Dave said. 'That should ease some tension. I've been waving my willy as much as I can at the police commissioner, but unfortunately he's been waving his back, so we've both been waving them at the Home Secretary, who has finally decided that I have the biggest. Which puts me in a good enough mood to apologize to you.' Sean cocked his head and looked at him. 'The bio-mule scenario. It's been at the back of our minds for a long time – if it could occur to us, then it would certainly occur to those who would wish us harm. And it would be a nightmare to guard against. Airport security today can stretch to full body scanning, checking passengers' shoes, taking biometric readings, but the one thing it doesn't do – yet – is take your temperature or analyse a blood sample. If Zara hadn't already been on our system because of her conviction, which meant her fingerprints would have given her away, she and Girl X would have just swanned through Immigration at Heathrow, no problem, and no one would ever have guessed what was in their blood.

'But as it is, the switched-airport scenario alerted us that something was going on. So we naturally paired it up with the Commonwealth Summit, which is the biggest security operation going on right now. And that meant we assumed a weapons-based scenario. A bio scenario would be too long-term – if the plotters were aiming at the Summit, they would use guns and explosives, not germs. So, to avoid distracting you, we didn't tell you about our bio-mule worries and con-centrated on finding weapons that go *bang*.'

And not a weapon that's as silent as it gets, Sean thought. *What noise does a germ make when it gets into your blood?*

'How do you know they aren't going to gatecrash the Summit and sneeze in someone's face and give them Ebola?' he asked.

Dave shook his head. 'The timing is out. Kath Buckingham and Rachel Cooke – the false identities being used by Zara and Girl X – were only in Nigeria for a week, and whatever got pumped into them out there, there's no known disease that would have had time to start showing symptoms – in other words, to make them infectious.'

'But it's brewing? Inside them?'

'Oh, yes. They're doubtless incubating the virus in their blood as we speak.'

Dave spoke so calmly that Sean stared at him to check he was getting this right. And then he saw the slight gleam of sweat on the guy's upper lip, the deadness in the eyes. Dave was acting like he didn't care, but it was merely a coping mechanism: in fact, he was absolutely fucking terrified. He had probably been thinking along the same lines as Sean: infection spreading through the capital at the speed of a cough.

'Blood can be mixed with anticoagulant and stored under refrigeration for up to six weeks, so it can easily be transported in a cooler box,' Dave went on. 'As you saw. I believe Zara was giving blood, as often as was safe without draining her completely, and that her blood will be transfused into more volunteers – perhaps under the skilled supervision of Ste, whose medical training was kindly paid for by the taxpayer . . . Makes you proud to be British, doesn't it?'

Dave's eyes were glazing as he looked deeper into the nightmare scenario, but he suddenly remembered himself and again gave the smile that didn't fool Sean for a second.

'But it's probably not Ebola. We've pulled up some research on the Sacred Cross Hospital, where the girls were in Lagos. It's a biorepository for tropical diseases, which means they have strains of numerous viruses in storage, for research. So we asked them what they currently have on the shelves. They have all the bad boys, including Ebola – Zika, dengue, West Nile – but those all require mosquitoes for transmission. However, they also have a particularly virulent strain of Lassa fever, which is transmitted by inhaling contaminated particles of rat urine in the air, and by contact with body fluids. So that's the likely contender.'

Sean thought over the very, very little he knew about diseases. 'So what's the – uh – incubation period?'

He remembered the MO using that phrase – the time it took between a bug getting into your body and the symptoms starting to show.

'That may be our first break. Lassa fever apparently comes in four strains, with incubation periods of between six and twenty-one days, but some genius has now combined two of the strains to produce a fifth. I got all kinds of technobabble about combining RNA strands . . .' He saw Sean's blank look and quickly got to the point. 'The new strain, which was in stock at the biorepository, is just as dangerous, transmitted through the air, including by coughing, and *extremely* infectious – about thirty per cent of exposed cases will become symptomatic – but it has a minimum incubation period of around twenty-one days. Which is why we aren't all being quarantined right now. The girls weren't in Nigeria for twenty-one days. If they were infected, then they'll be dangerous, but they're not dangerous *yet*.'

Sean thought back to the hidden camera showing Emma logging on to her computer . . . and the way she had suddenly folded double. 'Emma was coughing.'

'She was, but so do lots of people for lots of other reasons. But yes, we're trying to find her, to bring her in – whether or not she's Girl X. We're done playing softly-softly. She'll be quarantined, and then we'll see what happens. And believe me, if you'd gone ahead and had sex with her, you'd be in a quarantine suit yourself right now. Ah, just who I was waiting for . . .'

A small team of guys dressed in white overalls were climbing out of a plain van that had come through the blockade. The leader came hurrying over, while Sean reflected that he had never been so glad *not* to have got lucky. The newcomer had his white hood pushed back and a surgical mask pulled down around his neck.

'You're the one in charge?' the newcomer asked brusquely. 'Peter Mirzoyan, Biohazard Response.'

'Pleased to meet you, Mr Mirzoyan. Before we go on, could you please describe the symptoms of Lassa fever to Fusilier Harker?'

Mirzoyan shot Sean a surprised look, maybe wondering why a mere Fusilier got the special treatment. He rattled off the description.

'Begin with fever and general weakness – victims might just think they've got the flu. After a few days – headache, sore throat, coughing, muscle pain, chest pain, nausea, vomiting, diarrhoea. Then they either get better, or it all gets worse and worse, progressing to severe dehydration, mental confusion and organ failure. At that point the lucky ones just go to bed, lapse into a coma and die. The unlucky ones – about a third – go on to start haemorrhaging in the stomach, intestines, kidneys, lungs, brain. Slow and painful. *Then* they die. But that is a *very* few – we're talking a mortality rate of one per cent, though that can go higher in an epidemic.'

Sean mentally translated 'mortality rate' as 'number of people who die'. One per cent? One in a hundred? Those were good odds.

Dave wasn't letting go. 'How much higher?'

Mirzoyan clicked his tongue in annoyance. 'In an epidemic – a massive number of cases all arising at once – I suppose it could get up to fifty per cent or so. Everyone's infection reinforces everyone else's. But that really is a worst-case scenario for a virus with a highly inflated reputation based solely on the unpleasantness of the symptoms . . .'

'One last question. I happen to know that at least one official biorepository has samples of a strain with a thirty-per-cent infection rate and a twenty-one-day incubation period. What happens if *that* gets loose?'

Mirzoyan was obviously only putting up with Dave because he had been told to. Numbers rattled off his tongue like a politician talking about NHS funding.

'Thirty per cent? Well, say one person develops symptoms. Thirty per cent of the people they then meet until they are contained, or dead, will develop symptoms themselves after twenty-one days. So if this person meets a hundred people on the day they become infectious, thirty of them will become infectious three weeks later. Thirty per cent of *their* contacts will then become infectious for as long as *they* are not contained – and so on.'

Thirty out of a hundred . . . Sean thought. Again, not so bad. Getting worse, but odds he was prepared to take.

ANDY McNAB

'And fifty per cent of them die,' Dave added.

Mirzoyan shrugged. 'As you say. So, the numbers over time are a simple GCSE maths problem. May we inspect the scene now?'

'I think you'd better. It's this way.'

Dave led Mirzoyan and his team away, giving Sean a last, lingering *Think about it* look as he went.

And Sean *was* thinking. Thirty out of a hundred? Maybe he didn't have GCSE maths, but even he could see . . .

Hang on . . .

He frowned. The maths problem was scratching at his consciousness.

Then his eyes flew wide open.

Fucking hell!

Those thirty cases came from one infected person. But if every one of those infected people met a hundred people each – that was thirty times one hundred. So they would meet three thousand people between them. And if thirty per cent of them got infectious – that was, what? Nine hundred people.

And those nine hundred infectious cases each met a further hundred people – which made ninety thousand contacts. Even just thirty per cent of that was . . .

He was running out of fingers. It was a lot.

This was getting way scarier.

He tried to picture that number of patients suddenly being dumped on a creaking NHS. Only, the number would actually be way higher, because they wouldn't all just neatly infect the set number of victims. Mirzoyan had said *until they were contained.* But how long would that take? They would just keep on doing it until they finally realized they had something worse than flu and got help. Or someone stopped them.

And even if only fifty per cent of them died . . . that was still way bigger than any terrorist strike so far that Sean was aware of.

And meanwhile panic would spread. One good front-page photo of someone vomiting blood, and the cities would be clearing. Every road and motorway grid-locked with cars heading out to the country.

Total breakdown of – well, everything.

Oh. Fucking. Hell!

A hand clapped hard on his shoulder and a familiar voice barked in his ear, 'When you're done staring into space, I understand we're meant to be taking down the OP . . . But first I think we should fill each other in.'

With his thoughts still whirling with images of plague apocalypse, Sean found himself staring, baffled, at Sergeant Phil Adams.

*

'We plonk down on the tarmac at Heathrow – next second I'm ordered to report to Knightsbridge barracks to hang around on standby.' Adams was in mufti, like Sean. They were standing in the shadow of one of the pillars of Wolsey. 'Then, out of the blue at oh stupid hundred hours, I get ordered to retrieve you two beauties and the gear.' He cocked his head. 'And you look like someone really just made your day. What's going on?'

So Sean gave Adams a brief report of everything he had just got from Dave and Mirzoyan. Adams's face went hard and expressionless, which was what it always did when he got really bad news.

'But the girls aren't infectious yet?'

'Dave says they aren't.'

Adams abruptly became businesslike. 'Then let's get the fuck out of Dodge before that changes. Take me to the OP – sorry, am I keeping you up, Fusilier Harker?'

A mighty yawn had stretched Sean's face.

'Sorry, Sergeant, long day. We're on the fourth level of Gladstone over there – but I'd better take you a roundabout route.' He poked his head round one of the vans to take a look at Kieran's crowd, over on the far side. 'That lot don't take kindly to authority figures and, no offence, you look . . . authority. Even when you're trying to be a civvy.'

'Lead on by whatever route seems best. But first . . .'

He put out a hand to touch Sean's elbow. It was the mate-iest thing he had ever done and Sean stared at him in disbelief.

Adams's voice was low and his eyes were hard. 'How did Wolston go down? Give me all the details.'

Sean bit his lip. He hadn't told Dave the full details. He hadn't even told Mitra. The old instincts were still there: *You do not grass on a mate.*

Adams clocked his hesitation. 'I can make it an order, Fusilier.'

It took a conscious act of will for Sean to remind himself that this was not grassing. This was reporting. And the purpose of a good report was to benefit everyone. He took the plunge. He would trust Adams with his life, and the sergeant knew more secrets about him than anyone else outside the Security Service. So he trusted Adams with this one, starting with him and Wolston cornered by a gunman in an alcove underground, all the way up to Wolston's little seizure. How he had just stood there with the knife that could have been a game-changer, and not done anything with it.

Adams gazed at him thoughtfully while Sean pressed on.

'And it's happened before. We didn't say, but . . . at the airport . . .'

He described Wolston's momentary brain freeze

before suddenly coming back to life and giving orders for dealing with the three gunmen. Adams's eyes grew colder. Sean wasn't sure if it was because of Wolston's actions, or because he was basically admitting to making an incomplete report the first time round.

But he was committed now. It was just tumbling out.

'And then – you remember when we were chasing those kids in the Wolf and he ordered an abort – I didn't think any more of it then, but now I wonder—'

'Enough.' Adams gazed into the night and breathed out. 'Shit.'

Sean didn't press him. He guessed Adams would say something more when he was ready. Sure enough:

'It happens, Harker, to the best of us. It's burn-out.' A pause. 'I'm not a doctor, I have no professional opinion to give – but I'd lay odds on that being the case.'

'Burn-out of what?' Sean asked. 'I mean, I know he's not a coward – it can't be courage—'

'Damn right it isn't!' Adams said. 'No. Not courage. It's . . . everything. Most people get by on about eighty per cent of the basic quota of nerves and energy that God gave them. That leaves them twenty per cent to call on when needed. But on top of that, inside most people there's always an emergency reserve. The army teaches you to go up to the full one hundred per cent,

and then to call on reserves if you have to go beyond.'
He sighed. 'But it also then gives you plenty of time to
replenish for the next incident. Only some people burn
up the hundred per cent and never give themselves a
chance to refill, so they go about their basic existence
on reserves. It means they have incredibly little extra to
call on when the shit goes down, and they can freeze up
at almost any time. And that, I think, is what probably
happened to Wolston in Afghanistan. Shit, it damn
near happened to me, but I had the sense to come down
with PTSD before it got really bad. People noticed and
they pulled me out. But Wolston's tougher than that, so
he was able to just keep going until . . . he couldn't.'

He clicked his tongue. 'Getting plugged could be
the best thing that ever happened to him. With the
right treatment he might even be able to return to service rather than be invalided out. Meanwhile we pity
him, but we don't condemn. Right?' He looked Sean
straight in the eye, and Sean gratefully returned the
favour.

'Right, Sergeant.'

'Let's go, then. I have a people carrier parked out
back. Is there much gear?'

'Nothing we can't all carry. We had to bring it in our
regular overnight bags, so it's portable—'

And then more sirens whooped through the night

air. Sean stared back at the square in dismay as another two vans pulled up and cops piled out of the back. These ones weren't SCO19, just regular bruisers, and they lined up in front of Wolsey. The shouts and catcalls from the Killaz immediately went up by about two hundred per cent.

'Oh, fucking hell!' Sean shouted. 'I said, *if they don't do anything stupid*!'

Dave suddenly appeared at the top of the stairs. As he strode over to the guy who looked like the most senior cop on site, his expression was furious. The guy wasn't backing down. Sean caught phrases like 'un-acceptable presence at a crime scene' and 'need to safe-guard civilian interests'. Hands were waving, fingers were jabbing in different directions. It looked like Dave was being told: *You're* in charge down *there*, *we're* in charge up *here*.

Maybe the Home Secretary had reconsidered willy size, on appeal.

The noise of the mob was getting louder, and there was something else in the warm night air – a tension that maybe no one not born on Littern Mills could have picked up. But Sean saw the next ten minutes laid out in front of him, clear as day.

'Shit,' he breathed. 'They're going to kick off. They're

going to do it. We need to get up to the OP, double quick.'

Adams shook his head. 'At this stage the OP can come to us. What's really sensitive up there – as opposed to just expensive?'

'Uh – the laptops? I suppose. Three of them. They've got all the int on them.'

'Then tell Mitra to pack them up and bring them the fuck down here right now. We can abandon the rest.'

Sean nodded and turned away to raise Mitra. He couldn't tear his eyes off the rows of cops across the square.

A ripple seemed to pass through the front line, and then they weren't just standing there any more, they were advancing.

The first bottles and stones started to fly through the air towards them.

The balconies of Gladstone were clearing. Law-abiding residents would be retreating into their flats and locking their doors. Others would be hurrying downstairs to join in.

The first Molotov cocktail blazed a trail through the air – a bottle half full of petrol with a flaming rag stuck down the neck. It smashed at the feet of a section of cops and they hurriedly pulled back, doing a dainty little dance around the liquid fire spreading over the concrete.

'*Stop it! Stop it, you stupid fucks!*'

Sean wasn't sure who it was shouting – until Adams put a hand on his shoulder, and he realized it was him. He blinked back furious tears. Just a couple of years ago, in another life, he would have been joining in – and that was what made it so painful now. He knew what a waste of space he had been back then, and he knew what he'd had to go through to wake up to reality. He wouldn't wish it on anyone else.

A fireball suddenly blossomed at the base of Gladstone. Sean heard the screams as a knot of Killaz scattered in all directions, away from a luckless kid who was enveloped in ripples of flame.

It was the easiest own goal to score if you were putting a Molotov cocktail together. All the petrol went up at once, bursting out of its bottle and spraying over whoever was holding it.

The cries of shock turned to screams of agony and terror, and the flames soon covered the kid completely. He staggered to his knees, then dropped onto his face.

Chapter 26

The Killaz fled to the edges of the square as cops ran forward with a fire blanket for the burning kid. They scooped up the body – alive or dead, it was impossible to tell – between them and hurried back across the square to the nearest ambulance.

The fire spread along the metal grille over the front of Lakhani's mini supermarket. Fire alarms split the air with their electronic screaming.

That's my home!

Sean didn't know if he'd said it out loud. He had never exactly loved the place – but a basic instinct to protect his territory took over.

And it was *fire*. When it came to fire, the little boy inside him was never far from the surface. Sean had been in fights and car chases. He had been nicked, he had done time. He had come under fire and he had killed in the line of duty. But it was *fire* that gave him nightmares.

'Fuckers!'

The shout came out of the dark, followed by more of the same as the Killaz grew in confidence. Figures began to move forward again, silhouetted against the flames. Sean's eyes narrowed. What were they doing? Their body language said something was up, but he could only imagine one thing, and that was impossible. Not even the Guyz, on their worst day, would think of—

'*This is for Adey!*'

Light sparked from a dozen cigarette lighters, and blossoms of flame flared in the mouths of a dozen Molotov cocktails. Then they flew towards the police.

Kieran had planned this. Under the cover of the bombardment, a couple of masked lads ran forward with one of the square's metal litter bins. They heaved it like a battering ram against Lakhani's grille. Sean could hear the metallic smashes across the square. One, two, three – and then the grille toppled forward.

More Molotov cocktails blazed as the lads hoisted the bin one more time and hurled it against Lakhani's window. The glass was tougher than the grille had been. It took several blows to knock out a hole the size of a dustbin, but that was all they needed.

The police decided that enough was enough. At a signal Sean didn't pick up on, they suddenly closed ranks and charged.

The Killaz only had a couple of petrol bombs left, but that was all that was needed. They shoved them through the hole, and flames spread across the floor of the supermarket, outlining boxes and shelves.

And the Killaz weren't the Guyz. Sean had known that, but now the sheer size of the difference finally sank in. In their own way, the Guyz had been looking out for the interests of Littern Mills. The Killaz didn't even have that. For them it was the kicks, and that was all. And revenge. Adey – the kid who had got the Molotov cocktail wrong, and was now either dead or badly burned in police custody – had to be avenged. To the Killaz, everything was *them* against *us*, even if they were the ones who'd started it, and even if other people were only trying to help.

'I will kill him. I will personally kill the little fuck . . .'

Adams held him back. 'You're going nowhere. Not your fight. Let the boys in blue have their fun.'

There was movement on the balconies of Gladstone again. Lights were coming on and people were moving out, more urgently than before. A fire alarm on the ground level would have gone off in every flat too. They were evacuating.

The Killaz had disappeared into the dark at the edge of the square, with the police hard on their tails. Sean guessed they would now run a chase through the maze of the jungle, where Kieran's lot had cornered Mitra earlier in the day. It was exactly what he would have done, back when he was on the wrong side of a good riot.

'Come on.' Adams hurried forward, beckoning Sean after him. 'We should look out for Mitra. It's just possible that an Asian man carrying three laptops from a burning building might need someone to vouch for him . . .'

Something gave inside Lakhani's. Light flashed and a fireball shot out of the shattered window, sending a lick of flame towards them. They both flinched, then Adams ran on. Sean stared into the heart of the inferno that now consumed the supermarket – until Adams yelled his name and the spell was broken.

Fuck this. He wasn't the kid afraid of fire any more. He was the trained soldier with a job to do.

The first inhabitants had reached the bottom of the stairs. Sean and Adams had to push their way up against the flow. Sean clocked the faces – frightened, worried, weary . . . and resigned. Even something like this, your home burning down, wasn't that much of a surprise on Littern Mills.

In the second-level stairwell they bumped into Mitra coming the other way, and they each grabbed a laptop.

'Let's get these somewhere they can do some good,' Adams said.

Back across the square, lines of cops had formed to herd the evacuees while they waited for the fire brigade to turn up. Adams had to get forceful with a couple of police officers and wave ID around to be let through to the cordoned-off area.

All the other towers were awake by now, the balconies again lined with onlookers gawking at a burning tower that wasn't theirs. The lads set down the laptops and watched the flames consume Sean's child-hood home. Mitra and Adams both saw how Sean was staring at the blaze, and had the sense not to try and say anything comforting.

Adams studied the scene across the square. 'Maybe I'm being paranoid, but I could almost believe they planned this. Evacuate all the inhabitants en masse and then send out your bio-mules. A few good coughs – infection left, right and centre.'

'Actually, that would be a very inefficient way of engineering contagion,' said a bored voice, just as Sean was starting to think, *Fucking hell, they could . . .*

The three soldiers turned round to see the biohazard man, Mirzoyan, with a couple of other white-suit fetishists, on a break.

'The open air is too well ventilated,' Mirzoyan went

on. 'To spread infection effectively, the space needs to be enclosed. If I was hatching this plot, I would infect my volunteers and then just send them to a gig, to a club, to a movie, to a game . . . that would do it.'

'Wouldn't the bleeding from the eyes and the coughs and the vomiting blood be a giveaway?' Sean asked.

The biohazard man smiled a small superior smile. 'Bleeding only affects a few victims. Most Lassa fever symptoms are internal – headaches, nausea, weakness – so they wouldn't show and they could be suppressed with drugs.'

'Well, that's you told,' Adams commented.

Sean opened his mouth, closed it again. Something Mirzoyan had said rang a bell, but Mitra broke his train of thought.

'Lassa fever?'

'Dave thinks that's what the girls were smuggling. In their blood. But we're still in the incubation period. They've got three weeks to become infectious.'

'Shit.' Mitra was quiet for a few seconds. 'This incubation thing . . . We know about the timescale – how?'

'Because Kath Buckingham and Rachel Cooke were only at the hospital for a week before they came home with us.' Sean was still trying to pin down the thing that was bothering him.

'And they are . . .'

'The false identities being used by Girl X and Zara at the hospital,' Sean said impatiently. Mitra looked doubtful. 'Got a problem?'

'If those were the identities being used at the hospital – I'll take Dave's word for that.' Mitra delved into his pocket for his phone and flipped up the images directory. His eyebrow went up as he nodded and showed the screen to Sean and Adams. 'Only, neither of those is the identity in Zara's false passport.'

The picture showed the main page of a passport. The photo was of Zara, but the name was yet another fake one. Beth Robinson.

While Sean and Adams took it in, Mitra thought for a minute, then flipped through the images more slowly. It was almost like he didn't want to produce visual evidence.

But he came to the one he wanted, dragged thumb and forefinger across it to enlarge, and showed it to Sean. It was another page from Zara's fake passport, and it had the entry stamp from Nigerian Immigration on it.

'And *she* entered Nigeria three weeks ago. Is that long enough for you?'

Minimum incubation period of around twenty-one days . . . That was what Dave had said. Zara had already had those twenty-one days.

Sean felt his guts go into freefall. This wasn't over. In fact, it was only just starting.

Adams had also joined the dots. 'Mitra, get over to Dave and push that passport pic into his face until he understands,' he ordered. 'We don't have three weeks' grace – this is happening *now*.'

'Me? And what are you going to do?'

'This has gone far enough. Dave plans to saturate this place with personnel to track down the girls, but we don't have time. From what you've told me, there's only one reliable informant, and the little cocksucker is currently leading a riot. So, Harker, you're with me. We're going to track him down and get answers.'

Chapter 27

Sean and Adams ran into the night, following the sound of fighting: the shouts and smashes, and the crackle of police radios.

Sure enough, it led them into the overgrown paths of the jungle. Depending on whether you really wanted a rumble or just to let off steam, it was here that you lured your enemy. Then you engaged them on your own terms. You planted ambushes, or turned and fought, or just disappeared into the dark.

The passages between the overgrown flowerbeds were pools of dark. Streetlights made it far enough down to show your head and shoulders, but your chest vanished into the darkness and you had no way of knowing where your feet were or what they might be about to step on.

Adams suddenly bent over double, swearing loudly as he tripped over a litter bin. Sean heard it rolling away over the concrete.

'Walk down the middle,' he said. 'Keep away from the edges.'

Orange light glimmered ahead and they came out into the open space of the playground. Sean's ears had already told him what they would find.

The Killaz were ranked along the far side, pelting a row of riot cops with stones, bottles and fragments of torn-up playground equipment. Sean and Adams lurked behind the police. They edged round the playground to get a gander at the rioters without attracting a baton charge of their own from the cops.

'So, which one's Kieran?' Adams asked.

Sean squinted, trying to see. There were several skinny types dressed in the Kieran uniform of sleeveless jacket, cap pulled down over the eyes, scarf over the face.

'That one . . . ?' he said, trying to be sure. 'Skinny fucker . . .'

'Focus, Harker. Try to narrow it down.'

'Third from the left . . . ?'

The kid in question hurled a bottle and the action made his hat fall off. He quickly scooped it up and jammed it back on, but it gave Sean long enough to see it wasn't their man. The kid had a crewcut.

'Nope, not him . . .'

'Fucksake, Harker, we've got a job to do.'

'I don't think it's any of them . . .' Out of the blue inspiration struck, and Sean pulled out his phone.

'Oh, right!' Adams exclaimed. 'He'll interrupt his busy social schedule to talk to you?'

'If he answers, and we don't see someone pick up, then he won't be any of them, will he?' Sean said as he called up the phone log and tapped Kieran's number. It rang twice, three times . . .

'*Yo, Sean, mate, how's it hanging?*'

Sean and Adams scanned the rows of rioters. None of them were on the phone. Adams rolled his eyes in disgust but kept quiet. He leaned in close to catch what Kieran was saying, jamming a finger into his other ear to block out the noise all around him. Sean could have put it on speaker, but people at the other end can always tell and no one likes the feeling of being listened in on.

'I need to talk to you,' Sean said. 'Where are you?'

'*Not so fast, mate!*' Kieran's chuckle was knowing and suspicious. '*You never know who might be listening in.*'

'OK, you know I'm local. Just give me somewhere the pigs won't know. I really need to talk.'

'*So, talk. It's what we're doing.*'

Sean drew a breath. How to put all this into words Kieran would understand? 'OK. The room. The room under Wolsey that the cops busted, right? That started all this.'

'*What about it?*'

'It was hot, but it's empty now. I heard some cops saying they think there's somewhere on the estate the goods have been taken to. Mate, we really need to find it before they do.'

'*You mean, another room stacked up with hot goods?*'

'Well, yeah.'

'*Sean, mate, you are full of it. There weren't no goods, were there? Hot goods don't get special attention from armed response and the Teletubbies.*'

'Teletubbies?' Sean said, baffled.

'*The wankers in white suits!*' Kieran snapped. '*What are they? Forensic experts? What have you got in there, mate? A dead body?*'

Sean opened his mouth to say something, but Kieran got there first.

'*Here's how it looks to me. You come to us talking about outside interests bringing their crap onto Littern Mills. Well, tell you straight, mate, I'm thinking that's what you've been doing.*'

'It's not like that—'

'*So tell me how it's like, and be quick because I'm seriously losing interest.*'

The best way of lying, Sean had learned a long time ago, is to tell the truth and let the other guy hear what their preconceptions make it come out as.

'Listen, you know how the Guyz went tits up? Getting involved in bombing? Well, it's the same thing again. Terrorists. Only I want to stop it happening.'

Sean saw Adams scowl at the glancing blow with the truth, but he didn't think he had a choice.

A pause, then Kieran was back, no longer sounding bored. '*Terrorists? On our manor?*'

'Yup—'

'*Well, fuck that. Once we've seen the pigs off we'll be turning our attention in that direction.*'

'But if you—'

'*Sean.*' Kieran sounded clipped and cold. '*I still respect you as one of the Guyz, but that could change. And no offence, mate, but you don't live on the estate any more, do you? You grew up here, you should understand. You're turning into a foreigner. We deal with our own problems. We don't get the pigs involved.*'

Sean tried one more time. 'Look, if you—'

'*OK, I've tried doing this the nice way. Here's the nasty way. Fuck off.*'

The line went dead.

Sean and Adams looked at each other.

'Nice try.' Adams's tone suggested he didn't think it had been. 'Give me thirty seconds with the little tosser and I'll debrainwash him . . .'

Sean tapped the phone in the palm of his hand.

'How does he know about the white suits?' he asked. Adams looked at him. 'The biohazard guys. They've stayed behind the vans. He could only see them if he's up close . . . or . . .'

They looked at each other.

'Or above,' Adams finished. 'The little shit's in Wolsey, looking down and having a laugh. Probably coordinating everything by phone.'

Chapter 28

'So here's what we do . . .' Adams was gasping as they sprinted back to the square, avoiding hidden traps on the pitch-black paths. 'We ID him from below. We each go up a different staircase and pincer him. And I dangle him by his ankles over the drop until he spills.'

'There could be a crowd of them,' Sean pointed out. 'Not that we couldn't handle one or two, but—'

'I repeat, he will be dangling by his ankles over the side. I guarantee immunity from interference from his mates.'

Sirens were whooping their way up the access road, laid down over the rumble of heavy diesel engines and the blue pulses of emergency lights. The fire brigade had arrived – two, three large tenders. The blaze in Gladstone was sending white and yellow flickers into the night.

The police cordon had been extended around the

base of Wolsey in all directions. No one could get in or out. There was already a small crowd of civilians gathered about the entrance to West Square, either passers-by who had wandered along for the entertainment or locals who had got out and found they couldn't get back in again. The cops moved aside to let the fire tenders in, but immediately closed up again as Sean and Adams tried to gain re-entry. A pair of officers blocked Adams off.

'Good morning, sir. We'll have to ask you—'

'We're here on business.' Adams flashed his ID, and nodded at Sean to do the same, making to move on without breaking step.

But the cops weren't shifting.

'Hang on, please, sir . . .' The guy deftly removed Adams's wallet from his hand and his mate shone a Maglite on it. Then they turned the beam on Sean's out-stretched wallet to compare.

'Royal Fusiliers?' The cop sounded disbelieving. 'What are you lot doing here?'

'There's no time to explain everything, Officer. You just need to let us through and you need to let us through *now*. I bet you get all kinds of cranks in your line, but a serving sergeant wouldn't be bullshitting you, would he?'

'Right you are, sir. No offence, but I'm going to have to call this in . . .'

'*Oh, for—*' Adams exploded. But he could see the other cop fingering his Taser, so he calmed down while the first cop turned away with deliberate slowness and tried to call up a superior officer.

Meanwhile, visibly seething, Adams tried to engage the second cop in a conversation that used facts and logic to make his point.

And Sean clocked all the onlookers who were clocking him and Adams trying to get some kind of clout with the cops. This was probably the last shreds of their security evaporating. It was a strange kind of relief. He could stop pretending to be undercover and just be a straight soldier again.

'Sean . . .'

It was so faint he thought he had imagined it, but then it came again – and there, on the edge of the onlookers, was Emma.

Sean stared at her, looked at Adams, who was still talking, looked back.

The fuck?

Her eyes were wide and pleading. She looked more tired and drawn than when he'd last seen her, a few hours earlier – but then, he supposed, that was also how he felt. She was beckoning him over.

He glanced at Adams again. Adams had never seen Emma, wouldn't recognize her now. But in front of all these people – and particularly in front of Emma – Sean couldn't just blurt out, *Sergeant, that's Emma Booth, and we still don't know if she's Girl X, and even if she isn't, she might still know something about Zara.*

Well, he could still talk to her, right?

He sidled away from Adams and the cop.

Emma flashed a tight, unhappy smile and led him away from the others. She reached out and took his hands in hers. 'I really need to talk, but . . .' She nodded back at the cordon. 'Sean, are you with these people?'

Sean ground his teeth together. What had she seen? Him and Adams showing ID to the police and obviously expecting to be taken seriously? But, hey, she *knew* he was in the army.

Basically he still had to act the innocent. If he still couldn't be one hundred per cent sure she was Girl X, it worked both ways: *she* couldn't be one hundred per cent sure he was on to her. By now she would be aware that he knew about Zara and Ste . . . but maybe not her.

And if she was just plain Emma Booth, then she was a fit civvy girl who he liked and who was in trouble, so he had to do what he could.

'Thought our army ID might work with the cops,' he said with a shrug. 'It was worth a try. Are you all right?'

She eyed him. 'OK . . .' She seemed to come to a decision. 'Look, I don't know exactly what's happening, but you were asking about Zara and . . . Oh, God, Sean, I have to tell someone. I don't know what else to do. There's no one else to turn to.'

'So, what's up?'

'She's in a bad way. A *really* bad way. She called me up, said she has to get help . . . Can I show you?'

O-o-o-kay! His smile grew fixed. So he was supposed to head off alone into the dark with a potential terrorist, no backup or support?

But, shit, if it was int . . . He was torn.

'Me?' He played for time. 'Sure, I'd like to help, but . . . but what can I do?'

'You're army. You're with . . .' She jerked her head at the cordon. 'You're on the inside. If the cops find her like she is, she'll just be busted. You might be able to have a word with someone . . . someone in authority . . . make them go easier on her . . . *Please*, Sean?'

Fuck, why can't this be simple?

'I . . .' He glanced back at Adams. 'I could bring the serge— my mate. He's senior to me. Authority will pay more attention.'

She shook her head abruptly. 'There's no way she'd trust a stranger.'

Bollocks.

He couldn't see any way out of this. He had a lead and he had to take it, even if he was heading into danger.

Sean took a step back towards Adams – and stopped. Adams and the cop still seemed to be locked in mind-to-mind combat. Would it really help if he interrupted? Or would he just be dragged into the interrogation and get bogged down again?

And if he said anything to show that Emma was a person of interest, then the cops would claim her, which would screw up the mission good and proper.

And meanwhile Emma would just push off, taking all the int in her head with her. She was trembling on her feet, poised to run away.

He couldn't wait any longer. He marched up to Adams and clapped him on the shoulder, just long enough to mutter in his ear: 'Gotta go – mission objective – I'll leave my phone on.' Then he about-turned and headed off before the cop or Adams could say anything.

Would leaving his phone on make any kind of difference? He didn't know. He did know phones could be tracked with the right equipment – which hopefully Dave had access to. He'd done what he could.

Sean and Emma slid away into the darkness.

They didn't talk much. Every sense of Sean's was

alert for danger, for any sign of a trap, for Ste and anyone else to come leaping out at him. But she was moving too fast and determinedly for it to be a set-up. At least, yet.

They took a circuitous route, away from the square, round the back of Coopersale Tower on the east side. With Coopersale in the way, you couldn't see the fire blazing away at the foot of Gladstone, and the bulk of the building blocked out most of the sounds.

Sean assumed Coopersale was where they were heading, or somewhere else on the estate, but then Emma began to curve back towards the rear of Gladstone. The tower grew out of a concrete apron that was covered with rubbish. On this side of the tower, where people weren't meant to be, at ground level there was a sheer concrete wall. The shops had no external back doors or windows. There was no sign of the fire that was blazing a few metres away.

Emma pulled aside a pile of boxes to reveal a crumbling hole, waist high – an even darker splodge on a dark background.

Sean whipped out his phone and switched on the torch so that he could crouch down and peer in. From this angle, all he could see was more concrete walls. He was sweating and he could feel his heart pounding. None of this felt good.

'She's in there?'

'It's always been our secret place.' Emma swung herself into the hole and dropped to the floor. When she turned to face him, he could see her from the shoulders down. 'See? It's not far. And there's lights on further along.'

Sean lowered himself almost to ground level and squinted in. She was standing in a short, dead-end passageway which led to the main underground passageway, as he had expected.

'And Zara's down here?'

He squeezed his eyes shut. It wasn't right, but he was having difficulty finding the words to say it. He had been on the go for nearly twenty-four hours, most of them spent upright. He was dead tired and his brain just wanted to shut down for the night. Zara was down here, under a burning building, and he was expected to go in and do something about it . . .

He couldn't see the fire, but with his face up to the hole he could smell it. There is something distinctive about the wrong sort of smoke. It's dirty and gritty and it scratches the inside of your lungs.

'*Yes!*' Emma kept her voice down. '*Please*, Sean? She's with some really dodgy types. I want to get to her.'

This was his last chance to stay in touch. His phone's

signal would be blocked in there. He thumbed up the text icon and started to type out to Adams.

Back of tower . . .

'Come *on*, Sean.' Emma turned and hurried off.
'Hey, wait!'

He looked at the screen. Fuck's sake, he hadn't even said *which* tower. Adams would have his balls for a sloppy report like that, and if he wasn't so brain dead, he wouldn't have even tried. He started to thumb back to specify which tower he meant.

But he couldn't afford to lose her. *Shit*.

So he hit SEND as was, and put the phone down next to the hole. Still out in the open; still – he hoped to God – trackable. Then he stuck his legs into the hole and dropped down after her.

The underground passageway was lit with the familiar dim lights in wire cages, made even hazier by the first faint hints of smoke. Like the place where Wolston had got shot, it was somewhere he had already been, earlier that day, and drawn a blank – because, as he now knew, there hadn't been anything the detector could have found.

Dave had said he was going to call in the pros to do this properly, now that their cover was blown. No sign of anyone else yet, though. Maybe they hadn't got round to this spot. Maybe events had overtaken them.

Sean was used to how the sublevels cut out surface noise, but he had never really appreciated it until now. His ears were still braced for the racket outside: the rioters chasing around the estate, the shouted orders and cries. Down here there was nothing. The building above cut out the sound just as efficiently as it did phone signals. Sean's imagination compensated for the absence by making up random fears.

And that was when his over-tired brain finally coughed up a question that needed an answer to make sense of all this. Emma had said Zara called her up? How, exactly?

'Emma . . .' he began as he caught up with her.

They were at a T-junction. The left and right passages looked identically empty. If Adams or anyone came this far after him, how would they know which way Sean had gone?

Emma darted down the left one. She had her back to Sean, so he fished his ID out of his wallet and quietly dropped it as he followed.

She had stopped at a door, pushing it open. It looked

like the twin of the one where he had listened in on Zara giving blood, right down to the wire ventilation mesh above.

'The fire's not getting any better,' she said in a loud whisper.

Which was true enough; it made Sean hurry forward the last few steps.

'Hey, babe! Look who I found for you!' Emma beckoned him in urgently.

The room was even barer than the last one Zara had occupied. Nothing to make it even remotely comfortable. Another concrete box with thick, heavy ducts running across the ceiling, and—

Oh, shit!

Zara, lying on a pallet by the wall. Her eyes were almost closed, and in the gloomy half-light the trickles of blood from her eyes and mouth were black and sticky. She peered up at him. 'Who's that?' she moaned. 'Em, I need a doctor!'

Sean grabbed up the front of his own shirt and buried his face in the cloth. It was the nearest he could get to a proper surgical mask but he had no idea how effective it would be. His brain had been running on pure reserves for a long time, and now they were almost used up; it was just shutting down. He ought to be doing something but he couldn't put his finger on it . . .

A blur of motion in the corner of his eye, and sheer instinct took over where conscious thought failed. He threw himself towards the wall as Emma lunged at him with a bloodstained transfusion needle.

Chapter 29

Sean hit the wall; Emma stumbled and slashed at the air where he had been.

She was between him and the door. In the moment it took for the last cobwebs to blow out of his head, she had locked it, standing with her back to it. Her grin reminded him of a hungry wild animal.

'Em . . .' Zara protested. Her weak voice dissolved into something that was a mixture of coughs and sobs.

'Shut up.' Emma slipped the key into a pocket and waved the needle at Sean. 'You know what's on this?'

His chest heaved as he sucked in breaths through the shirt. He couldn't see any point in pretending any more. 'Gonna guess Lassa fever.' The shirt muffled his voice. 'Version five.'

'Clever boy.'

Anyone else, especially any other girl with her slight build, and he would have just decked her, and that

299

would have been that. But the thing in her hand focused his mind like it was hypnotic. If it broke his skin, it was basically game over for him. And his skin was just as thin as hers.

Zara had slumped back onto her pallet. He'd had no idea that everything would be so quick. She hadn't looked this bad when he watched her being evacuated from the other room a few hours ago. But now, with her blood leaking like that, there was no doubt in his mind that she had reached the end.

'I don't want to do this any more, Em,' she mumbled. 'It hurts too much. I want a doctor, please . . .'

'This is what we both signed up for,' Emma said. She was speaking to Zara but didn't look away from Sean. Her voice was calm, but the grin was fixed and her eyes had a glint that spoke of madness. 'You know that, Zee. So do I. Remember what they said? There'll be doubts. It's just our human nature. It's to be expected. We just hang on that little bit longer . . .' She must have been holding herself back while she kept up the charade, because she suddenly dissolved into a fit of lung-wrenching coughing. But she still managed to keep the needle up, waving it and jabbing it randomly at the air in front of her in case Sean tried to make a break for it.

He wasn't trying any such thing. He had his back

pressed against the far wall and his shirt pressed even further up his nostrils.

'So who fed you that load of crap?' he asked. 'Someone who isn't here, by the look of it. Must be nice to know they're one hundred per cent behind you. Decent of them.'

The fit passed. Emma drew some breaths, then straightened up and pulled back her sleeve. A fresh white bandage was wrapped neatly around her elbow. 'Don't even try, Sean. You'll never understand. Have you worked it out yet?'

He nodded. As long as she was talking, she wasn't attacking him with that needle. And there was still the chance of finding out more.

'You got infected with something,' he said, 'which we think was probably the three-week extra-nasty Lassa fever, and you've both been giving blood so that Ste can . . . what? Infect other people? Who?'

She giggled. 'I don't know!' She held her hands wide open, smiling innocently, and for a second he thought he could close the gap between them, grab her wrists, nut her hard to knock her out. But then the needle was back in front of her, held out like a duelling sword.

'I don't know,' she repeated. 'That's what's so clever. Right, Zee?'

Zara had collapsed onto her side, barely twitching

but sobbing very faintly. Sean clocked the look of compassion that flitted over Emma's face – a remnant of a time when they were just two ordinary BFFs, before this mad self-righteousness had taken over.

'That's how I know this is right,' she said. 'Ste told us. Bombs aren't the way. Think about it. It's wrong when the Americans take out a leader with a drone, and simultaneously wipe out twenty innocent people as collateral. But our brothers do the same. The London bombs – how could they be justified? What had those people on the bus or the Tube done to them?'

Her eyes were going glassy with the glorious vision, and Sean thought he recognized the smooth tones of Fayez in the rhythm and inflection of her words.

'But plague – plague is in the hands of God! You let off a bomb on a crowded train and everyone dies. But you release a virus, and who knows? One person will die and the one standing next to them will live. Their lives and deaths are exclusively in the hands of God, where they belong. By choosing to offer up our lives, we are giving God a weapon that is guaranteed to strike down the ones only he has chosen. *He* chooses! Not us! It's fair. It's just. We were booking up tickets to events, shows, games – anything where there would be people. We would move among them as the instruments of God. I bought so many tickets . . . And Ste will put the blood he took off us into other people like me, and *they* will buy tickets . . . And . . . And . . .'

Over his shirt Sean stared at Emma, wide-eyed, as the wave of half-baked religious crap dried up. And remembered watching her on the laptop back at the OP. That's what she had been doing. Buying tickets. It had looked harmless at the time . . .

'Emma,' he blurted, 'how the *fuck* did you end up like this?'

Her glowing smile dissolved into a snarl. 'How did *I*? How did *you*? I wasn't lying when I said we had a crush on you, Sean. You were bad, and we loved it. You didn't give a fuck. You weren't going to be told by anyone. And then what happened? You only went into the army! The *army*! Just like that, one day you're with us, the next you're with them. Do you know what that did to the people here in your old home? Do you have any idea how much we despise you now?

'And then Ste introduced me and Zara to some guys he had met at college.'

The snarl began to fade back into the happy glow again. 'No one's ever given a shit about us, but here's these guys treating us like princesses without wanting to get into our pants. They showed us, Sean. It's like . . . it's like righteousness is on the other side of a door. Open that door and light will shine into the world!

But you *can't* open that door because the system that *you* work for is like this massive *dead weight* slumped against it. We have to make that weight *shift*. Then the door will open and righteousness will shine into the world. Everyone will see it.'

She smiled knowingly, but immediately dissolved into another cough. Maybe illness, maybe smoke. It was creeping into the room through the vent over the door, and it had got stronger in the last few minutes.

'It comes quickly,' she said quietly, like she was mentioning it to someone else in passing. 'Quicker than we thought. No one really knew how this new strain would work. Ste will tell them for next time.'

'Emma. Reality check. You're going to die, and it's going to be slow and painful, and then you'll be gone and that'll be it.'

Sean wasn't sure why he was saying this. It was already too late to save her. If she went the same way as Zara, then within hours she would be leaking blood from everywhere.

'Yeah, I know life on Littern Mills is crap. But I'm living proof you can get out . . .'

The knowing smile came back, and she let the needle drop. Once again she was holding out her hands, and they were empty.

'I know I'll suffer pain, like Zee. I'm not looking

forward to it. But it will only be for a while. Death takes everyone – but mine will have meaning. Let's not kid ourselves, Sean. You're taller and stronger than me. You probably know twenty different ways to kill me. You can escape this room and report everything I've said to your superiors. Maybe they'll be able to stop Ste, maybe they won't. But I can absolutely guarantee you won't leave without being infected yourself.' She grinned and then gnashed her teeth. 'I can break your skin without a needle. C'mon. What's keeping you? Let's *both* choose to lay down our lives for what we believe in!'

'Thought you were leaving it up to God,' Sean said. His mind was in overdrive.

Ste. He was the one who had radicalized the girls – but someone had also got to him. Ste would tell *them*, she had said. So Ste had someone above him, the ones who had masterminded this. Fayez? Jaz? And maybe others.

And where was Ste now? There was no cooler box here. He still had that bad blood, ready to pump into more volunteers. Another stroke of genius for their random God.

Emma screamed and ran at him, mouth wide open and teeth bared. Sean sidestepped quickly and tried to make a break for the door before he remembered she had the key. Shit!

Emma swung round and lunged at him again – with another scream that turned into a wild laugh as they both stumbled in different directions. He backed away and cast about for some kind of weapon – anything at all in the room that he could use to put a bit of distance between him and Emma's teeth.

There was nothing except his own limbs. His legs were longer than her arms. So when Emma ran at him again, he ducked down on bended knee, balanced on one foot, and lashed out with the other in a sidekick into her stomach. Her scream turned into a sudden choke and she bent double. Her body folded over his leg and dragged them both to the floor. She twitched feebly, gasping for breath in huge whoops, while he struggled to drag his foot free. The needle was within arm's reach. She scrabbled for it while he got to his feet, and then he brought his heel down as hard as he could on the back of her hand. He felt bones break through the sound of a different kind of scream.

But the key was still in Emma's pocket. He felt the room swim around him. Shit, on top of the exhaustion and trying not to panic about being trapped in a burning building, he was hyperventilating. Meanwhile Emma was up again, ignoring the agony of her broken hand as she flung herself towards him. She no longer had the needle, but her teeth caught in a loose fold of his shirt. She hadn't been joking about biting. He hammered on the top of her head with his elbow, and she fell to her knees.

Sean blundered backwards, and fell to his knees himself. They sized each other up through the haze, face to face across a distance of a couple of metres. They braced themselves for the next, possibly final, lunge. He stared into the hate-filled, twisted face, and for a moment his heart broke for the girl who had ended up like this.

A red beam lanced through the smoke behind her. Sean traced its source to the grille above the door at the same time as the crack of a shot filled the room. The round punched through her heart and burst out of her chest in a red spray that Sean tried to avoid, scrambling away as fast as he could. She crumpled into a heap, face still contorted.

'*Harker!*' He recognized Adams's voice. '*Get away from the door!*'

''S OK,' he mumbled. He started to crawl towards Emma's body. 'I've got—'

The door blew in with a snap of plastic explosive that sent a shock through his whole body, before he could finish with 'a key'. It was a stunning blow. Sean hit the concrete, and his dazed mind thought how nice it would be to lie there for the rest of his life, cold grit pressed against his face.

Strong hands lifted him up and he felt his arm being wrapped around Adams's neck. A masked SAS man approached Zara cautiously, MP5 at the ready.

She twitched and looked up through eyes that were caked with fresh blood. 'Can you get me a doctor?' It came out as a whispered sob.

'Let's see how you can walk,' Adams said to Sean, his voice firm but kind. Sean's feet made vague walking movements beneath him. His head was still ringing from the explosion, but his legs remembered what to do when they were pressed into solid ground, and he could carry about half his weight as Adams led him towards the door.

Pure muscle memory made him flinch as a rattle of shots burst out behind him. He whipped his head round. The SAS man was turning away from Zara's still form and lowering his weapon. His body blocked Zara from view. Sean stared at him in shock. The SAS guy met his gaze calmly, eyes unblinking through his goggles.

'The fuck . . .' Sean whispered. They had just shot her? Put her down?

'Better all round,' Adams muttered. 'Come on, soldier. Let's get you out of here.'

Chapter 30

'They're still out there,' Sean mumbled. They were shambling along through the smoky haze towards the stairs. The SAS guy in the gas mask led the way, un-affected by the smoke. 'They've got poisoned blood in a cooler box. We've got to get them . . .'

'Yeah, I heard. You can tell your story from a safe distance to someone who can do something about it. Come along.'

From a safe distance . . . ? Sean thought fuzzily. And then: *Oh, yeah, right.*

What else had been in the air in that room? What else was now polluting his lungs, on top of all that smoke, getting into his bloodstream that way?

He couldn't deal with that right now. He mentally filed it away under things to totally freak out about later.

Adams's arm was strong around his shoulders. 'I

have your phone, I have your ID – but *back of tower*? What kind of report is that? Hey?'

'A crap one, Sergeant,' Sean mumbled between coughs. He knew that Adams was keeping him talking to make him stay with it, and he was grateful for it. Smoke was thick in the corridor, and Sean's muzzy head found time to be puzzled by it. The fire was on the ground level and there should be fire doors, even in a place like Littern Mills. Weren't they working?

But then they were at the stairs that led up to the square. Slightly cleaner air gusted in their faces, and Sean's head cleared a bit as they stumbled up.

'But you still found me?' he asked.

Adams grinned without humour. 'I did. I got past plod, I was making my way up the stairs as planned, and there was your little prick of a friend coming down the other way. So that speeded up the process of dangling him by his ankles. His friends were disinclined to get in my way. Your weird Littern Mills telepathy seemed to work on him – he guessed you meant the hole at the back of Gladstone. So I borrowed our pal in the mask here, and off we went. Thanks to your phone we found the hole.'

'You tracked it?'

Adams shot him a strange look. 'Do I look like 007?

I *called* it. And when I heard it go off, I thought only one of my lads would have a crappy ringtone like that.'

The gate stood open, and Sean and Adams staggered out into the air and the tentative light of a new day. Sean had never been happier to see the Littern Mills estate.

By the time they were halfway back to the cordon across the square, Sean felt he could walk on his own again. He disengaged himself from the sergeant's supporting arm and looked around at the devastation.

The fire had well and truly caught. The entire ground level of Gladstone was alight. The populations of the other three towers were being escorted down their stairwells and away from the square.

He could only watch. He knew, deep down, that he would get around to caring about this. A lot. For the time being it was like someone else was seeing it on his behalf. His thoughts just couldn't stretch beyond this present point into the future.

The police vans were still clustered at the base of Wolsey. Fire tenders were drawn up in front of Gladstone, but there wasn't much sign of the firemen doing their stuff. And what the fuck was that *singing*? He must be hearing things.

But he wasn't. He was hearing a chorus of teen boys'

voices tunelessly singing '*Let it burn, let it burn*' to the tune of *Let It Go*. The cops had got on top of the Killaz by sheer weight of numbers, and the gang were being rounded up around the estate. Every new arrest was brought forward to be squeezed into one of the police vans, and each one added his voice to the song.

Kieran was next in line for the back of a van, hands cuffed behind him, face battered and bruised. He was singing along with the rest of them – until he clocked Adams approaching. His defiant grin turned to fury and he lunged forward.

'That fucker there!' Kieran howled. 'He's the one you should be arresting! He abused my civil liberties!'

The cops didn't seem to care, and Kieran was bundled in with the rest of his mates, still protesting. The chorus had got to '*I never liked the building anyway . . .*'

'It's possible he fell against some unmoving objects in the course of our interview,' Adams said, deadpan. 'Now, let's get the alert put out for Ste . . .'

As they approached the vans, Sean spotted Dave and a fireman with a station manager's helmet – white, with a single thin black stripe. They stood side by side, looking at the fire, and the fireman's body language was absolutely rigid with fury. Sean suddenly thought: *Why aren't they doing anything to put out the fire? Why are they letting it all just fucking burn?*

Mitra came forward to meet them, and Sean could tell from his face that it was bad news. But it was Adams who held up a hand, stopping Mitra in his tracks, five metres away.

'Harker and I are in our own personal biohazard zone. Don't come any closer. What's happening?'

Mitra stared at them. 'You're—'

'I asked you a question, Fusilier!' Adams snapped. It was rare for him to snap when a sarcastic word could do so much more. Sean guessed he was feeling – or rather, trying hard *not* to feel – exactly like *he* did at the thought of the Lassa virus colonizing his blood vessels and body organs . . .

Mitra held up the screen of his phone. 'We've made local radio and we're breaking news on a lot of websites. They're saying the fire brigade have been forbidden to approach until, quote, details of dangerous chemicals stored illegally in the basement can be verified, unquote. Sorry, Stenders. They're just letting it take its course. They're just going to let the fire destroy it all.'

'Sterilization. It makes sense. They'll just burn out the passages,' Adams said after a moment. 'It probably won't bring the building down. They won't let it all go . . .'

Sean didn't bother saying anything. He was surprised to feel tears pricking the back of his eyes, and he blinked them away before anyone could notice.

Adams was probably right – this wasn't exactly a 9/11 scenario. But it was the *principle*. That was his childhood home over there, with flames licking as high as the second-floor balcony, and columns of smoke scorching their way up to the roof.

Then another thought hit him.

Shit, I hope Mum isn't listening to the news . . .

'Sergeant Adams! Fusilier Harker!' Dave was striding towards them. He came to a stop a safe distance away. His face was tired and haggard, with the shadow of a dark-haired man who hasn't shaved for twenty-four hours. He looked pretty much like Sean felt. 'Two white females have been reported eliminated. Please confirm their identities.'

Sean straightened. He knew how to make a report, even if it was only to a civilian, and a spook.

'Zara Mann and Emma Booth,' he said, 'and I can confirm that Emma was Girl X.'

Dave's face was impassive, but he ground one fist into the palm of his other hand. *The bastard's pleased*, Sean thought. *He's got a result.*

'And the others?'

Sean shook his head. 'No sign of Ste or Fayez or Jaz. Ste's still somewhere with a case full of their infected blood . . .'

'Understood. We'll get him, and that cooler box.

You two just stand there until we can get you your own special isolation ambulance.' Dave turned away. 'Shit, this square's going to be a forensics nightmare. Once the fire's gone down, before the civilians get here, we'll have to get our people to retrieve the bodies . . .'

'Yeah, it's tough at the top,' Adams said as Dave hurried away. 'Bastard.'

Sean nodded wearily; then, without asking permission, he sank down to squat on the cool concrete paving, drawing his legs up and resting his elbows on his knees.

Adams sat down next to him. 'How are you feeling, Stenders?'

The question from an army colleague didn't mean the same thing as it meant to civilians. A civvy might have understood it as an invitation to discuss his deepest thoughts, his emotions on watching Gladstone burn; the trauma of having to beat up a girl who, only hours ago, he had felt close to.

Sean knew that Adams genuinely cared for his well-being, but when a sergeant asked a question like that, it meant only one thing: *Are you battle fit or not?*

And as long as you knew you could still get up and put one foot in front of the other and charge the enemy, there was only one acceptable answer.

'I'm fine, Sergeant.' Honesty made him add: 'Beat,

though. And kind of, you know, hoping I don't have Lassa fever.'

'Yeah, that could put a serious dent in both our social lives. The wife's already making plans for Christmas.'

But Sean saw the grim set of Adams's jaw. When it came to the deep-rooted terror that they might actually be infected, neither of them was fooling the other. He pictured that single, lethal shot that had torn through Emma's chest. Puncturing the skin that was designed to keep the blood in, expelling a spurt of it out through a neat little hole in aerosol form, for him to breathe . . . *Shit, thanks, SAS guy.*

Adams grunted and thumped his chest. 'I feel like I could cough for Britain after all that smoke, but under the circumstances I'd be locked up in an isolation ward quicker than you can say Jack Robinson. Mitra! Make yourself useful! Tell the ambulance people there's a couple of guys here suffering smoke inhalation. See if you can wangle a couple of O_2 cylinders to clear out our lungs.'

Mitra hurried off towards the ambulances while Adams pulled out his phone and called up the search box.

'Let's see what delights await us.' He began to type

out: '*Treat . . . ing . . . la . . . laryngitis? Lawns? Laser burns?* Strange – Lassa fever isn't in the dropdown box.'

Sean wasn't sure he wanted to know. If the only end was like Zara's, then he would do it himself before it got that far, quickly and privately. While they waited, he ran his eyes over the ghouls at the edges of the square, as close as they could get to the action. Every few seconds there was a pinprick flash as some moron recorded the scene on their phone. Sean wondered if #LitternMillsfire was trending yet.

And if so, what they all made of the two guys sitting on their own a short distance away from everyone else.

He glared back at the crowd. He couldn't make out any faces – just got general impressions of movement. Rubberneckers. Bunch of wankers trading a good night's sleep for a spectacle.

He wasn't quite sure why one particular movement caught his eye, but it did. It was sheer instinct.

He followed the movement with his head.

'*Ribavirin seems to be an effective treatment for Lassa fever if given early on in the course of clinical illness,*' Adams quoted. 'And that's the World Health Organiz-ation. Not one hundred per cent happy about that *seems*, but— Something up?'

Sean just nodded in the direction of the anomaly.

Until then, he had only seen the top of the guy's head. Now he was walking through a small gap in the crowd. Sean caught a glimpse of a black hoodie over a wiry body. The guy was wearing a small backpack.

Adams had once been in the gangs, and the instinct was still in him. He put into words what Sean was feeling.

'Everyone's gathered around to watch and he's strolling casually away.'

'People can just walk, Sergeant.'

'Sure they can, but that isn't just walking. It's proceeding.'

And Sean noticed another thing. No cooler box, but still . . .

'He's the same size and shape as Ste . . .' he said.

Chapter 31

Adams came alert like a cat spotting something small crawling across the room.

'You say? So where's he been hiding all this time? Not his flat.'

'He's lost the cooler box,' Sean said after thinking for a moment. He had last seen Ste five hours ago. That was plenty of time to get well away from the estate, so something had kept him here. 'Maybe he had to package up the contents in a special way for that rucksack. Then sterilize wherever he went. Get rid of forensics.'

'Get orders, communicate with his muckers . . .' Adams continued the line of thought. 'Or just plain wait for an opportunity when everyone was distracted . . . Maybe someone should ask him . . .'

They both shot a look at the ranks of police and emergency services, and read each other's mind.

'We're nearer,' Sean said.

'He'll just get away if we take our eyes off to report him.'

'And he'll just run the moment he thinks someone's on to him.'

'Looks like it's you and me, Fusilier.'

They casually climbed to their feet. No one in the emergency services clocked them, and Mitra was still arguing with the ambulance guys.

They drifted towards the edge of the square.

'Just try not to cough on anyone,' Adams said.

'Permission to cough on the suspect, Sergeant?'

'If he's our man, Fusilier, you have my permission to French-kiss him.'

The suspect was heading away from West Square and towards the low-level apartments.

They let him keep about thirty metres ahead as they walked down what was officially a 'boulevard' – a wide concrete alleyway with flowerbeds down the middle and split-level maisonettes on either side.

They slowly stepped up their speed – until Adams suddenly put a hand across Sean's chest to slow him down a little. He gestured at the ground, and Sean saw what had almost given them away. The streetlights were still on, and they cast faint shadows that were almost long enough to overtake the walker. If Ste looked down, he'd know he was being followed. At the moment he seemed to have no idea they were there: he still had his hood up, and – never mind how cool it looks in Jedi Academy – doing that cuts off fifty per cent of your peripheral vision. Sean had learned that at a very early age, and still had the scar just above his hairline to prove it.

Adams held up his hand, all his fingers extended. Then he started to count down from five. Sean clenched his fists and raised himself onto the tips of his toes, ready to spring forward when the count reached zero. They would close the space between themselves and the guy in a couple of seconds, and it would all be over before he could go for any kind of weapon.

But as they reached three, the man was passing a side alley off the boulevard. He suddenly ducked left and pelted away.

'*Shit!*'

Without a break, the two were after him. There was no point pretending now. Their feet slapped on the concrete slabs. The guy risked a glance back, which was stupid of him. You can't run at top speed if you're looking backwards, and the action and the flow of air made his hood fall back. Sean recognized the profile – and the shiner. Yup, it was Ste.

Who suddenly vanished altogether.

'*Bollocks!*' They skidded to a halt, and Sean made

them backtrack a few paces. He had forgotten this. Every pair of units had a narrow pathway between them, the walls so tight that, walking along, his shoulders brushed against them. It was some Council Tax dodge to classify the apartments as semis rather than terraced, or something like that.

The distant sound of running echoed back at them, and they could see Ste's silhouette getting smaller and smaller ahead. He had a good lead, and they were both too well built to run at speed down a narrow gap like that.

'Run down to the end,' Sean ordered, gesturing to the side. 'Turn left, take the third left again. The *third*.'

Adams stared at him through the twilight, but then just bowed to local knowledge. 'Understood.' He ran off, twice as fast as before.

Sean was already heading the other way.

Sean and Adams and Ste were taking three different directions, but they were all now heading for the same point. Ste wouldn't be able to run as fast down that passage as in the open, but he was running in a straight line to get there, while Adams and Sean had to run round three sides of a rectangle. So they needed that extra speed.

The passage that Ste had taken cut across two more boulevards and ended at the third. In theory he could turn left or right into any of them. But Sean knew he wouldn't. The first was decorated with flowerbeds in raised concrete squares that made it impossible to run down safely at speed. The second was currently being re-laid, so the concrete slabs were up and it was a lethal mix of cracked stone and sandy pits.

So the third boulevard it was.

Sean tore right into the west end of the third boulevard, just in time to catch the dark figure breaking for it in an easterly direction, and then skidding to a halt as Adams appeared at the far end. Ste turned, ran the other way, and saw Sean charging at him.

For a moment he crouched, caught in indecision. It meant that he lost important seconds as they got closer. Then he fumbled at his waist below his hoodie. Sean and Adams both recognized the body language and stepped up their pace.

He was tugging at something in his waistband and making jerking movements with his elbow. The gun tucked down inside his belt must have got caught – probably the front sight snagging on his trousers.

Sean and Adams were metres away.

Ste ripped the gun free, staggered, looked from one to the other, and must have thought Sean was marginally closer: that was the direction in which he pointed the gun.

Sean's vision zoomed in on the small black circle at the end of the barrel. He was too committed to feel fear or to swerve. It was do or die – an expression he had never really understood until now. The one thing he couldn't do was duck aside or back off. And if Ste killed him – well, Adams would get him a second later, and Sean would be spared a long, slow, painful Lassa-fever death.

He let out a roar – the yell they had all been taught in bayonet training. It gave you a psychological boost to spur you onwards, as well as making your enemy freeze and stop in their tracks – just before you jammed six inches of steel into their guts. Sean saw the gun flash in the shaking hand, heard the single shot, felt something pluck his right bicep with a light touch, somewhere between a red-hot poker and an icicle.

And then Sean cannoned into Ste and they flew backwards, Sean's arms locking them together, just in time for Adams to hit them from behind, equally hard. Ste, caught in the middle, let out a bellow of pain and crumpled. The gun hit the ground with a metal clatter. Adams dragged him up again to deliver a final knockout blow to his terrified face.

They stared at each other, panting, bent over with hands on knees.

Adams switched his gaze to Sean's arm. 'You're hit.'

'Yeah?' He didn't feel hit. He just felt that weird burning. He was still too high on adrenalin to care. He cocked his right arm to look at it, and winced. 'OK . . .'

It could have been a lot worse. The round had skimmed his skin, just below the end of his short sleeve. There was a red, jagged gash that was slowly weeping fluid. It didn't look much more than a graze, but he dimly knew that it was going to hurt, a lot.

'Piece of piss.' Adams straightened up and took Sean's arm with a light touch that didn't go with his words. He rotated it gently, examining it from all angles. 'I've seen people more wounded by an unkind remark. Get a bandage on it and it'll be fine. *Don't* touch it – infection. Now, give me a hand? Let's see what we have.'

Between them they rolled Ste over – Sean's arm was starting to throb now – and Adams released the backpack. He delved cautiously into it.

'Feels cold . . .' He pulled out a package. 'Because . . .'

It was a blood pack, strapped between a pair of freezer blocks with elastic bands.

There were more. Adams counted them out one by one: '. . . four, five, six. How much blood do you think they squeezed out of the girls in the time available? Shit, no wonder Zara was feeling so crap. Even if they gave equal amounts and allowed for recovery, they would be down to five or six pints each. A lot more than an armful.'

Sean was starting to feel more and more light-headed. Maybe some of it was down to the satisfaction of getting Ste. And adrenalin crash. And exhaustion. Fuck – how long was it now since he'd been able to just stop? And when was it going to end?

Adams took it in at a glance. 'Sit,' he ordered, and Sean gratefully dropped down onto the ground, watching the plumes of smoke from Gladstone, picked out in streaks of pink and red and orange by the rising sun. It was close on dawn. Shit, where had the time gone?

'I'm just the newcomer to this mission, Fusilier. You may have the pleasure of calling this in.'

'Thanks, Sergeant. That's Harker . . .'

He gave it a few seconds, and tried again. 'That's Harker?' He frowned, puzzled, at Adams.

The sergeant shrugged. 'Dave and Mitra have probably stood down. Radios all packed away. They think it's all over.'

'Lazy tossers.'

Sean tried to reach for the phone in his right pocket, and found that his arm had seized up, though it still wasn't doing anything more than weep a little. He reached across his body and clumsily pulled out his phone with his left hand. It was only then that he realized a text had come in without him noticing. He had been too busy with other things.

> bet ur still in bed lazybones i got
> 2gether with shaz&jen&were at
> the shard now watching the sun
> come up over the city its beautiful

'Glad for you, Mum.'

He wondered whether he should call her, or just let her pick up the news. Shit, he'd have to call her. Once she knew what had been going on here, she'd be worried sick. And she didn't deserve that. And when was he going to tell her – if ever – that he'd never come home for any kind of holiday? How about never?

But he also had a job to do first. He dialled up Dave's number and pressed CALL.

Chapter 32

'Well, fuck me, look who it isn't!'

Ravi Mitra stood outside the briefing room, wearing military T-shirt and MTP trousers, like Sean. Shit, it felt good. After three weeks in the isolation ward, wearing civvies and watching wall-to-wall daytime fucking TV and eating food pushed at him through a little airlock, it had been like putting his skin back on. He had stopped off at barracks just long enough to kit up for the day, and then it was off to the briefing to rejoin the lads.

Mitra winked. 'Good to have you back, Stenders. So you're all clear?'

'Footloose and Lassa free,' Sean said solemnly. 'But the unprotected sex is still off, Kama Sutra.'

'Well, shit. And I was saving myself and everything.' Mitra pushed the door open. 'Guess who?'

The lads welcomed him back the only way they

could. As Sean stood in the doorway, the platoon started coughing, very loudly and pointedly.

He held up a finger from each hand to encompass the whole room. 'And swivel!' he shouted.

Then he couldn't suppress the grin any longer. He pulled back a chair and plonked his arse down next to Chewie West. They bumped knuckles, and then quickly came to attention as Lieutenant Franklin and Sergeant Adams entered the room, together with an officer Sean didn't know.

No one coughed for Adams, fresh out of the isolation unit next to Sean. No one would have dared, even if he wasn't flanked by a pair of Ruperts. The glint in his eye challenged them to try it.

'As you were.' Franklin stood at ease at the front, and acknowledged Sean with a nod. 'Welcome back, Fusilier.'

'Good to be here, sir.'

Franklin carried on addressing the rest of the room, giving them the sitrep on things Sean had only heard about second hand for the last three weeks. Well, there was no better way to catch up than to dive in at the deep end. For the first time since they had parted company in Lagos the platoon was together again—

Except, of course, that it wasn't. Sean's mind was picking out the absences in the room. For all his good intentions, it was hard to concentrate. He'd had all that time in isolation to process it in his mind, but he had known that being back on base would bring it home.

Shitey Bright was dead. Sean had missed his funeral.

Joe Wolston was alive and still in Headley Court, according to the last report. Getting the help and healing he needed for mind and body – maybe coming back, maybe not. Still too soon to say. Still, Sean knew there were openings for disabled veterans. Quartermaster, and the like. He hoped Wolston would take one of them if the army decided on an honourable discharge. Or would it just be too painful for him, being surrounded by active soldiers but unable to be part of it?

Maybe it would have been better for Wolston to call it quits when he got back from Afghanistan, Sean often thought, rather than put his head down and keep going, ending his career on a covert op of questionable success . . .

In one respect, the op *had* succeeded – because the plot had failed. Sean had been told that the blood in Ste's backpack, strapped to the freezer blocks, was the amount the experts calculated the girls could have given in the time available. So there was none still AWOL. No secret stashes of contaminated blood to be put into other volunteers.

But in other respects . . .

All Sean knew for sure was that the op had produced two dead civilian females and one live male. He had no idea if Ste was giving MI5 anything, and MI5 wouldn't be telling Sean if he was. He knew that Ste would not be seeing the light of day for a long time, but there was still Fayez, and Jaz, and Omar, aka *Clarkson*, and the completely different pair of gunmen who had held up the air traffic controller and got the flight diverted to Southend.

Whichever way you looked at it, the people behind Bright's death – people who thought it would be a good idea to flood the country they lived in with a deadly tropical disease – were still at liberty.

Had the operation produced int that could track them down? Sean knew he'd probably never know.

He was glad it wasn't the final marker on his own career.

He suddenly realized that the other Rupert, the stranger – a captain – was speaking. Sean had missed the intro. He forced himself to pay attention just as the guy said:

'. . . and so it is my job now to brief you on the basics of radicalization . . .'

The fuck! Sean quickly wiped the look of dismay off his face, but he knew Adams had clocked it, even if no one else had. Their eyes met for a fraction of a second, and Sean sat up a little straighter. Maybe he would learn something. Before the operation started he'd had a quickie intro to radicalization from Dave; he'd had a lot of time to think about it since – and practical experience of all the theory the captain was handing out now. But there were still gaps. He still didn't have an answer to the question he had put to Emma: *How the fuck did you end up like this?*

'It is a mistake to think that religion will necessarily be a factor . . .'

OK, so the captain was giving them what Sean had already got from Dave. He thought back to the plane. If he'd been told that there were two terrorists on board, then he might well have picked Okwute and someone like him. Not the girls. And even after Dave's briefing, even after he had all the right info in his head, he'd still got it badly wrong with Emma. And nearly died as a result.

Anyone would have said Emma and Zara had better prospects than the teenage car thief a couple of years older than them who lived in the flat opposite. Sean wondered what would have happened if whoever first got hold of them, whoever helped them take that tiny first step on the path, had got hold of *him* instead.

He liked to think he would have told them to piss

off. But would he have recognized that first small step for what it was?

His old gang mates Copper and Matt hadn't.

Sean had been out of it, first in the YOI, then in the army, when they got radicalized. It had been by right wingers, white supremacists, not Muslims – but the starting conditions had been identical. Result: one dead, one in jail for a very long time, ringleaders still not caught. There were people out there recruiting for whatever cause, and somehow places like Littern Mills were feeding the demand for whoever wanted it.

'So just remember this, gentlemen.' The captain was winding up. 'If anyone starts being simplistic about radicalization – if they say it's all down to Muslims, or immigrants, or any one group that is slightly different from any other – ignore them. Newspapers, social media, politicians, even superior officers – *ignore them*. They're *wrong*. Radicalization does *not* fit into neat pigeonholes. It is everywhere and it can strike anywhere. Be aware, and never be afraid to challenge it.' A last smile. 'I think I've engendered the right level of paranoia in your men, Lieutenant Franklin. Thank you for your time.'

The room came to attention as he marched out, and Franklin took over with details of that afternoon's exercise. Sean looked forward to putting his body through some hard paces again and not having to use his mind. Maybe one day he'd even get that holiday in Tenerife.

Because whenever his mind *did* flip into operation, he still thought back to Zara and Emma, and everything that had happened, and the burning question still flashed up time and time again: *How the fuck did it come to this?*

The captain had told them to be aware. Well, Sean was aware.

And he was ready for a fight.

Read on for an extract
from the first book in
the **STREET SOLDIER** series.

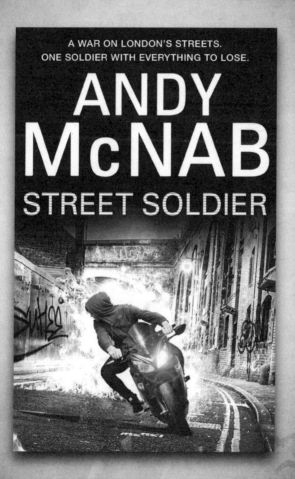

A WAR ON LONDON'S STREETS.
ONE SOLDIER WITH EVERYTHING TO LOSE.

ANDY McNAB

STREET SOLDIER

Undercover, under threat – only Sean Harker
can save the streets from all-out war.

Chapter 1

A helicopter roared in enemy airspace. Its searchlight speared out of the warm night and swept over the rooftop. Sean Harker swore and ducked into the shadow of an air vent.

He pressed himself against the rough, damp brick. He had dressed for the darkness, as per orders. Black jeans, black top, black hood pulled over his blond hair. If the light caught him, nothing would stand out more in its merciless glare than someone who was obviously trying not to be seen.

But it was just a routine patrol, not looking for anyone in particular. The light moved on and the helicopter didn't react to him. It disappeared into the darkness.

Sean stayed where he was until he saw Matt emerge from the shadow of another vent. Then he stepped out, just as Curly crept from behind the small generator shed. Sean had spent half the night crouching down, and his thighs cramped. He flexed his arms and back and gazed out across the graffiti'd maze of rooftops and alleys. Then he and Curly looked to Matt for orders. Matt jerked his head, and the three of them silently gathered together by the skylight.

One of its panels was cranked open, and fumes of oil and petrol and ganja rose up from the workshop into the summer night. Sean took a deep breath through his nose. They were the smells of his childhood.

The vehicle workshop was all lit up and the security shutters were down. Men in grimy overalls lounged in an office behind a glass partition, catching a last smoke and a drink before heading off. Even if they had looked up, they wouldn't have seen the three lurkers. They would be looking out of a brightly lit space into the night.

Finally it looked like they were leaving. One of them stood by the keypad to the security alarm, ready to tap in the code. Matt gave Sean the nod and Sean delved into his pocket for his phone. He had already loaded up the recording app. Slowly, so that no one down there would spot a sudden movement out of the corner of their eye, he stretched his hand through the open panel, holding the phone out to catch the sounds below.

Bleep, bleep, bleep. The electronic tones echoed around the workshop – they had the recording. They could play it back at their leisure to work out the code. Then they could let themselves in, switch off the alarm, and they'd have all the time in the world to get what they had come for.

Sean grinned at the others and began to withdraw the phone. Matt gave an approving thumbs up. A grinning Curly went further and gave him a nudge.

Sean's hand bumped against the frame of the skylight and the phone was knocked out of his fingers. He made a futile grab at thin air at the same time as he heard it hit the concrete floor.

Perhaps even that wouldn't have been so bad if he hadn't instinctively hissed, '*Shit!*'

A cry came from below. Curly and Matt flung themselves flat, away from the skylight. Sean was frozen for only a second longer, but it was long enough to be caught by the searching torchlight. More shouting below – not in English, but he got the gist of it. *There's someone on the roof!*

Running footsteps echoed. Without a word the three pelted towards the top of the fire escape, a vertical iron ladder with safety hoops around it . . .

And skidded to a halt. The workshop's back door was right by the bottom of the ladder and it was just opening. They wouldn't get down before the work crew emerged.

Sean ran over to the far side of the building. There was no escape here – it was a sheer drop into the forecourt. The only other way was the narrow alley at the back of the shop. It couldn't be more than three metres wide.

'Oh shit oh shit oh shit . . .' Curly was muttering.

Matt cuffed him on the head. 'OK.' He backed away from the edge. 'They're gonna come up one by one. We're just going to have to pick them off one at a time—'

'No. No need,' Sean said. They stared at him. 'They only saw me. They don't know anyone else is here.'

'So what?' Matt demanded. 'We just let them take you? Fuck that!'

'No.' Sean shook his head emphatically, and pointed at the vents where they had hidden. 'Get back there.' He felt the excitement rise within him. A tense, nervous thrill, like his lungs and his stomach and his balls were all cramping into a tight knot. It was scary and weird and *good*. 'Go on!'

He grinned and ran back to the top of the fire escape. The first of the work crew had his foot on the bottom rung.

'Wankers!' Sean shouted, and ducked out of sight. He turned quickly to face the others. 'Guys. I can do this. Hide over there.' He jerked his thumb at the air vents. Matt took a breath, about to argue. Sean looked him in the eye. 'Please?'

Curly turned to Matt for orders. Matt just stared at Sean like he was mad, but he could see it was their only option. Slowly, not taking his eyes off Sean, he backed into the shadows, with Curly at his side.

Sean bounced on his toes, and felt his heart thud inside him. And as he heard footsteps on the iron rungs, he began to run back across the roof towards the alley.

His long legs ate up the distance in a few paces. He drew a deep breath into his lungs, leaped onto the low wall with a single bound, and flung his lean, six-foot frame into the darkness. Air soared around him . . .

. . . Except that he wasn't going to make it. He was dropping faster than the far wall was approaching. It was only three metres away, but he had picked a really bad time to learn that three metres was further than it looked.

His arms began to windmill, striving for that little extra momentum.

'*Shi-i-i-t . . .*'

His torso thumped into the wall with an impact that knocked the breath from his body. He flung his arms forward to get a hold. Pain flared in his armpits as his weight ground them into the sharp edge of the roof.

But he wasn't falling any more. With an effort, he hooked his elbows over the top of the wall, dug his toes into the cracks and levered himself up until he could fall forward onto the flat roof on the other side.

He rolled onto his back, stared up at the night sky, and laughed. Pain stabbed through every bruised rib and he didn't care. '*Ha!*'

Angry, baffled yells behind him made him grin. The work crew lined the edge of their roof. They were three metres away and might as well have been on the other side of the city.

'You little shit!' one of them shouted. Another seemed like he might seriously try and jump over, but then he looked down and thought better of it. If Sean could barely do it with a run-up, no way was it possible from a standing start. None of the men had noticed the other two figures, still in the shadows on the other side of the roof.

But now one of them was fumbling inside his coat for . . .

Shit! Sean pushed himself to his feet and was running for cover even before he was upright. If the guy was armed, he wasn't going to hang around.

He ducked down behind the coaming of an aircon unit, breathing heavily. He hadn't thought much beyond this point, and had no idea if you could get down from this place. If there were skylights, then he would break in, risk the alarms, and smash his way out of a window downstairs before reinforcements arrived.

But he had to be quick. He only had a couple of minutes before they sent people down to ground level, and then back up inside the building.

He needn't have worried. His eyes lit on the railings at the top of a fire escape – a proper one: a metal staircase winding its way down into the next alley. He charged towards it, hearing the angry shout from across the way.

Sean threw himself down the metal stairs and kept his grip on the iron railing long enough to fling himself in the direction of the main road. The pain in his ribs he told to piss off, and for the time being it obeyed. The alley was an obstacle course of overturned bins and sagging boxes, all vomiting their contents across his path. Sean half ran, half hurdled, his whole life shrunk down to one aim: get to the main road; get out of here.

He burst out into the road like a cannon ball. The pavement was lined with the turning-out crowd – people heading home from a late screening or a restaurant. The air was rich with the sweet aroma of fast food. Faces loomed in front of him and then whipped away, just as shouts rose up behind him. *Shit*. They were still on his tail. At least they probably wouldn't start shooting in front of all these witnesses.

Sean put his head down and urged himself on.